BID MY
SOUL
FAREWELL

BID MY
SOUL
FAREWELL

BETH REVIS

RAZORBILL

RAZORBILL

An imprint of Penguin Random House LLC
Penguin.com

First published in the United States of America by Razorbill,
an imprint of Penguin Random House LLC, 2019

Visit us online at penguinrandomhouse.com

LIBRARY OF CONGRESS CATALOGING-IN-PUBLICATION DATA
Names: Revis, Beth, author.
Title: Bid my soul farewell / Beth Revis.
Description: [New York] : Razorbill, 2019. | Series: Give the dark my love ; book 2
Audience: Ages 12 up. | Audience: Grades 7 up.
Summary: Told in two voices, Grey hopes to revitalize plague-ravaged Lunar Island, but knows that his alliance with the emperor threatens his love for necromancer Nedra, who wants to keep her revenant sister with her even as she tries to free the souls of the dead.
Identifiers: LCCN 2019023069 | ISBN 9781595147196 (hardcover)
ISBN 9781101627860 (epub)
Subjects: CYAC: Alchemy—Fiction. | Magic—Fiction. | Sisters—Fiction. |
Soul—Fiction. | Good and evil—Fiction. | Fantasy.
Classification: LCC PZ7.R3284 Bi 2019 | DDC [Fic]—dc23
LC record available at https://lccn.loc.gov/2019023069

Printed in the United States of America

ISBN 9781595147196

1 3 5 7 9 10 8 6 4 2

To Corwin,
who always knows how to
fix my broken heart.

Dei gratia.

"Tyranny, like hell, is not easily conquered."

—Thomas Paine

BID MY SOUL FAREWELL

ONE

Nedra

THE GOVERNOR'S CASTLE rose into the dark at the top of Northface Harbor. All the streets in the city converged there, at the base of the imposing mansion.

The road was empty. Except for me and my dead.

My revenants walked beside me, an army of corpses. They bore wounds that I would have to heal with alchemy. Dead flesh could not knit back together on its own. Blood splattered their faces—the black blood was theirs, the red blood was from those who opposed us.

None of it was Governor Adelaide's. Her blood was on my hands alone.

I bowed my head, my teeth clenched as I strode down the cobblestone road. Grey was somewhere behind me, still at the castle. He had thought—I flinched, even though he wasn't there to see—he had thought that killing Adelaide would be the end. That stopping the plague would be enough.

I reached blindly to my right, feeling for my sister, gripping her left wrist to make sure that she was still by my side. Her skin was cold and clammy, no life pulsing in her veins.

None of this could end until she was whole and alive again.

The road evened out, and I almost stumbled on the curb. I looked up—and there, past my sister, were the iron gates of the Yūgen Alchemical Academy. I could see through the moonless night the dark outlines of the buildings I had lived among for a year—the library

1

where I had researched, the dormitory where I had slept. The administration building. I had danced along the rooftop beneath the clock tower with Grey, before everything had changed. I had worked in the basement with Master Ostrum. I had gone deep into the earth at the very foundation of that building, and pulled from the shadows the severed, bony hand that formed the foundation of my iron crucible.

I turned sharply toward the gates that protected the school. My revenants sensed my intentions, following me without needing any directions.

The heavy gates were locked, just as they had been the first time I'd arrived at the academy. *I want in*, I thought, and every single one of my revenants heard my desire.

My army of the undead had fought tirelessly for me tonight, helping me invade the governor's castle and destroy the necromancer who'd caused the plague that had killed my family and thousands more. But the dead cannot tire. They worked as one, swarming and pushing against the iron bars. The gates were old, and the hinges rusted. With a groan and a clatter, the iron gates gave way, clattering to the brick walkway beneath them.

I knew there were students at the academy, guards, teachers, and staff, but none dared approach as I and my undead army strode down the gravel pathway that cut right through the center of the school grounds. I wondered, though, if they watched from the darkened windows.

I forced my shoulders down, my spine straight, my chin forward.

Let them watch me. Let them fear me, if they must. I did not need their thanks for all I had done for them tonight.

I had never had it before.

The administration building wasn't locked; everyone on campus felt safe behind the iron gates that kept the city out. I pushed open the door, my revenants streaming behind me as I made my way downstairs to Master Ostrum's office.

The last time I'd been here, Master Ostrum had just been arrested. As a descendant of the most infamous necromancer in history, Bennum Wellebourne, Master Ostrum was plagued by suspicion. He was never a necromancer, even though he'd secretly kept books on the fourth alchemy and a crucible cage made from Wellebourne's own mummified hand. After he was taken, I'd snuck into Master Ostrum's office, stolen the crucible cage, and left, expecting never to return.

His office was boarded up now, two wooden planks forming an *X* over the door, nailed into the frame. The broken glass window in the door had not been repaired; jagged edges poked up like teeth in a gaping maw all around the frame.

Let me in, I thought, and my revenants surged forward, using their primal strength to rip the boards down and then step back, allowing me entry.

The room was dark. In the basement of the administration building, there were no windows to the outside. But even with the dim light from the hallway, I could tell that there was nothing left for me here.

I tried to swallow down my bitter disappointment. A part of me had hoped that there would be something else here in this room. I was so used to Master Ostrum providing me with the answers I needed. But the books on the shelves were all gone. The desk and chair were empty. There was ash and broken glass and splinters on the floor, debris from Master Ostrum's arrest.

My sister's empty body moved closer to me, hearing my unspoken call for her comfort. Of all my revenants, she was the one most covered in gore. She had fought the hardest. I rested my forehead against hers and wondered if some of the blood that flaked onto me was Master Ostrum's.

Governor Adelaide had had him arrested under suspicion of necromancy, but she had known he was innocent. His execution was a way to get to me. His dead body had been raised and forced to fight me in an attempt by Adelaide to take my crucible. I touched the iron bead at my neck again. While most other crucibles were large, souls did not take up much space. My necromancy crucible was a hollow sphere I could barely squeeze a fingertip into. Size had nothing to do with power, though. I had defeated Adelaide. But doing so meant that Master Ostrum had returned to death fully.

He was gone.

I looked around the empty room.

And so was my last hope of finding something here that could restore my sister's soul.

The events of the night were catching up with me, a tide rolling in, drowning the false hope I'd fabricated.

I started to leave, my feet crunching the broken glass. But a piece of cloth, dark blue and almost invisible in the shadows, caught my eye. I bent down to examine it.

Master Ostrum's coat.

I held the cloth close to me. I could almost still smell his cologne, bergamot oil musty against the wool. My hand gripped the material, my knuckles shaking. It wasn't *fair*. He had been a hard man, but a good one. He had wanted to help others. He had wanted to help me.

And he'd been killed for it.

Tears sprang to my eyes. Master Ostrum had been nothing like my father, but the place that ached inside me was close to the same hollow spot where Papa's love had been. The injustice of his senseless murder reminded me too much of the injustice of the plague itself. Governor Adelaide had been so eager and willing to slaughter anyone, seeing them only as potential puppets in an undead army she could use to overthrow the Emperor.

I looked down at my hand, clenching the blue cloth. Earlier tonight, that hand had been wrapped around a sword. It had pushed the blade through the governor's heart.

No. *I* had done that.

I had watched her die.

I had wanted her to die.

My chin tilted up. *Should I feel regret?* I thought dully.

I didn't.

Cursing, I tossed Master Ostrum's coat to the ground.

It thunked.

I crouched to the floor, rifling through the pockets. There was some spare change, a handkerchief, and inside the front inner pocket was a small book. My heart thudded—I recognized the slender volume.

On my very first day at Northface Harbor, I had shown this little book to Master Ostrum. I snorted bitterly at my memory of the day. I'd been so proud of the journal, the handwritten text by my great-grandmother that listed the herbs and common treatments for illnesses in the north. Master Ostrum had graciously considered it "homeopathic," but I knew now that most of the things my great-grandmother had listed had been weak compared to modern medicinal alchemy. I flipped through the pages.

This journal had first sparked my love and interest in medicinal alchemy, and that spark turned into a flame as the Wasting Death spread throughout the north. It had led me here, to Yūgen, to Master Ostrum, to Grey. And then it had led me back home. I'd returned to my village as a medical student with a golden crucible used to help heal the sick, but I left it a necromancer with an iron bead around my neck.

A flash of deep black caught my eye. I flipped back to the page—fresh ink stained the margin. Master Ostrum's handwriting.

I sucked in a breath.

I held the book up to the open doorway, using the dim light from the hall to read. Passages were underlined; notes littered the margins, especially near the end, where my great-grandmother had interviewed people who had lived through Bennum Wellebourne's revolt.

Master Ostrum's single-minded focus had been to find a cure for the Wasting Death, and he had known early on that it was necromantic in origin. I had to assume he saw something in this journal that hinted about the cause or the solution to the plague, or other signs of necromancy at work.

I gripped the book and stood up. Maybe I would still be able to find the answers I needed.

"Let's go home," I said aloud to my revenants. They followed me as I left the office behind, as I strode past the iron lump of Wellebourne's statue, through the gates, and back into the city.

This was not home.

It would never be home again.

TWO

Grey

I BENT DOWN, ignoring the way my muscles burned with exertion. My body wanted to shut down, but my mind feared the silence sleep would bring. I kept my gaze focused on the soldier's chest, the shiny brass buttons, the crisp lines of the wool coat, as I slipped my hands under his shoulders and heaved his body up. I stared at the starched collar, not the lolling head. I focused on the tangled gilded threads of his epaulette, not the sword embedded in his flesh.

I dragged the soldier's body down the hall, dark crimson smearing a trail on the white marble.

When I had arrived at the castle with Nedra and her army, I had been horrified at the way her revenants attacked. But if I was honest, I'd also been in awe of how efficiently they cut a swath through the highly trained Emperor's Guard.

What I hadn't thought about was how heavy the corpses would be when we cleared them from the hall.

The human body was not designed to be moved after death. It was awkward and unevenly weighted. When death felled a man, the earth should swallow him.

Bile rose in my throat.

When death felled a man, he should not stand again.

"This the last of them?" a small man with wire-rimmed glasses asked me. He held a clipboard, and I wondered if he intended to take a census of the dead.

"As far as I know," I replied. Servants in black coats with green trim moved wearily, carting the bodies of the fallen from the halls and toward a wagon outside, where they could be transported to the pauper's grave in the clear-cut forest at the center of the island.

The man nodded. "Just the tower, then." He looked around, squinting. It wasn't until his eyes landed on me that I realized he had been looking for volunteers. The other servants were busy loading up the last of the soldiers.

"I'm not a—" I started, but the man had already turned, leading me back into the castle. I sighed, the weight of exhaustion sinking in.

I could walk away. But when I looked behind me, to the open door and the night sky beyond, all I could think was that *she* was out there. Nedra. She had left through that door, and I did not want to follow her.

So I followed the man.

"Who are you, anyway?" he asked me as I fell into step behind him.

"A student at Yūgen," I answered, although I wasn't sure that was true anymore. I had still been arrested, even if it had been by a corrupt, traitorous governor. I wondered if saving the Emperor would have any kind of bearing on my status.

"Linden's boy," the man said after looking me up and down. We mounted the stairs leading to the old tower.

"Yeah." My father was high on the council, much more accustomed to walking the halls of the palace than I was.

The man made a derisive snorting sound that seemed utterly incongruous with his short, mousy stature. "I'm Hamish Hamlayton," he said, pausing in front of the iron doors that had been locked earlier, trapping the Emperor behind them. "City planning."

"Grey—gori," I said awkwardly, then repeated my name more clearly. "Greggori. Astor."

"Yes," Hamish said, but his attention was elsewhere. His rounded shoulders hunched a little, reminding me of the rats we kept caged at Yūgen for alchemical experiments, the ones that stood on their hind legs and sniffed the air, their lips curling over their fangs.

I wondered how such a man had not only found himself on the governing council, but become something of a leader in clearing out the bodies. Hamish held the door open for me and caught my curious look. I was still trying to place him; I thought I'd known most of Father's fellow councilmen. "City planning," he said again, stressing the words. "Streets and sewers."

It clicked then. Father had often mocked the role. City planning was the least respected position on the council, a near-thankless task with twice the work and none of the prestige other council members enjoyed.

I stepped inside the room that had been used to imprison the Emperor. It smelled sharply of metal—unsurprising, as iron covered the walls, a remnant of when the chamber had been used to imprison Bennum Wellebourne, the original traitor of Lunar Island. But the metallic twinge was so sharp I could almost taste it.

Blood, I realized, looking down at the floor. It pooled on the dark metal, drying and sticky, clinging to my boots.

My eyes followed the lamplight flickering on the bodies.

The one closest to me was a man. Strange, wasn't it, that I had spent every evening in his office for a year, that I had sat across from his desk and recited my lessons like a good lad, that I had spoken to him more than my own father, and yet, in death, I almost didn't recognize him. How could the escape of a soul change a body so much? But it had. It made Master Ostrum's face slacker, his eyes duller. He didn't look asleep, as I'd often heard death described.

He just looked dead.

"Did you know him?" Hamish asked, hefting another body around and positioning it so that he could drag it down the stairs and to the hallway.

"Yes," I said simply.

Hamish thumped down the stairs, then paused, waiting for me. I picked up Master Ostrum from under the shoulders, struggling with his limp weight and the joints in his body that were already stiffening. He was larger than me, and I staggered under his weight, but I would not let his body bounce on the steps and drag along the floor like the one Hamish was weighed down with. Master Ostrum deserved more than that. I could give him so little now, but I at least had respect.

By the time I reached the cart in the hall, hefting Master Ostrum's body up, Hamish was waiting for me. I finally saw which body he had moved so callously out of the iron chamber.

Governor Adelaide's lifeless eyes stared up at the ceiling, one lid half-opened, squinting up at the ceiling. Someone had removed the sword Nedra had used to kill her, but the wound remained, a stain of black-burgundy across her dress.

Master Ostrum no longer looked like himself in death. But when Nedra had plunged the sword into Adelaide's chest, piercing the governor's heart and watching the life drain from her, Nedra had not looked like herself either.

THREE

Nedra

THE DOORS OF the quarantine hospital swung open as I mounted the front steps. A dozen or so people rushed out, led by a middle-aged man—Dannix, the living father of one of my revenants. He ran down the steps, straight past me and to Ronan, his son whom I had raised from the dead the night I became a necromancer.

The other people followed Dannix's lead, running into the crowd of revenants and reaching for their dead loved ones. I paused, and so the revenants paused. My eyes went to Ronan, who stood awkwardly in his father's embrace. Dannix pulled back from the hug, wiping a globule of drying blood from his son's face, then picking at his hair, where gore clung to the dark strands. He gagged as he withdrew a chunk of flesh that must have been severed from a soldier during the battle.

Dannix whirled around on me. "Where did you take my son?" he roared, advancing.

Calm, I told my revenants. I did not need them to protect me from a single angry man.

"You made him get up in the middle of the night, you forced him like he was in some sort of trance to follow you, and you come back hours later like *this*?" he said, thrusting his hand, smeared with old blood, at me.

"I needed Ronan's help," I said evenly. I looked out at the other living people, each simmering with rage but too afraid to stand up to me as Dannix did, their eyes sliding away from mine as I met their gaze coolly. "I needed all their help."

"To fight a battle?" Dannix shouted incredulously.

"Yes," I said. I turned and headed back up the stairs toward the hospital. My revenants followed, even Ronan, and Dannix scrambled after us. He grabbed his son by the wrist and dragged him closer to me.

"He's a child," he hissed at me, anger seething through his voice.

I didn't pause, but my look made Dannix stumble back. "Don't be simple," I sneered. "He was no longer a boy the second he died."

The look on the man's face was as shocked and horrified as the one Governor Adelaide had given me as I sliced into her heart with a steel blade. A part of me wished I could wrap the spoken words around my fingers, like I could grasp a soul, and slip them back past my own lips, swallowing them down forever. But of course, I could not. I let the silence hang between us as Ronan slipped his hand free of his father's grip and followed me through the open mahogany doors into the hospital. Once all the dead were inside, the living followed.

I headed to the stairs leading up to the clock tower, the place I had claimed as my own. I knew that there was a bed with blankets waiting for me beneath the steady ticking of the giant clock, but the idea of climbing all those stairs suddenly wearied me. I pushed the exhaustion away, but I could not summon the strength to mount the steps.

"You can't just do this!" Dannix was not yet done with me. He strode across the tiled floor, stopping several meters before he reached me. "I'm his father! If you want to wage war on the Empire like Wellebourne, fine, but not with my son!"

I stared at him coldly, and I could see his courage falter. Every single one of my revenants turned to face him, their dead eyes leveled on his face, twisted with rage. I strode forward, and my revenants parted before me, each one moving in perfect sync. I stepped uncomfortably close to Dannix, and he backed away from me, stopping abruptly against the stone wall. I could smell his breath, count the individual hairs sprouting from his cheeks.

I felt rather than heard the warning from my revenants. Not about Dannix and his silly fight with me, but a real threat. I whirled away from the angry man, striding back to the mahogany door, my exhaustion forgotten for the moment.

Small ships floated on the black water, their bows pointed toward the quarantine hospital. Six—no, eight.

"What are they doing?" Dannix had followed me outside.

Set a watch, I whispered silently in my mind, the words echoing in the minds of all my revenants. They streamed out in formation, some along the steps, others heading around the shore on either side of the hospital's island. In moments, I had eyes watching each direction.

"Are those ships going to dock?" Dannix asked. "What do they want?"

"It's a warning," I whispered. I hoped.

News of the battle at the castle must have traveled quickly. Why else would they be here, now? It did not matter that I had killed a necromancer. I *was* a necromancer. I had stopped the plague, but did these people in their threatening ships know that? Did they care?

"Are they going to attack?" Dannix asked warily.

The ships didn't move.

"Not tonight," I said finally, turning to go back inside.

In truth, however, my certainty was false. I could only hope that, at least for now, their fear of me outweighed their indignation. Because that was the only weapon I had left.

Fear.

FOUR

Grey

I JUMPED AT a sound I didn't recognize, so startled that I burst from sleep. Light flooded the room, blinding me. I struggled to sit up, a weight sliding off my body. Heavy damask. My brain fought through the fog of exhaustion.

I was in a bed. A large, ornate bed, with heavy drapes that had been flung open by a servant.

"Master Astor," the servant said, no hint of humor at the rhyme. "You have been summoned."

"Summoned?" I looked around the room. After the bodies had been cleared from the palace, Hamish, the city planner, had offered me a bed here. I had accepted, too exhausted to think of where else I could sleep. I'd left Yūgen Academy in cuffs; I couldn't very well stroll into my dormitory room. And my parents' home was not a home to me. It never had been. When I'd first left for Yūgen, I'd sworn to never spend another night there.

"His Imperial Majesty has summoned you," the servant pressed again.

Finally, his words sank in. The Emperor. Wanted me. I looked down at myself. I'd been so bone-weary last night that I had collapsed on the blue-and-gold-damask-covered bed, pausing only to strip off my blood-crusted shirt and pants. I sat on the silk sheets in nothing but my undergarments, and, when I looked back, I could see I'd stained the luxurious cloth with the previous day's grime.

14

"We have time for ablutions," the servant said in a lower voice. "But we should hurry," he added.

After quickly cleaning and dressing in a set of simple, borrowed clothes the servant produced for me, I rushed down the hall. The servant allowed me to go first, as was proper, but subtly touched my elbow when it was time to turn down a different corridor. He cleared his throat when we reached an ornately carved mahogany door with a shining brass knob. Another servant stepped out and led me inside a bedroom cast in shadows.

"Is he here?" a voice said from behind the dark curtains of the bed.

My eyes adjusted to the dim light slowly as I padded across the thick carpet. This was not at all like the bedroom I'd been given. Five or six times larger, with a full-size table on one side, floor-to-ceiling windows hidden by silken drapes, and a desk, behind which stood a secretary with a quill at the ready. The room held nearly two dozen servants and nobles and yet did not feel crowded at all.

A man close to my age—the Emperor—lay propped up on pillows in the center of an enormous bed, the four posts scraping the ceiling and holding back velvet drapes spangled with gold thread. I finally met the Emperor's eyes. His face was pale and wan, his cheeks sunken. I was reminded harshly of the last time I'd seen him—groveling on the floor, a prisoner for months, subject to Governor Adelaide's whims. He somehow looked smaller and weaker here, surrounded by pillows, than he had on the iron floor.

"Greggori Astor," the Emperor said in a soft voice that still commanded respect.

Emperor Auguste gazed out at the council members assembled in the room with hooded eyes. There were more than thirty men and women on the regular council, but less than half were gathered here now.

"I have learned," Emperor Auguste said, his voice growing stronger as he spoke, "that I cannot trust this colony to be ruled under a regent. Not when the regent is someone like Adelaide, and her council mostly made of vipers."

He coughed, his body falling against the pillows, but his eyes were sharp as they roved around the room. "You all know the law. I had chosen Governor Adelaide because her opposition, Lord Anton, was openly proposing secession. I had made it clear when I overrode the vote and appointed Adelaide that such proceedings would not be tolerated. And yet most of the council was so busy trying to undermine my authority that they neglected to see Adelaide was a necromancer poisoning the very people they were supposed to protect."

The full impact of his words settled on me. All of the council members who'd voted for Anton, including my father, weren't here. My stomach sank. Was Father even now in the dungeons below, awaiting trial for treason?

As if reading my thoughts, the Emperor continued. "The council members whose selfish neglect led to this disaster on Lunar Island *will* face punishment." He paused, his eyes skimming the crowd, resting on no one in particular. "The ones fully in support of Adelaide's blasphemous necromancy or who openly advocated for rebellion obviously must be dealt with first. We've arrested five." He rattled the names off quickly—none of them Linden Astor, who I knew had been integral in gathering supporters to break from the Empire. "I am not certain we've weeded out every threat, but know that the remaining traitors who occupied council seats *will* be found and tried for their crimes against the Empire."

My eyes darted around the room at the remaining council members. I wondered if the woman by the door shifted because she was afraid of being found out, or because she was simply uncomfortable. I

16

wondered if the man standing to my left didn't meet my eyes because he had something to hide, or because his mind was elsewhere.

"Sir," a man near the window said, taking a step closer to the Emperor's bed. "What about . . . ?" He glanced around at the other council members in the room. I recognized him from one of Father's dinners—Finip Brundl; he did something with exportation tariffs. When he didn't continue, the Emperor waved his hand at him impatiently. "What about the necromancer?" Finip said, all in a rush.

A chill descended on the room. I kept my eyes trained on the Emperor, whose stony expression betrayed no hint of his thoughts.

"What about her?" the Emperor asked without inflection.

"She's—" Finip turned to the window, which faced the bay. "She's out there still, Your Imperial Majesty. She's violated every law of the Empire and our gods, and yet no charge has been made against her. You yourself saw the evidence of her crime—"

The Emperor silenced Finip with a flick of his fingers. "I saw the evidence," he said in a clear, strong voice, "when she used her undead revenants to *save* me."

Hope surged in my heart for Nedra.

"But you are correct, Brundl," the Emperor continued. Finip looked taken aback that the Emperor knew his name. "What kind of leader would I be to allow a murdering necromancer to go free merely because she saved my life?" His eyes drifted as he contemplated his next words. "We must have a trial," he said, his voice so low that, had it not been silent in the room, I doubted anyone would have heard him.

After a moment, he glanced up. "You may all go," the Emperor said.

The council members hurried to the door. Finip Brundl was among the last to leave. Another man gripped his elbow, whispering in a low undertone, "Don't press it."

I started to the door.

"Not you." Emperor Auguste's full attention was on me, his piercing eyes trained on me. "Stay." My feet rooted to the floor.

Finip glared at me before the servant shut the door in his face.

The Emperor smiled and nodded to a chair beside his bed. I hesitated—his gleaming white teeth seemed both an invitation and a threat.

I sat. "Are you . . . recovering well?"

"No," the Emperor said. I blinked, unaccustomed to such brutal honesty.

"I was locked away for half a year, forced to live on nothing but scraps, with barely a ray of sunlight touching my skin. I am not well," the Emperor elaborated, emphasizing the last sentence. He coughed again, dry and raspy. "But neither is this colony, and that is my sole concern right now."

Father was wrong, I thought. He always acted as if every person in authority held power only for the glory and riches, but it seemed like the Emperor actually cared.

"It's not just Adelaide's necromancy, although the plague she cursed this land with was a disaster deadlier and more tragic than any I've yet seen," the Emperor continued. "It would be naive of me to think that Lunar Island's problems are limited to one necromancer with a lust for power."

Nedra had been the one to show me just how bad things could be on our island. At Yūgen, the lads like Tomus had popularized and romanticized rebellion, but I knew they were just parroting what their fathers were saying. It was easy for the rich who wanted to be richer to blame tariffs rather than their own faults or bad luck. Nedra had shown me true poverty, desperation, and hopelessness. In the factories and the hospital, and, I assumed, throughout the north. Those people had actually had a reason for rebellion. They had so little, and that was before the plague. Now they had even less, and it wasn't hard to imagine that rage might fill the hole death had left behind.

The Emperor looked up at me, thin red veins standing out against the whites of his eyes. We were close to the same age, but the Emperor's eyes looked ancient. And sad. "There is no one on this island that I trust," he said, his voice clearer.

I must surely be among those who did not merit trust. Not only was my father a marked man, but although I had worked to free the Emperor, I had also fought beside a necromancer.

"What will you do with the traitors?" I asked, careful to keep my tone neutral.

The Emperor's eyes did not waver from mine. "I don't know," he said finally. "People are angry. Whenever there is a tragedy—and with the plague, there were thousands of tragedies—people look for someone to blame."

"They should blame Adelaide," I spat.

"And they would have. She would have hung for her crimes. Just as anyone who practices necromancy should."

Nedra's name was unspoken between us.

"She's not like Adelaide," I said quickly. "She's not trying to—"

The Emperor's cold gaze settled on me. "Necromancy is forbidden."

Necromancy was against every law of gods and man. The punishment was death. Once, hundreds of years ago, it had been merely taboo, a dangerous pastime of alchemists who no longer feared the wrath of vengeful gods. After Bennum Wellebourne's revolt against the Empire using an army of the undead, it became the highest crime, the worst form of treachery.

"You're going to put Nedra on trial," I said. It wasn't a question.

"I will be fair," the Emperor promised.

But that was the problem. *Fair* was recognizing Nedra had broken the law. *Fair* was a noose.

The Emperor allowed me to see a bit of emotion on his face, and I was surprised to recognize regret etched in the deep set of his brow. "I'm not ignorant of how she helped me," he said finally. "But surely you must see that I have to uphold the law. I can . . . delay the inevitable. Perhaps indefinitely." He sighed. "But perhaps not."

"She has an army." The words tumbled out.

Emperor Auguste raised an eyebrow.

"I mean," I continued, "she has revenants. Lots of them. You saw them. She could have taken the whole castle last night. She could have killed you. She could have claimed the whole island."

"But she didn't, is that your point?"

I chewed on my lip. That was my point. Nedra could have used her army of the dead for evil. But instead, she had freed the Emperor and left. Back to her island. With her dead.

"Before they were her subjects, they were mine," the Emperor said. "Necromancy is worse than treason. It betrays both the Empire and the gods." He paused, looking at me. "But I understand what you're getting at. Nedra is not a direct threat to me or the Empire. Our resources will focus on finding the traitorous seeds of rebellion first instead."

People like my father.

We sat in silence for several moments. I wondered if the Emperor was waiting to see whether I would try to defend Father the way I had Nedra. I did not speak.

"What does it take," the Emperor said eventually, breaking the silence, "for a girl to choose to be a monster?"

"I don't think it's a choice," I said softly.

The Emperor looked at me, surprise in his eyes. "Of course it is."

FIVE

Nedra

PAPA USED TO read to Ernesta and me every night before bed. One of Nessie's favorite books was a collection of short stories—fairy tales, really—that Papa would read aloud to us long after the age we outgrew them. Of all the stories, Papa loved "The Boy-Monster" the best, but Nessie always tried to get him to skip it. There was no kissing in that story.

Usually Papa did nothing but read the story and tell us good night. But I remember one night that was different. "In the deep, dark woods," Papa said, his voice sonorous. Every story in the book started with those words. "There lived a boy who was a monster."

"And everyone hated him and then he died and no one cared because he was a monster, the end," Ernesta said. "Can't we read anything else?"

"No. This is my favorite story of all time." I stuck my tongue out at her.

Papa lowered the book, giving Nessie a quizzical look. "Is that what you think this story is about?" he asked.

Nessie had this way of cocking her eyebrow and glaring at someone that usually made the kids our age cower in fear. But Papa just wrinkled his nose at her and tapped her lightly on the head with the book. "'The Boy-Monster' isn't about a boy who's a monster," he said. "It's not about a monster at all."

Nessie rolled her eyes, but I said, "So what's the story about, then?"

"The other people in the forest. They're the real monsters." Papa flipped the book's pages to the illustration in the middle of the story. It showed a shadow of something hulking, with horns and fur, but the picture's main focus was a group of people—mostly children but several adults—all shouting at the monster just beyond the page, pointing their fingers and sneering at him. One person held a stone, his arm cocked to hurl it at the monster. A woodcutter gripped her axe, her jaw set with steely determination.

"The monster isn't real," Papa said. "You both get that, right?"

I leaned up in bed, staring at the picture on the page. Of course the monster was real. I could see his shadow.

Papa subtly adjusted the book so I could see it better, but he spoke to both of us. "The monster is just someone who's different. That's why there's no picture of him in the book. Because we make monsters of men by our imaginations alone."

"He's different because he has horns and claws and fangs and eats people," Nessie pointed out.

"Where in the story does it say that?" Papa challenged. He dropped the book on Nessie's bed and nudged it closer to her when she didn't pick it up.

I ran through the story in my head. Certainly the villagers and people in the forest *called* the boy a monster and said he did terrible things, but in the story itself, he didn't actually *do* anything bad. He stole bread, not a child, to eat, and only because he was cold and hungry. Nowhere in the story did the boy have fangs or horns or claws—only the hint of them in the shadowy illustration.

The only reason I had thought the story was about a monster was because of the title and the way the other characters described the boy. Was that all it took to make a monster? A label and the accusations of others?

"The story is a lesson," Papa said, taking the book from Nessie and closing it. "All stories are. Not like in your textbooks during class, but lessons on how to be human."

Nessie laughed. "Good thing I'm a natural," she said, flicking her braid over her shoulder.

"Even if the boy were a monster," Papa continued, "imagine how the story would be different if the villagers hadn't been so scared."

"You can't turn off fear," I said. My voice was softer than Nessie's, because Nessie was never scared of anything.

"I think you can," Papa said.

I know now that he was right. You can burn fear away after every nightmare you've ever had comes true.

Papa patted the book and then stood up. "Treating someone with fear when they are merely different from you is one of the worst things you can do. Perhaps the only thing worse than fear is apathy. Fear makes us do horrible things to people. Apathy makes us allow horrible things to happen to them. When we act in fear—or when we *don't* act out of apathy—that is when we become the monster."

The first thing I heard when I woke up in the morning were the whispers of my revenants, who had stood in silent guard all night long, informing me that the ships still surrounded the island.

I was the monster now, no matter what Papa had said.

And it was time for me to invoke some fear. Or, at least, *more* of it. A bitter smile curved my lips. That was why they were here, after all. Men, when afraid, lashed out. They needed to remind me— they needed to remind *themselves*—that they were not scared of my undead army.

And I needed to remind them that they should be.

Outside, a few of the living people who'd stayed with their raised dead were shivering in the early morning light.

"They're local," Dannix told me when I approached. He stood near his son, Ronan, who was stationed at the top of the steps in front of the big mahogany doors leading into the quarantine hospital. Ernesta stayed silently by my side. The rest of my revenants spanned the perimeter of the island.

When I didn't answer him, Dannix said, pointing, "Those are fishing boats. They've got markings from the cliff villages."

It was true, although these southern villages were hardly worthy of the label. They were more akin to a cluster of transient men and women who lived primarily on their boats, only occasionally dwelling in the shacks beneath the cliffs to the southern side of the island.

"I thought the Emperor might come to arrest you," Dannix continued in a low voice. "But these are not the Emperor's men. They're from Lunar Island. They're our people."

"I don't have a people," I said. I stopped having a people the day they picked up stones and drove me and my sister back into our house, trapping us inside with the rotting, plague-ridden corpses of my parents.

I reached out with my mind to the ten nearest revenants. *Go*, I ordered them, knowing that they understood my intention.

"Hey!" Dannix shouted as Ronan followed the other revenants silently down the steps toward the red lacquered boat I had acquired from the Emperor's men weeks ago.

"Go inside if you can't bear to watch," I said in a cold voice, and Dannix silenced. I could feel his apprehension swirling around him like mist, but I ignored him, watching my revenants instead. They hurried down the steps, boarding the Emperor's boat. Within moments, they were sailing toward the smaller fishing boats, cutting through the cold gray waves like a blade.

A high-pitched whistle blared. A signal to the other ships. My revenants watching at the back of the island let me know that the ships there were heading to the front. Eleven boats against my one. Forty or so sailors against my ten.

It was hardly a fair fight. My smile curved deeper.

Before the reinforcements from the back could reach my red ship, it had drawn beside the closest fishing boats. Distantly, I could hear the fishermen shouting at my revenants, warning them to stay back. My ship cut closer. The fishing boats did not have cannons or defense, but the men lit torches and hurled them toward the red ship.

Let it burn, I told my revenants in my mind. My body was a tightly coiled spring. I would do nothing. I would let these men destroy themselves.

The revenants on the deck stood still as flames leapt across the wood, each one of them staring down a different fishing boat.

And then the fire reached the black powder for the cannons.

The Emperor's boat exploded in a deafening burst of red and yellow and orange. Heavy black smoke billowed over the ship, the stench so acrid I could smell it from where I stood at the top of the stairs. The boat cracked in half, timbers splintering, and my revenants, limp like dolls, were catapulted into the air before smashing against the waves and sinking down, down, down. Over the reverberating sound of the crackling, burning boards I could hear the men on the fishing boats cheering as my beautiful red warship sank beneath the cold water of the bay.

"No!" Dannix gasped, his eyes searching the wreckage.

"Peace," I said, somewhat impatiently.

"But my son—!"

"You cannot kill what is already dead."

Dannix's mouth snapped shut, his teeth clacking together.

Ronan, Dannix's boy, was one of the first to crest the debris-ridden waves. His head bobbed out of the dark water, and he started to swim to the closest ship. I bit my lip in anticipation, eagerly scanning the water. My revenants' hands reached up from the waves, digging their fingers into the wood of the nearest ship, dragging their bodies up.

Sailors on the other boats started shouting and pointing as my undead crawled like cursed spiders over the hull of the first ship. The sailors aboard the chosen vessel screamed, throwing objects down in an attempt to dislodge the revenants crawling closer and closer to their deck. One man swept a lit torch down, hoping to divert my undead, but instead, the black-tar-sealed wood caught fire, flames licking down to the water.

My revenants pulled themselves over the railing, landing on the deck of the first boat, water streaming from their bodies, the droplets turning to steam as the fire spread.

The sailors leapt into the water, ignoring the dangers of the sinking red warship, the splintering debris, the fire smoking at the water's lip. The water churned as they swam furiously toward the other boats. Their panic drove them to frenzy when my revenants followed them into the water, but they were swimming back to me, not chasing the sailors.

By the time Ronan and the others mounted the steps, my warship had sunk beneath the waves and the fishing boat was alight with flames. It would be gone soon enough.

Two ships sacrificed for one message. Still, effective. I hoped.

SIX

Grey

HAMISH HAMLAYTON SPOTTED me in the corridor after I left the Emperor's bedroom. "Do you need help?" he asked.

I couldn't hide my self-deprecating smirk. If he only knew the thoughts and worries churning in my mind. But I understood what he meant. "This place is a bit of a labyrinth."

He nodded. "Back to your rooms?" he asked.

I hesitated. "Actually, could you take me to the chapel?" I'd been there once before, when I was a boy and my father had volunteered my services as a candle bearer during an Empire Day service. I'd never been very religious, even then, but when Nedra had felt hopeless, she'd found some sort of peace at the Yūgen chapel. I didn't know if she ever found answers there, but if I couldn't feel closer to the gods, perhaps I could feel closer to her.

We turned again and then went down a set of stairs to the ground floor, walking in relative silence until Hamish stopped in front of an arched wooden door.

I pushed it open, then turned back to Hamish. "Thank you," I said.

Hamish looked at me with consternation, as if he wanted to tell me something important but couldn't find the right words. Finally, he said, "The Emperor has condemned all homes and lands held by . . ."

"Traitors," I supplied, biting off the word.

Hamish nodded. "They're to go to temporary control of the closest relative. Your father's estates . . . I'm handling the paperwork myself. I'll expedite the process as they go to you."

"Thank you," I said, because I could think of nothing else to say.

"It's fallen on me to allocate residencies. The Emperor made note that you're to stay in the palace as long as you like," Hamish added. "I just wanted to make sure you knew you didn't have to."

I frowned. Before I could answer, Hamish nodded in farewell and strode back down the hall.

The chapel jutted out from the main castle, three sides in the center of the courtyard. The clear windows along the west and east walls looked out onto flowering sakoola trees, the soft yellow petals dancing on the light breeze outside. The north wall was dominated by the circular eye window, shades of blue and green and brown juxtaposed with dark gray grout, symbolic of Oryous's eye ever watching over us. Colorful light from the stained glass played with the shadows at my feet.

I took a step closer to the center of the chapel, my shoes echoing on the stone.

I didn't know what to do.

I was raised to claim a religion but not to believe in it. My family was Oryon because the Emperor was; everyone in the Empire was. We prayed at funerals and hosted holy day feasts.

But there was never a moment in my life when I had felt there was no one I could turn to but the gods.

What did Nedra say when she prayed? Did she find answers or only more questions?

I closed my eyes, but that felt ridiculous. I opened them but had nowhere to look. Finally, frustrated, I turned on my heel and strode back to the door.

But I stopped, my hand on the iron loop of a handle. I didn't want to go back to the rooms the Emperor had allowed me in the castle. I didn't want to go back to Yūgen, a place that had so easily turned its back on Nedra. I didn't want to go back to the house I had been raised in; my father was a traitor on the run, and there was no memory there I wanted to relive.

I wanted to go home, but the only home I had left was Nedra herself.

And I wasn't sure she wanted me.

SEVEN

Nedra

WITH THE THREAT of the fishing boats gone—for now, at least—
I returned to my clock tower. I kept only Nessie near me, a silent
watcher as I opened my great-grandmother's journal. The gears of the
massive clock ticked by while I slowly turned the pages, examining
Master Ostrum's notes in the margins.

The scribbled words were frustratingly vague. I had no doubt
that they had meant something to him, and, likely, Master Ostrum
had planned on sharing what he'd discovered with me, the only student he'd shared his dark theories with. But phrases like "refer to
Whitmore's" or "418" or "similar to the effects in Almand's theory"
meant very little to me, and I couldn't see their connection to necromancy. The numbers likely referred to other books or papers, but I
didn't know which ones.

I kept reading anyway. It was a slim hope, to find something hidden within the text I'd read dozens of times, but it was the only hope
I had left.

"Why aren't you like them?" I asked softly, even though I knew
Nessie couldn't answer me. She was the first person I had raised, and
perhaps I had irrevocably damaged her soul when I tried to pull it
back from Death. But none of my other revenants were an empty shell.
They weren't the humans they once had been either, but they were, at
the very least, *more*. If I couldn't make Ernesta exactly as she had been
before she died, a vivid flame of life, I would settle for a spark.

I wasn't sure how much time had passed when I finally came across a page that'd been circled in Master Ostrum's heavy hand, highlighting a list of medical tools. I'd read the passage before—I'd read the entire journal over and over before coming to Yūgen. But it was only now that I'd learned necromancy that I realized it was important.

Dowsing rod—locate fluids
Pendulum—draw out poison
Stone hammer—eradicate bile
Crystal shard—rejuvenation
Plaster of willow—heal a sprain
Orcine sinew straps—reduce a tumor

I examined the passage, trying to see why Master Ostrum would bother marking it. The nearly illegible word he'd scribbled in the margin seemed to say "collector" or maybe "collection," and I wondered if he was referring to something in his own collection of inherited objects from Bennum Wellebourne.

Most of the items on the list were, at best, weak substitutions for actual medicine. I stared at the list for several long moments, wondering, praying for understanding.

No answer came.

I tossed the little book onto my desk. It landed facedown, and for a moment, I felt bad for mistreating it. I was still, after everything, my father's daughter. I brushed my fingertips over the leather, feeling the insignia stamped into the back. A rising sun with six pointed spikes to represent the six original tribes that joined together to form the start of the Allyrian Empire. This notebook had been imported from the mainland, probably from the capital city of Miraband, like most of the small luxury items in those early days of the colony, before Lunar Island had set up its own manufacturing.

It wasn't the book's fault—or Master Ostrum's—that there was nothing here that could help me. It was a feeble hope, anyway, the kind easiest to break.

If I wanted answers, I'd have to find them myself.

My hand ached as I clutched my tiny iron crucible. Not my right hand—my left hand, the one that had been obliterated when I'd become a necromancer. I winced in pain as I lifted my residual limb. The flesh ended above my elbow, scars stretching over the too-pink skin at the end. But a shadow hand extended past that, a dark hand made of nothing. I could see it. My revenants could see it. But no one else.

What else could I see, now that I was a necromancer?

I turned to my twin sister. "Fetch me a mirror."

Without a word she spun on her heel and raced down the spiral staircase. She could sense the urgency in my command, and it took her only moments to return, her feet pounding up the stairs. She had ripped a gilt-framed mirror from a wall within the hospital so forcefully that plaster clung to the edges. She set it down in front of me, and for a moment we were both reflected in the smudged surface. Even though she was the one who'd lost her life, I looked like a ghost next to her, my hair a shock of white after my battle with Governor Adelaide, a stark contrast to her solid black tresses.

We used to be so similar that sometimes even our own mother couldn't tell us apart. But it was more than just the hair now. Her eyes were hollow; mine were bright. Her skin was ashen but unblemished; mine was haggard from lack of sleep. Her body was cool to the touch. I still had my fire.

I turned to the mirror. I had never tried to see my own soul before. I looked now.

It was harder to see a soul in a living person. Life filters the light. But souls were easiest to glimpse in the eyes since light clung to the irises. And there . . . *there.* A bit of gold sparkling in my own brown eyes, trailing across my skin, swirling over my heart.

Unconsciously, I raised my right hand, tugging my shirt down and exposing my breast, the heart that lay under it, the light that seemed a bit more visible there.

I cast my eyes to my residual limb, the arm Death had taken. I held it in front of me. The shadow arm did not reflect in the mirror.

I had used this shadow arm to pull the souls from Governor Adelaide's crucible, breaking it and ending the plague. I had used it to grasp the governor's own soul, forcing her to be still as I drove a sword through her heart. I had dipped the incorporeal fingers into corpses, pulling up the dregs of their souls to reanimate them.

Now I let my shadowy fingers trail along my skin. I shuddered, my throat gagging at my own touch. So *cold.*

Tears sprang into my eyes—not of sorrow, but of horror. I wanted nothing more than to break free of my own touch. But I was so full of soul, of life. Could I . . . ? I glanced at Nessie. Could I give something of myself to her?

I forced myself to stay still. My shadow hand paused over my heart. I glanced at the mirror. My own eyes were wide with terror, sweat beading on my forehead. I swallowed, hard.

And I plunged my hand into my skin.

EIGHT

Nedra

MY MOUTH DROPPED open, but I choked on air, unable to scream the way my body instinctively longed to. The sensation split my mind in two: part of me deeply aware of the *wrongness* of the shadow entering my own body, sliding between my muscles, fingering through my ribs; the other part of me insatiably hungry for the sensation, relishing the way the shadow seemed to feed upon my life.

When my hand brushed against my heart, it stopped beating.

The color drained from my face. In the mirror, I could see myself. Dying.

Some part of me had enough life left to pull my hand back, and the shadow withdrew. My heart beat—once—tentatively, as if unsure of how to operate. Then another thud, stronger, defiant.

I gasped for air.

My living body pulled at the shoulder attached to the shadow arm, revolting against my brain that whispered death would give me peace. I forced my shadow arm to withdraw more slowly than felt natural, and when the fingers finally pulled away from my skin, they were twined around a single golden thread.

Not my whole soul, but a piece of it. A living person was a tapestry of light; I could afford to unravel this one string. It remained connected on one end to my heart; the other end floated as if being lifted by an ethereal breeze.

I pulled my iron crucible closer with my right arm. I knew if I just held the thread of light to my sister's empty body, it would fade to nothing. Souls had to travel through the crucible before my necromantic powers could affect them.

And—my breath caught. Deep within the blood iron, I could sense the near-invisible traces of my family, irrevocably entwined with the metal. I could not touch them. Not with my flesh, not with my shadow arm. But perhaps . . .

I poised the thread of my own soul over the crucible's lip, then used my shadow hand to push it inside.

My mind filled with—not images, exactly, but *feelings*, impossible to put into words. Chaos tumbled through me, as if the thread of my soul had opened a floodgate of hundreds of different ideas and memories and emotions and tastes and scents and hopes and nightmares and fears and loves. They swarmed over me, filling me up, drowning out *myself* with *other*.

I felt what it was to die—over and over, from each of my revenants. I felt the loves they lost, the hopes that died with their bodies. I experienced each soul that had passed through my crucible.

Somewhere, deep, deep in my mind, I thought, *Further in*.

My parents and my sister had been the first souls to touch my crucible. They were the furthest away.

The thread of my soul dove deeper.

It swirled in a tornado of echoes, unable to pick apart the three individual souls of the people I loved the most, unable to find a way through to my sister. My parents were already barely a whisper within the crucible; how could I find them amid such *noise*?

Love.

I homed in on that feeling, the familiar feeling of my parents' love for me, my sister's hand in my own, family dinners, laughter by the fire, my father's voice as he read aloud to us at night, my mother's arms wrapped around me, the belief that this was eternal, the security and sense of safety that existed by their mere presence.

And I found them.

The other souls faded to silence.

My soul found my parents' souls. Nothing conscious—I could not talk to them, but I could feel them.

I could feel their love.

I sobbed, my back bending and my chest caving in with the overwhelming emotion of it all.

And then I felt Nessie.

Her soul was stronger—there was more of it within the crucible. The iron had been forged with my parents' ashes, but it was bound together by my sister's soul, whole and freshly freed from her body at its formation.

Neddie, she said, her voice clear and loud in my mind.

Take it, I thought, shoving my own bit of soul toward the incorporeal presence that I sensed was the truest part of her left. I felt resistance, though I wasn't sure if it was her or the crucible or the limits of my untrained power. I was operating so blindly, relying on instinct. *Let it be enough, let* me *be enough, please, please*—

And then the shell of my sister's body twitched. My eyes grew round as Ernesta stepped closer. Her face—for the first time since she had died—took on life. Her eyes shot to mine, and I knew—I *knew*— she was seeing me, *really* seeing me, as clear and present and true as anything.

I wanted to spin around and grab her, hug her to me. But I was careful to keep the strand of my soul in the crucible. It was the lifeline, the connection between us.

"Neddie," Ernesta said, hope and wonder in her voice. Her voice. From her lips.

She was back with me.

And then her eyes filled with a horror deeper than any I'd ever seen before.

"Nedra," she gasped, her voice already weaker. I turned to the thread of my soul that connected us—it was dimming. I shivered, suddenly aware of the cold.

"No," Ernesta said.

At first I thought she meant, "No, it's too soon to go." Because already the light was fading from her eyes, the life evaporating from her body. I could see her consciousness slipping away.

But then the darkness touched me, and I felt the source of Nessie's terror. Without my noticing, black had begun to stain the golden thread of light from my heart, creeping up from the base of my crucible. Fear washed over me.

"Don't," Nessie said, the word barely a whisper.

And then she was hollow again, nothing more than a shell with no hint of her own soul.

I stared down at the thread that extended from my heart into the iron crucible. It was turning the deepest kind of black, an utter absence of light, the kind of blackness that shouldn't exist.

My body shuddered.

It was so *cold*.

The blackness stretched out, swallowing the once-golden thread. I watched, as if entranced, as the darkness traveled the length of the thread.

And up toward my heart.

The moment the black touched my skin, my body seized so violently that I fell out of my chair. The mirror on the table slid down, smashing against the tabletop and sending shards of silvery glass over my body. A sliver sliced into my cheek and blood flowed out, so hot it seemed to steam against my icy skin.

My eyes darted to Ernesta. For a moment—for a single, shining moment—she had been herself.

But now her body stared at me impassively, watching me die.

I could die, I realized somewhat dully. And Death did not, in this moment, feel like an enemy. My heart slowed. *I am dying.*

Don't, I heard Nessie's whisper again, only a memory. But it was enough. I *pulled* with my shadow hand, wrenching the black thread free.

I had watched my parents die, I had carved runes upon their cold flesh, I had torn my sister's soul free of its body, and I had held the soul of a living person in place while I killed her. *I would not succumb to this.*

Death would never claim me so easily.

The black strand fizzled in my shadow arm, writhing like a snake whose head had been sliced off, twitching violently in the throes of death.

Then it stilled and faded to nothing.

I panted on the ground, the silvery shards of the broken mirror scattered on the floor around me. I had torn myself away from the dark power, but at what cost? Had I just lost a bit of my own soul for one moment with Nessie?

If I tried it again, would I be able to break free?

NINE

Nedra

MY BACK CRACKED and my neck popped as I tried to remind my body what life was like.

Ernesta stared at me.

For all it had cost me, I had had my Nessie back. I pushed up off my knees, standing up slowly, then reached for my sister.

I raised my right hand to my chest, feeling the place where my heart was. There should be a scar there, physical evidence of what I had lost. But the skin was smooth.

Brushing aside the splintered shards of the broken mirror, I peered into my crucible.

I could see the souls inside more clearly now, picking out the presence of my parents and sister almost immediately. I wondered if it was because my power had strengthened from practicing, or because I had simply grown closer to Death that I was able to see impossibly into the tiny space, discerning the imperceptible shifts of light.

But there . . . in the very center of the crucible, built into its base . . .

Utter black swirled.

It wasn't simply darkness, although that would be the easiest way to describe it. This black was more than just the absence of light. It was its own being. And it felt strangely powerful. Much like lightning crackles with electricity, there was . . . more to the black inside my crucible.

I snatched my hand away. Was that the price? To free my sister's soul, would I have to sacrifice my own?

I stared at Nessie. She couldn't answer me.

But my revenants could.

I concentrated, sensing who was closest. A young woman named Kessel was just outside the hospital, standing on the steps leading to the bay.

Come here, I ordered her, and immediately she raced inside, up the stairs, and straight to me.

I knew every revenant on my island. Kessel was a young woman of nineteen, born in a village to the north but living in the slums of Blackdocks for most of her life. I knew that she had lost her family at a young age, and the two women who formed her team at the loom in the weaving factory had become her sisters. I had felt her pain at watching them die, months before she herself fell to the plague. The bitter regret at being raised without them lingered in my own heart. Every time I drew close to Kessel, I could feel the names of her sisters weaving through her thoughts, as tangible as the threads they once wound round the pegs of the loom.

And yet, as she stood in front of me now, I sensed nothing.

"Kessel?" I said.

She blinked at me. Finally: "Yes?"

"Who were your sisters?" I asked.

"I have no sisters," she said flatly.

"I mean the women you worked with. Your friends."

Blink. "Mora. Bellamae." She spoke their names with no emotion behind them, as if she were answering a mathematical problem.

Silence blossomed between us when I didn't answer. Before, Kessel thought of her dearest friends with the same sort of constancy that I thought of Nessie, her knife-sharp love for them never far from her mind. But now they were just syllables dripping from a dead tongue.

I frowned, then reached forward and touched Kessel with my shadow arm, the dark fingers dipping beneath her mottled skin. My connection to my necromantic powers was always amplified when I used my arm. Where I would usually feel her thoughts, I heard instead a low, guttural moan resonating through her soul.

"Kessel," I whispered. "Is something . . . wrong?"

It was a foolish question.

Kessel's eyes stared at me, tracking my movements as I paced, trying to figure out what was wrong. I could tell that she was struggling to speak.

Then her gaze flicked to Nessie.

"Oh," I breathed. "Oh no."

I reached forward, cupping Kessel's face and drawing her attention back to me. "You're fading away, too," I said. Just like Nessie.

But Kessel couldn't answer my question, and I didn't understand why. While the few necromancy books I'd read had mentioned revenants, none of them had talked about their well-being. Revenants were a sidenote, barely a concern beyond what they could be used for. So perhaps this was just a natural progression. The souls of the dead burning out within their bodies like a dying fire.

I remembered then a lecture that Mama had given me after a neighbor's house had burned to the ground.

"It's because the windows and doors were open," Mama had told Nessie and me. "If our house ever catches on fire," she'd instructed, "get out as quickly as possible. But if you can, close the doors behind you. Fire spreads faster when the doors and windows are open."

My mind flashed to a different house fire, the one I had started, the one that had burned Mama up, and Papa, too. I wished I'd remembered that lesson then.

A body is a house where the soul can live. While alive, the doors and windows are closed up, keeping the soul inside. But once the body dies, all the doors and windows open and the soul escapes.

When I raised Kessel—when I raised all my revenants—I put their souls back inside their bodies. But I hadn't realized that a dead body probably couldn't hold on to a soul, at least not forever. Death left the door open, and the souls were evaporating like smoke.

Kessel's eyes drifted back to Ernesta, silent and still. Tentatively, I tried to sense my other revenants, scattered around the island. How had I not noticed the growing silence before? But it was true—their voices were like distant echoes, slowly losing what tiny spark of life they'd had before.

My revenants were all emptying, becoming as hollow as my twin sister.

"Please," Kessel said, drawing me back to her.

What? I asked within my mind.

Don't let me be like her, Kessel said, her eyes still on Nessie. Communication was easier when we didn't speak aloud. *Please kill me, really kill me, before I become a monster.*

"She's not a monster!" I roared, stepping away from Kessel. She didn't answer me. I knew the dead couldn't lie, and I wondered, then, if they could be lied to.

I took a deep, steadying breath. "I want to help you. All of you."

I sat down, and Kessel followed suit, crossing her legs beneath her. I held out my crucible. "What is the black?"

We have to pass through it, her voice echoed in my mind. *Each of us, when you raise us. We pass through the iron.* A hint of a smile crossed her face at the memory. *And the darkness.* The smile was gone. She raised her gaze to meet mine. *The black is power. And it's old.*

"Old? My crucible isn't that old, it's—"

Parts of it are old.

I sucked in a breath. A part of my crucible *was* old—the crucible cage that had melded with my parents' ashes and my sister's soul to make the iron bead. I thought of the larger-than-life portrait of Bennum Wellebourne in the lobby of the hospital. He had sacrificed his own hand to make that crucible cage.

"It was just flesh and bone," I said. "There's no power in that, no black."

Kessel shook her head. *You're wrong.*

I stared at the little bead. What did Wellebourne do to make that crucible cage so dark that my revenants, who had defied death, feared it?

It's hungry. Kessel's voice was so soft that I wasn't sure if she'd spoken aloud.

My head shot up at the word.

Starving, she added. *We feel the ache, deep inside, when we pass through. It's so hungry. It wants to devour.*

Why did none of them tell me this before? I wondered. But I knew the answer already. I hadn't been asking the right question.

"How did you escape it?" I asked. "You had to pass through the black, you said, but if it's so ravenous, how did you escape?"

It doesn't want to eat us, Kessel said slowly. *It wants none of the revenants—it doesn't care about us. It wants power.*

She stared at me.

It wants you.

TEN

Grey

I WAS LATE for the council meeting. I hadn't thought I was expected to attend, but a servant came to fetch me, and I raced after. One did not ignore imperial summons. I burst into the council chamber, breathless. All eyes turned to me, and I nervously wiped damp hair out of my face as I stepped inside.

The only thing more out of place in this room than me was the bed. It stood at one end of the table, covered in pillows and draped in silk while the Emperor lounged on it. He was still pale, his skin a yellowish tone that crept into the whites of his eyes. His cheeks were sunken, and he looked as if he were struggling to remain upright, even propped up by a dozen down pillows.

"Here," a servant said, tugging my sleeve toward a seat positioned against the wall, closer to the Emperor than the council table, but not close enough that it appeared as if I had been given preferential treatment.

The Emperor broke the awkward silence. "We begin."

The council members all turned their full attention to him. "As we plan the best ways to meet the needs of the citizens of Lunar Island, one thing is clear: We need change," he said, struggling to speak loudly. "The old policies failed our people. Let us see how the council meets this . . . unusual circumstance."

He settled back on the pillow and glanced at me. I squirmed uncomfortably. It was rare for anyone to be a witness to a council meeting who wasn't actually on the council.

At first, no one spoke. The lead members of the council, including the chair, were all missing, having fled after the Emperor took over Governor Adelaide's position. Hamish finally spoke up. For such an inconspicuous man, he seemed determined to plow forward and carry on as if this were a normal governing day. "Our first priority will be filling the seats of the council members who are missing," he started, turning to the rest of the council.

"No." The Emperor's voice was weaker now, but everyone heard him. "I need the people to see that I am a strong leader. There will be no point in establishing a council if the people don't believe in me—they won't believe in my council either. I must speak before them, show the people that I support them."

Hamish winced. "But Your Imperial Majesty," he started. "You have been so unwell . . ."

The Emperor leveled him with an unreadable gaze, his eyes cold and steady. "Do you really think they care whether or not I've been ill? They saw me as a tyrant. They wanted to overthrow me. And for what reason?"

Finip Brundl dared to answer him. "Taxes and levies," he said. After a heartbeat, he added, "At least, that's how the people feel."

"They are the same taxes that all the colonies face. And you reap the same rewards from paying them. The streets are paved with granite from Siber. The trade routes are protected from pirates by my Imperial fleet. New medicine, textbooks for your schools, protection of the guards—all of this is what your taxes pay for."

I saw the little muscle in Finip's jaw clench, but he didn't speak again.

"But you're right," the Emperor continued. "They don't understand. So I must show the people that their Emperor cares about them."

"Perhaps an article in the news sheets?" one woman suggested.

"The north," I said.

Everyone turned to me. I hadn't realized I'd spoken so loudly, but now it felt as if I'd shouted the words.

"Do continue," the Emperor drawled.

I took in a shaking breath. "The north needs to see that we care, too. They were hit the hardest by the plague. And, frankly, they see the least benefit of the Empire's aid. The roads aren't paved in the north. The farmers and villages are struggling to survive."

"You have extensive experience in the north?" the Emperor asked.

I felt my cheeks burning. The truth was that, no, I had not been farther north than the quarantine hospital or the pauper's grave in the center of the island. I suddenly remembered Hart, which *did* have paved streets, at least by Father's description of it.

The Emperor turned away from me, toward the council, and continued on as if I'd not interrupted. "Before we unravel the socio-economic issues in one area, let's consider a quicker solution to the immediate problem at hand. Morale is low. We need a celebration," he said. "A rally of sorts."

"You want to throw a party?" Several of the members of council shifted uncomfortably in their seats with Hamish's countering of the Emperor's words, but he didn't back down. "Our people are still recovering from the plague."

"That's it," the Emperor said, sitting up and shaking a finger at Hamish in approval. "We should celebrate the medical alchemists who worked so hard to fight the plague, and we should celebrate the survivors."

"Perhaps a memorial for the dead . . ." Prinna, the councilwoman of finance, suggested.

Emperor Auguste shook his head, dismissing her suggestion. "No mourning. We must move forward. And to do that, we need to bring joy back to Lunar Island."

"It would be, at best, merely a bandage to dire feelings of anger and distress," Hamish started.

"I know." The Emperor's voice was stronger now. "This is not a solution to all of Lunar Island's problems. I want to assure you—assure all my people—that I am not merely going to throw a party and run back to the mainland. I want to strengthen the people's morale, and prove to them that I am not a weak man hiding in confinement as the news sheets claimed."

His eyes drifted to me. "And," he added, "let's follow Astor's suggestion as well. The north needs revitalization, as you say." He paused, contemplating. "How would you feel about going there?"

It took several beats for me to realize he was waiting for my answer. "Me?"

He nodded. "We need a face of change. Someone new, someone young, someone energized. Someone the people can trust."

"I don't . . . I don't have any experience," I started, looking around me.

"This isn't about experience," the Emperor said. "It's about appearances. We need someone the people will trust. Frankly, that excludes the council and anyone who's already established in politics."

"But . . ."

"My secretary can handle all the details," the Emperor said, turning away from me. "Meanwhile . . ." He snapped his fingers. A steward came forward, spilling a pile of heavy linen paper on the table. I strained to see more. Each of the large papers bore a heavy wax seal beribboned and gilded—the sign of the Emperor himself.

Hamish picked up the top page. "Decrees for state buildings?" he asked. His frown deepened. "Orphanages, a new wing to the hospital, market stands . . ."

"Our coffers are empty," Prinna said. "The banks cannot lend the government any more—"

"This is being paid for from my personal treasury," the Emperor said. He smiled as the council applauded his generosity.

"But where are they to go?" Hamish said. "This one—a new orphanage in Blackdocks. We'll have to condemn a factory, I think, or—"

"Make it work," the Emperor ordered. "We must give this to the people."

Hamish nodded silently, his eyes still on the papers. As city planner, he would be responsible for finding ways to make the buildings fit into the already crowded city. It would be difficult, but surely worthwhile.

Prinna shook her head, the ends of her hair bouncing off her cheeks.

"You have something to add?" the Emperor said coldly.

I saw the councilwoman of finance clench and unclench her fists under the table. She took a deep breath, but when she spoke, her words were loud and clear. "If our people must celebrate, let them do so with a hanging!" she declared. "What about the necromancer? Surely that is a crime that takes priority over a few new buildings and a *party*?"

My back stiffened. Out of the corner of my eye, I noticed the Emperor glance at me.

"My mind is heavy in regard to Nedra Brysstain," Emperor Auguste finally said. "She violated the law against necromancy, but she also used it to free me. It is not a simple matter."

"The law is clear—" Prinna started.

"It is." The Emperor cut her off so smoothly that Prinna's teeth clacked together as she snapped her jaw closed. "The law of the land and the law of the gods are both very clear: We must not suffer a necromancer to live among us."

No one looked at me.

This is it, I thought. *He's going to demand her arrest. She's going to be hung.*

"Council is dismissed," the Emperor said. A secretary rang a brass bell, letting it toll once before silencing the clapper with his gloved hand. The council got up from the table, muttering to one another in low tones. I stood, awkwardly, because everyone else was standing. I tried lingering, but I couldn't catch the Emperor's eye. I followed the council out into the hall, then made my way back to my rooms.

Could the Emperor condemn to death the person who had saved his life? By law, he should, but . . .

He made the laws.

ELEVEN

Nedra

My hand spread over my great-grandmother's journal as I tried to reorient myself. I remembered when I first found it. I had wanted, even then, to be an alchemist. While Nessie picked a new dream every day, mine was indelible. When I first opened the soft leather cover, my fingers brushed against the faded illustrations of herbs, the recipes for potions, the history of medicine. I turned the pages reverently, feeling the same sort of awe I felt during holy day services.

My grandmother—my father's mother—had still been alive then.

"You remind me of her," Granny had told me. "Just as stubborn, and just as hungry."

"Hungry?"

"For knowledge. For answers." Granny had laughed. She'd been cooking something—I remembered that we had this conversation in the kitchen, and that it was warm and it smelled of home. I wished I could remember the details more clearly. That had been one of my last conversations with her.

"My ma, she loved learning. That's why she loved Pa's book cart. She always said she married him for his books and not his looks." She laughed then. I could still hear the echoes of the joyous sound in my ears. I closed my eyes, leaning into the memory.

"And you," Granny had said, turning and pointing the wooden spoon at Nessie. "You're just like my ma's sister, Aunt Mabry."

"In what way?" Nessie said. Our great-aunt Mabry had died before we were born.

"Carefree." Granny snorted. "Careless."

Nessie had giggled.

"No one could ever tell Aunt Mabry what to do. She never did get married, never did settle down. No man or woman could tame her. She'd come home long enough to earn a little money, then she'd be off again, doing some adventure or another. Sailed halfway around the world."

Nessie had leaned back. "That'll be Ned, not me," she'd said. "I'm not going anywhere."

"Neither am I," I said glumly.

Granny had shaken her head. "No, my love," she told me. "You'll go places. But you'll always come home."

"You'll always come back to us!" Nessie had said in a singsong voice. Then she stuck her tongue out at me. "And I'll have to bail you out like Great-Grandmother had to save Great-Aunt Mabry."

"Like that's going to happen." I'd snorted. Even then, Nessie was already notorious in the village for her array of dramatic love stories and her aspirations of grandeur. "We both know that I'm going to be the one to have to save you from yourself."

The memory faded from my mind. I squeezed my eyes shut, trying hard to remember what else had been said. What scents popped up from Granny's cast-iron frying pan? What sounds were in the background—Mama? Papa? But as I tried to hold on to every detail, they slipped away, water through my open fingers, and I was left with cold reality.

I opened my eyes, and my gaze settled on Nessie.

She stared blankly back at me.

"I'll still save you," I whispered.

TWELVE

Nedra

I HEADED OUTSIDE, needing fresh air. There was very little land on the tiny island; I could easily walk the perimeter in fifteen minutes. But while the southern side of the island ended on the gray stone steps that led directly into the bay, the northern side had a small grassy lawn, a few scraggly trees, and swampy marshlands.

Before I had made the quarantine hospital my home, this lawn held nothing more than a few tables for the alchemists and potion makers to relax and eat lunch between shifts. Now it was something of a playground. It hadn't been the revenants who'd used ropes and planks to make swings in the trees or who'd cleared a space for a maypole. It had been the parents of the children raised from the dead.

As far as children's playgrounds went, it wasn't bad. It was just . . . quiet.

I stood by the door, watching the children play. Two girls used a tightly wrapped wad of cloth as a ball, kicking it back and forth between them. A little boy fluttered the ribbon of the maypole. Most of the parents—living people unable to let go of their children—stood to the side, close together, their attention focused on their individual offspring.

Ernesta stood behind me, as constant as my shadow. When one of the parents—Dannix—broke away from the group and approached me, his eyes kept flicking to Nessie. No one liked my twin—not the living, not the dead. She was some strange in-between that made them all uneasy.

Ronan followed his father, a silent shadow. "Go play," Dannix told his son when he noticed him. While his father watched, Ronan plastered a smile on his face and ran to the swings. As soon as Dannix turned away, though, the emotion faded from Ronan's countenance and he let the swing he sat on still.

Dannix's attention was on me. "I've been wanting to speak with you," he said, a note of trepidation marring his voice. I watched him coolly. "Last night, I woke up to Ro standing over me."

I didn't speak. I had learned that most people wanted to fill the silence, if I just let them.

"He was staring at me," Dannix said again, his voice pitched a bit higher, a bit more frantic. "I said, 'Do you need something?' And do you know what he said to me?"

I shook my head. Dannix's gaze shifted to Nessie again, then back to me.

"He said, 'Don't worry. I won't leave you like Mother or Jax.' And there was just . . ." He struggled to find the words. "There was something terrifying about the way he said it." He exhaled, his confession voiced. "'Don't worry. I won't leave you,'" he repeated in a high-pitched monotone.

I looked past Dannix, toward Ronan, still sitting on the swing, still waiting. I knew—because he was my revenant, because I had held his soul in my hand—I *knew* that he really wanted to be free. But he was a bird sitting willingly in his open cage.

He would never leave his father behind. It was his choice to be here. He would hold on as long as he could. I had given him the same choice as all the others, and just because he was a child didn't mean he didn't understand what he chose. Even now, all he had to do was tell me he wanted to let go, and I would release his soul from his body.

BETH REVIS

Dannix turned to me. "I don't know which is worse. Losing him, or having him back."

"I'm not sure either," I said softly.

Dannix's mouth dropped open at my words. I did not elaborate.

"It's not *fair*." Dannix spit the words out bitterly. Neither Nessie nor I responded. We both knew it wasn't fair. Death wasn't a children's game with rules that must be observed. It simply was.

When I didn't answer him, Dannix turned his back to me, watching his son. After a few moments, he spoke without turning to face me. "He's quieter now."

I thought of Kessel, and the way she had seemingly forgotten her sisters.

The dead were fading away to nothing.

I realized now why Dannix kept looking to Nessie. He was probably afraid that his son would become like her.

"Tell me there's still hope," Dannix said softly. "Even if it's untrue. Tell me there's hope, and I'll believe you."

I took a step closer to Dannix, not breaking eye contact, and waited to speak until I knew his attention was fully on my words. "There is hope," I said. "As long as the body can stand in front of me, there is hope for the soul."

Dannix's whole body sagged in relief.

But mine coiled with anxiety. I closed my eyes, reaching for my revenants. Their voices were quieter than before, but not yet silent. There was Ollah, and Kessel, and Nixah, and Kent. I sifted through each one of them, reassuring myself that they were still there. And that they still wanted this.

They had all come back from the dead for a different reason. Some, like Ronan, had a living loved one to stay beside. Some had been afraid of death. Some had longed for more time, more chances. Some had just wanted to stay.

I felt the fear inside of them, too, the unease as they grew aware of what they had lost. They could tell they were fading. But while they did not want the empty life I had given Nessie, they were not ready to let go of the one I had given them.

Which meant that I couldn't give up either. I had to save them all.

THIRTEEN

Grey

I TOOK THE long way back to my rooms, and when I arrived, Hamish Hamlayton was already waiting for me. I remembered the way he'd bit back his words at the chapel; it seemed he'd finally worked up the courage to speak his mind.

"Astor," he said by way of greeting.

"What do you need?" I asked.

Hamish cocked an eyebrow at me. "Do you understand what happened in the council chambers?"

Was he talking about Nedra, and the way the Emperor hadn't set a firm order for her arrest? "I understand enough," I said.

"Your father knew the game," Hamish started.

"This is no game," I said. "And I am not my father."

Rather than excuse himself at my obvious dismissal, Hamish leaned against my wall. "Why are you trying to help the north?" he asked softly. "You do realize it's going to be an almost impossible task to revitalize the economy of an entire region? Why are you setting yourself up for something that could fail so easily?"

"The north needs support," I said.

"I know," Hamish said. "That's why I've had propositions in the works for years to rebuild the infrastructure there."

"But then why—" I started.

"Why haven't they gone through? You tell me." He crossed his arms over his chest.

I tried to find the answer in his inscrutable face. Had delays in progress happened because Governor Adelaide blocked them? Had people like my father stood in the way?

"You don't know how this works," Hamish said, his voice almost gratingly sympathetic. "So what makes you think you can do anything?"

I rolled back my shoulders. "I'm at least going to try," I said firmly. "Maybe the Emperor is right. Maybe the situation needs new eyes; maybe making a show of helping will mean that eventually *actual* help comes." I paused, suddenly thinking of Nedra. Thinking of all the times I hadn't bothered to ask her about what it was like for her at home, how I never offered to go with her to the villages, how I neglected to notice the poor. "At least it's something," I said, my voice quiet as I remembered all the nothing I had done.

A sharp knock interrupted us. I opened the door, and a tall, thin man with wire-frame spectacles entered. He carried a sheaf of papers in his arms, bound by a leather wrap. "I'm Alyn Trublon," he said hurriedly. When I blinked blankly at him, he added, "The Emperor's travel secretary." His gaze turned to Hamish.

"I'll see myself out," Hamish said, heading to the door. Just before he closed it, he shot me a look of what could've been suspicion or pity.

Alyn went straight to my desk, unrolling the leather wrap and spreading out the papers. "These are your expenditures," he said, handing me a small envelope. When I peeked inside, I saw bank credit notes, each worth a hundred allyras. This wasn't exactly a fortune, but more than my parents gave me in a year's allowance. "Accommodations have already been arranged for Hart," Alyn continued, either ignoring or not noticing my expression. "And the Emperor has allocated you a cabin on board his private cruiser, which is being used to transport guards."

"I'm sorry," I said, finally able to get a word in edgewise. "What's happening?"

Alyn leaned back, adjusting his bifocals. "I was told you're helping spearhead the initiative to revitalize the northern economies," he said.

"I—er."

"You can take it up with His Imperial Majesty." Alyn shuffled through the papers. "You should arrive in Miraband—"

"Miraband?"

"The capital," Alyn said in a flat voice.

"I *know* Miraband is the capital," I snapped. It was also on the mainland, and about a week's journey away.

"The Emperor oversees all operations of the Empire," Allyn said. His voice was slower now, as if he thought I was simple. "But the Allyrian Empire is vast, so he allocates tasks to committees. You must get approval by the trade commission for any imports and exports prior to presenting them to Emperor Auguste."

My obvious lack of understanding caused Alyn to—finally—pause. "You are Greggori Astor?" he asked.

I nodded.

"At the council meeting, you proposed that the north needed aid?"

I nodded again.

"The Emperor has allowed you the opportunity to prove yourself," Alyn said. "You are to take a selection of local goods from the markets at Hart, then present them to the travel commission in Miraband for approval on new exports."

"I had, er, thought perhaps funds could just be sent to the northern villages," I said. "A type of welfare."

Alyn leveled me with a cold gaze. "And how would that help?"

I wanted to protest—surely giving aid would help the north recover quicker—but Alyn's cold stare made me feel as if I were simply not intelligent enough to see why it was such a bad idea. "Right, you're right, er—I just. This is happening rather suddenly."

Alyn started to gather his papers. "I am simply a facilitator. Whether or not you actually choose to accept the task is up to you."

I started to say more, but the travel secretary was already sweeping through the doorway. I stared down at the papers he'd left behind.

"I guess I'm going on a trip," I muttered. The door closed with an audible click, and I examined the travel documents. The schedule would have me back in time for the proposed rally the Emperor had mentioned at the council meeting. *That's why this is happening so quickly*, I thought. *The Emperor needs me to bring him the information before the rally.* I had to admit that if he was able to tell everyone that not only had plans been made, but already carried through, it would surely help my cause. Actions— even if they meant I would be sailing across the sea and back in a few weeks' time—would speak far louder than promises.

The door opened again, and I spun around, a question on my lips for Alyn. But my voice died away as His Imperial Majesty, Emperor Auguste, entered. His face was still wan, but his gait seemed stronger. As he stepped fully into the room, I noticed that he was using a silver-tipped cane for balance.

"I see Alyn's been here," he said casually.

"Ye-es," I was able to stammer out.

"He's quick. I meant to speak to you first."

"I'm sorry?" I was unsure of how to respond.

The Emperor shot me a small smile. "And did he explain the mission I've set out for you?"

"A bit," I said.

"I've done this sort of thing with other colonies before," Emperor Auguste said. "Find something to export across the Empire, and an entire colony's economics can change overnight. Although, I usually allow more time to prepare." He leaned against the cane, looking at me with a sympathetic smile. Even he seemed to feel that the timeline of this endeavor was ambitious, to say the least.

"Perhaps . . ." I started, then steeled myself. "Perhaps it would be better to send someone more experienced."

The smile faded. "Who would you suggest?"

I wished I'd paid more attention at Father's dinners. "Desminde," I offered tentatively, remembering the name of one of the governors of Hart who'd retired and moved to Northface Harbor.

"Campbell Desminde?" the Emperor asked. "He's among the fugitives."

I swallowed, thinking of the happy, rotund man. He had not struck me as a rebel, but I supposed now that many of my father's closest compatriots were.

"Prinna, then?" I'd seen her just this day at the council meeting, and as the councilwoman of finance . . .

The Emperor was already shaking his head. "It should be you. You were the one at the council meeting who expressed interest in aiding the north. And I meant what I said before: I think you could inspire the people."

His eyes searched mine, as if he wanted me to figure something out, something he couldn't say. When I didn't reply, he continued. "I had a lot of time to think in that prison."

I didn't know how to respond to that either.

"For the most part, people don't want this." The Emperor paused, gesturing to himself with his free hand. "The power," he clarified at my confused look. "People don't want the power that comes with ruling, because it also comes with an enormous responsibility. These people," he continued, "the council members who fled, the commoners who have been speaking out, all of them—they have not been happy. And their unhappiness is my fault. I am their Emperor. Had I solved their problems, they never would have felt the need to betray me."

Which was why we had to hurry now. Trade news would give the people hope after the plague. And it might just be enough to distract them from wanting to seek vengeance on a certain necromancer. I glanced down at my travel papers. There was nothing in them that said I had to go alone. If I could convince Nedra to come with me . . . She could get lost in the vast city of Miraband. She could hide.

I almost laughed at myself. Convincing Nedra to come with me would be more daunting than changing the economic system of the entire island. Maybe I could leverage the situation, though.

"I noticed you haven't arrested Nedra yet," I said, choosing my words carefully.

The Emperor arched his eyebrow at me. "Should I?"

"No!" I said immediately. "No, I mean . . . If I get new trade for the north and begin enacting the kind of change the people have wanted all along . . . could you pardon Nedra?"

The Emperor cocked his head. "A pardon . . ." he said, his voice low. "For a necromancer?"

My fingers clutched the papers, and I knew no matter what the Emperor said, the best solution would be to get Nedra into hiding.

"I do not relish the idea of hanging the girl who saved me," the Emperor finally conceded. "However, I could not refuse justice if it were demanded. But if you are successful, and the people are perhaps . . . distracted by their change in situation, then I will not order a death the people do not request."

I let go of my breath, feeling my shoulders visibly sag in relief. It wasn't a guarantee of Nedra's pardon, but I had never expected that. But I could buy her more time, and buy myself the opportunity to convince Ned to get to safety. And the idea of actually *doing* something eased some of the weight of guilt that had settled in my chest. I hadn't done enough to stop the plague before. I hadn't been able to save Nedra; I had let ignorance be my excuse to remain idly passive. This, at least, was *something*.

"So will you do this for me?" the Emperor asked, indicating the travel papers in my hands.

I swallowed. "Yes," I said, my voice cracking.

FOURTEEN

Nedra

I WATCHED THE children silently playing, going through the motions with methodic intent that belied the usual boisterous chaos of youth. A scream sliced the air, and a tawny, pale bird shot like an arrow from the north tower of the hospital. A squirrel near the trees stiffened, its front paws splayed, its body frozen with indecision.

I watched the bird of prey descend. The dead children I had raised stopped their pretend play and turned to watch as well—what I focused on, they focused on. Their living parents, not privy to our connection, followed their offspring's eyes.

At the very last moment, the squirrel somehow mustered the courage to run; it feinted left then darted right, toward the trees. The bird—an awlspring—changed course, wheeling in the air, heading deeper into the forest. The squirrel zoomed around a tree and the awlspring, so focused on its prey, slammed into the trunk.

We all heard the crunch of its broken neck.

"Stupid bird," Torva, one of the mothers, muttered, turning away as the tawny feathered body dropped to the forest floor, motionless.

My father used to say much the same thing. Awlsprings were vicious hunters but notoriously myopic. Papa saw two collide in mid-air once, both so intent on the same prey they had not seen the other.

I strode forward. One by one, my child revenants followed me into the trees, filing behind me as surely as if the awlspring had been a new corpse for me to raise. I felt the revenants inside the hospital drawn to me, but I mentally pushed them back; this would not take long. A few of the parents jogged to catch up with us.

"What is it?" Torva asked. There was fear in her voice. Odd. It was just a bird.

"I have an idea," I said to no one in particular as I bent and scooped the still-warm body of the awlspring in my hands. My revenants watched me, a dozen childish eyes that knew too well what I planned to do. They expressed fear, too, but unlike Torva it was not painted on their faces, but hidden in the whispers through our mental connection. Unlike Torva, their fears were valid.

I could not experiment on the living; the thought of doing so felt wrong. And I did not want to risk hurting my revenants by experimenting on them. I knew they would let me—they could deny me nothing—but that made it worse, somehow. How could I risk harming someone who trusted me with their soul, someone who I knew so intimately? I had tried to turn my powers on myself, but that . . . I shuddered. Not only had it cost me a piece of my soul, but it had pushed me deeper into the very darkness I did not want to succumb to. That power had felt addicting, but also blinding. No. I couldn't do that.

But here was a fresh corpse—not human, true, but dead—and perhaps I could learn something from it.

Go play, I ordered the children. *Let your living believe the lie.*

They returned to the ball and the swings, the maypole and the sandbox. Their parents, comforted by the facade of normalcy, followed.

The dead awlspring was lighter than I'd supposed it would be. The feathers made it deceptively large, but I could feel the thin, bony body through the down. Its head flopped, and I shifted my hand so it looked as if it were sleeping in my grasp. I cradled the bird as I mounted the iron spiral staircase leading to my clock tower.

And behind me every step of the way was Ernesta.

If she were really here, really herself, she would be mourning the dead bird. She loved animals. She'd held a funeral for the barn cat Papa had refused to name. She would have cried at the awlspring's senseless, sudden death.

As I laid the bird's body on my worktable, Nessie stepped back into the corner, unblinking, uncaring.

I spread the awlspring's wings out, exposing its breast.

Animals did not have souls, but they had a life force, which was much the same thing. I shifted my vision as I reached with my shadow hand to touch my crucible. While human life wove like golden light, animal life had a deeper color, more bronze than gold, and the wilder the animal was, the darker the light. This was no pet dog or work animal. The freshly killed awlspring had just a glimmer of dark bronze streaming from its chest.

My hand clenched. I wished I had more books. I should have been able to study necromancy as much as I'd studied medicinal alchemy. But the only texts I had were old and worn, two solitary books that did not answer the questions that shrouded my necromantic curiosity.

I pulled my iron crucible from the chain I wore around my neck, letting the little bead rest in my shadow hand. It was easier to see the darkness swirling in the heart of it. Was that because I had seen it before and knew where to look, or was it because the inky depths were spreading?

I tipped my shadow hand to the side, letting the necromantic crucible fall into the palm of my hand made of flesh. Stretching out the shadow arm, I twined the threads of bronze light from the dead awlspring through my incorporeal fingers, tugging it up.

A human soul had thoughts and memories and something of the essence of the person it emitted from. An animal's life force was not so clean. Feelings flitted through me, matching what the bird knew—flight, taste, hunger, rest, hunting. This bird lived its life with wings at the ready.

The bronze light dripped through my shadow fingers, leaking down, trying to escape my grasp. I plunged the light into the iron crucible, watching as the threads of it swirled down, spiraling into the dark center.

Cold shot through me like lightning. Out of the corner of my eye, I watched Ernesta. I had taken some of the light from my soul and given it to her, and for a moment, she'd woken up. Would the life of a dying bird give her a minute more? Could I somehow channel it through my crucible and into my sister?

The bird's life force touched the darkness that swirled in the base of my crucible. I could pull it through and raise the bird from the dead, simple enough. Instead, I fed the light of the bird's soul to the blackness, pushing it toward Ernesta's soul. The black overflowed from my crucible, spilling toward the bird, filling the little dead body, replacing the light that I had taken.

Like frost spreading on my village's fishing pond, cold crackled out, fracturing fractals spreading impossibly up and up. The bronze threads of light were no longer wispy like fog, but hard and brittle. And black. The glowing life of the bird seemed to cave in on itself, turning into a nothingness that absorbed warmth and light. As it crackled up out of the crucible it curved around, the edge of it sharp as a blade as it pierced the lifeless body of the awlspring.

Still I pushed the bird's light through my crucible toward Ernesta, willingly trading what remained of its life for a moment of hers. The bird's body was now consumed by the black.

One claw twitched.

I straightened, focused on the bird's body. The other claw moved, then a wing. The darkness didn't sink into the bird's skin; it crackled over its corpse. The tawny white spines of the bird's larger feathers turned black with crimson seeping from the veins.

The bird's eyes were already onyx beads, but they seemed harder now as the awlspring blinked slowly. It righted itself, the move somehow graceful despite the awkward position in which it had been laid. The claws—now obsidian and serrated—scarred my wooden table.

I did not take my eyes off the bird as I reached for a knife.

The awlspring cocked its head, staring at me. I was connected with every living thing I had raised, but this was different.

Sunlight gleamed off the bird's feathers, each one razor sharp. Its curved beak could have been made of steel, the tip sharpened more than that of a sword. The awlspring opened its beak in a silent scream, and a forked tongue flicked out.

I glanced behind me. Nessie stood where she always stood, but her face did not seem so impassive as before. Had the experiment been successful? Had the lingering energy within the bird reawakened my sister's soul? My heart lurched. There was true expression in her eyes.

But it was fear.

I turned around. In that brief moment, the bird had moved silently closer, its talons gripping the edge of my table, the wood cracking from the impossible force. The bird craned its head closer, its onyx eyes boring into me.

I reached out with my connection to the dead for the bird. As before, I sensed only emotions, no concrete thought. But the feeling from the bird was no longer varied and touched by its life. It felt only one thing.

Hunger.

Ravenous, bone-deep starvation. Its only desire was to feed. Its entire being was insatiable.

Entranced, I stared at the blackness that slimed its way through the awlspring's now razor-edged feathers.

The hunger started to fill me.

The bird clucked, a sound of motherly affection.

My crucible was still in my shadow hand. I lifted it up. The black spiraled at the base, flickers like flame licking at the light. The dark energy was infecting me, *corrupting* me. I wanted to *devour*, consume the light, the life, the souls swirling in my crucible, and leave nothing at all behind but the dark.

I licked my lips and tasted copper. Blood smeared my teeth—I had not even realized I was biting my lip so hard.

"No."

The word was whispered so softly that I almost didn't hear it through my starved focus. But I knew my sister's voice.

In my shadow hand was my crucible. A feast beckoned me, begging me to succumb to the darkness and destroy the souls I had so lovingly gathered. They were all right there, in the crucible, strings of light I could devour and be filled with power.

But in my other hand was a knife.

Before I could hesitate, I slammed the knife through the core of the bird, pinning it to the wooden table, acting on instinct more than knowledge. If I had truly raised this bird from the dead, the blade would not kill it. The dead cannot die. But the awlspring's life energy had burned up in Nessie like oil in a lamp, and now it was nothing but a puppet of the dark, a toy easily broken. I wished I understood more, could *do* more than simply kill this experiment gone awry.

The thing screeched with an otherworldly scream, its beak opening impossibly wide, its claws spread and grasping, its wings twisting and curling like burned paper, the black gore beneath the blade staining the cracked wood.

FIFTEEN

Nedra

A BOAT COMES.

I heard the warning from my revenants. With the burning of the fishing boat, I'd hoped that others would be deterred from acting out foolish threats. Fortunately, I'd not been so simple as to eliminate a watch. I raced down the stairs, calling my revenants to me, so that when I burst through the mahogany doors moments later, the full force of my undead army stood behind me.

But it was not a Cliffside fishing boat.

It was an Imperial cruiser, the black lacquer shining against gilded highlights carved into the delicate frame. It was a bigger ship than any local one, with at least a dozen or so cabins belowdecks, and three large, rectangular sails beneath a silk Allyrian flag snapping in the wind.

My fist clenched. I had known the Emperor would come for me eventually. It did not matter that I had saved him, had saved this whole island; I had committed treason of the highest order.

I felt my rage pouring into my revenants.

He should have sent more than one ship.

All of us, as one, focused on the black cruiser slipping through the waves, heading straight to us. For a moment, I regretted giving up the warship and the cannons.

And then I saw the man leaning out over the bow, his arm raised in greeting. "Grey?" I whispered breathlessly.

The boat landed, and a gangplank lowered to the steps. Only Grey departed, but the ship remained docked to my island. I went down a few steps to greet him.

My knees trembled, and I stopped, waiting for him to reach me. Why weren't my legs cooperating? Why was my heart beating so chaotically? I sensed my revenants retreating. With the threat gone, they faded back into the quarantine hospital. I tried to seep some of the dead calm inside of them into my tight chest.

And then he was right in front of me.

He'd been grinning so widely that I could see the flash of white teeth from the boat, but now his expression sobered.

"Nedra," he said, his voice low.

I couldn't seem to move. When he had left me before—no, when *I* had walked away from *him*—I had believed there was no coming back from that choice.

But he was here now.

"What are you doing here?" I blurted out.

The corners of his lips twitched. "Hi," he said.

The wind blew my hair into my face, strands of white flickering across my vision. "Well, come in," I said, turning on my heel and leading the way inside.

SIXTEEN

Grey

I FORCED MYSELF to follow Nedra into the quarantine hospital. My body was reacting as if I were expecting a fight—muscles clenched, fists tight, jaw hard. I made myself breathe, swallow. There would be no fight.

Not one I could win, anyway.

The revenants that had been scattered over the steps were disappearing deeper in the quarantine hospital. All except for Nedra's twin, Ernesta. She stood beside the iron spiral staircase leading to the clock tower. She watched me.

I was never really comfortable with the way Nedra's dead twin sister stared at me. The problem was that Ernesta looked so very much like my Ned. Same nose, same lips. Same olive skin, smooth over high cheekbones.

The only difference was in her eyes. Nedra's burned with intention. Ernesta's were hollow, empty caves.

I turned to Ned. She was so different now—one arm amputated, her hair paper white, her cheeks sunken, her eyes fierce. No—that wasn't different. Her eyes were always sharp, like the edge of a blade. I just wasn't used to that razor gaze being directed at me.

"Um," I said.

"Eloquent as always, Grey," Nedra said, but she smiled, and the tight coil inside me finally released. She might have an army of the undead, but she was still Nedra. She still called me by the name she had given me.

"I wasn't sure if you'd ever come here again," she said in almost a whisper.

"I wasn't sure if you'd want me to." I took a step closer. I couldn't read her expression. "I meant what I said before."

Nedra frowned.

"When I said I loved you," I told her. "I meant that. Truly."

Nedra stiffened. "I seem to recall you had a 'but' with that. You loved me, *but* . . ."

"I can still love you, even if I don't agree with everything you do."

Nedra's eyes drifted to the floor, her head shaking almost imperceptibly. "That may be so, but can you still care about me if you don't agree with what I am?"

I crossed the distance between us, putting my hands on her cheeks and turning her face toward mine. "I love *you*," I said, hoping she could see the truth I could never deny. *And I want to save you*, I didn't dare add.

A flicker of a smile crossed over her lips. "I'd like to believe that," she said sorrowfully. She took a step away from me, then jerked her head to the spiral staircase leading to the clock tower. I followed her up. She moved with ease, while I struggled to catch my breath as we reached the top.

Nedra had turned the clock tower room into her private domain. With ticking gears on one side, connected by pistons to the milky glass of the clockface, the area had a steady heartbeat that Nedra seemed to find comforting. One corner was littered with blankets and cushions piled atop a mattress; the other had a worktable half-drowned with wax from melted candles.

"When I saw the ship," Nedra said, "I wondered if the Emperor had decided to arrest me."

I rolled my shoulders, trying to ease the tension in my body. "He will," I said. "I don't know when. I don't think he wants to, but the people may force his hand. Necromancy—you knew it was illegal."

"Laws don't change whether something is right or wrong," Nedra insisted.

"But that won't matter," I shot back. "You'll be arrested and tried for the highest crime in the Empire." And we both knew she was guilty.

Nedra's chin tilted up. "He could try."

I had to make her see reason. "Nedra, anyone who was even loosely tied to the rebellion—whether they were on Governor Adelaide's side or not—has run. The dungeons will be full of traitors. The Emperor can't just ignore your crimes, even if you used them to save him. The people want answers." But more than that, they wanted someone to pay for the plague, and they didn't care who.

"Arrests have happened already?" Nedra asked. She eyed me. "Your father?"

"He managed to escape." I was careful to keep all emotion from my voice.

"But . . ."

"He and Mother likely went to Doisha. We have an estate there as well. And the Empire doesn't reach quite that far."

She noticed my use of "likely," the uncertainty that I tried to hide. My parents had left me behind. But she only said, "I can't imagine you in Doisha."

"Oh, don't worry. I wasn't invited."

She spared me any further comment. Her eyes grew distant, and her hand reached unconsciously for the iron bead she wore around her neck. How cruel it was that her parents, who loved and were loved, were gone, while mine were alive and happy, probably on the beaches of sunny Doisha, drinking wine and laughing about their escape.

"So you're alone at your house?" Nedra asked, changing the topic for me.

"The Emperor gave me rooms at the palace."

Her eyes dropped. I wondered if she was going to invite me to stay here instead. I wondered what I would say if she did. When she didn't speak, though, I said, "I'm actually leaving for a trip now."

Her gaze shot to me, and I felt a pang in my heart.

"I'm heading to Hart first," I said. "And then the mainland. The Emperor gave me a special task, to find ways to help revitalize the economy of the north. I'm going to try, Nedra. I could make a real difference. I—" I paused, trying to think of the right words. "I want to help. I want to do some good." *For them, because I failed you*, I thought.

What I most wanted was to convince Nedra to come with me— just her, and not her revenants. If I could do that, perhaps I could get her to Doisha, like my parents, or somewhere else that the Empire couldn't reach.

I opened my mouth to speak, my eyes falling on the little workstation Nedra had set up for herself, littered with books, candles, paper, and quills. And—

I cursed, loudly. "What *is* that?"

Nedra stood and strolled over to me. "An awlspring," she said, looking down at the mangled body, covered in black slime, pinned to her wooden desk with a dagger. "Or, it used to be."

My eyes drank in every detail, even though I wanted to look away. Perhaps the form was originally that of an awlspring, but it no longer resembled the delicate raptor. Its claws were twisted and black, its beak mangled and no longer even, as if someone had taken the top and the bottom and yanked them in different directions. The eyes were lined in red, and even though the creature was dead, it seemed to stare at me with anger and malicious hate.

Nedra grasped the hilt of the knife and jerked it from the table. Black oozed off the blade, and she wiped it carelessly against a dirty rag on the desk before using the cloth to wipe the table's surface and wrap the body up, letting it drop unceremoniously into a metal waste bin. The body thudded and splattered in the container.

SEVENTEEN

Nedra

GREY'S EYES KEPT darting to the waste bin, where the dead awlspring was half-hidden by the black-stained rag.

I drew closer to him, anticipation twisting my stomach, ready for the moment when Grey would once again demand that I choose between him and necromancy.

And I knew the answer I would give.

But rather than an order, he simply asked, "Why?"

I blinked, confused. "Why?"

"Why don't you let them go?" he asked, nodding toward the door, to all the revenants I'd raised beyond it. "You don't need them. If you just let them go back to their graves . . ."

My jaw clenched. "You don't get to tell me to give up my sister."

Grey shook his head. "No, I mean . . . what about the others? Keep your twin, I can understand that, but the others . . . It makes things so much worse. People fear your army."

"I like them afraid." Why couldn't Grey see that? I *needed* the people afraid of me, because once their fear ran out, they would attack. That's what had happened with the ships from Cliffside, that's what would happen, eventually, with the Emperor and his men. I *had* to make sure their fear outweighed their anger. It was my only hope.

He reached out, grabbing my wrist, his grip warm but firm. "I mean it, Nedra. You're in danger."

"You think I don't know that?" I jerked away from him. I had watched the boats burn. "That's *why* I need an army." It was the only chance I had to defend myself.

"I can take you away. Ernesta, too, if I have to. I can take you both, hide you somewhere the Empire can't reach you."

His voice trailed off as I shook my head. "Grey, you don't understand."

"So help me to see," he said.

I stood up, sighing. I needed air. I walked past Grey and moved to the door that led outside, to the little balcony in front of the clockface. Grey followed me, his steps small, his knuckles white as he gripped the thin railing, the only thing that protected him from a drop to the bricks below.

"What's that?" he said, pointing to the charred remains of the ships that I'd destroyed earlier.

"The reason I need an army of the undead to protect me."

Grey turned to me, searching my eyes. "You're not like that," he said, confident. "You wouldn't keep other people from freedom just to protect yourself."

"I'm not," I said quietly. "Grey, the plague . . . It took away so much from so many. I had a chance to right some wrong in the world."

He shook his head, disappointment flickering in his face. "This isn't right."

"You don't get to decide that."

"And you do?"

"No," I answered. "*They* do. I brought my revenants back because they *wanted* to be brought back. The plague was murder. If I didn't bring them back after, when I could, when they wanted it, how is that different?"

Grey was silent for a long moment. "They're not your responsibility," he said finally.

I looked away, my eyes scanning the horizon as if there was something in the distance that could make Grey see the situation from my point of view. The clock tower faced the city, and to the right, across the sea, was the mainland of the Allyrian Empire. I looked to the left. Leaning against the railing, I pointed. "What's out there?" I asked.

"The pauper's grave?" Grey asked. We couldn't quite see the land cleared to make room for the graves of those killed by the plague from this angle. I imagined that I could see a glow there, like a setting sun over the thousands of corpses, but then I looked past it. "No," I said. "Farther out."

"The sea?"

"And?"

"A few islands." Grey paused, thinking. "And a lot more sea."

A row of islands trailed like a ribbon from the mainland up to Lunar Island. Most were so small cartographers didn't bother putting them on maps; they just swept the words "the Stellar Chain" over the area and let ship captains figure it out for themselves. The tiniest ones weren't always there; sometimes the waves washed over them, sometimes not. Ships avoided these little, rocky islands; it was too easy to scrape a hull against the jagged stones. No one bothered with the ones north of Lunar Island—there was nothing past the end of the Stellar Chain. Once the rocks were gone, they were replaced by icebergs, floating in the cold blue waves.

But the fishing was good there.

"My father told me about some fishermen who went north, around the Stellar Chain," I said, my voice soft as I remembered the way Papa told his stories, between bites of Mama's best roast chicken at the supper table, the room warmed by the wood-fueled stove, our laughter sprinkled more generously over our meal than salt.

"North? Why?" Grey asked.

"The orcines," I said. "They like the cold, but they sun themselves on the rocks in the winter. And their pelts . . ."

Grey nodded. Orcine pelts made the best coats; their fur was sleek and black, waterproof and warm. For a while, half a century ago, orcine pelts made the north rich again. Then the orcine grew harder and harder to hunt, and the icy north too dangerous to risk trying.

"Papa told me about a group of fishermen who sailed out there. The sea was rough, but they needed to eat. They had to hunt."

Grey was quiet. I imagined my father's warm voice telling the story I'd heard countless times as I recalled it to Grey. "They made it to one of the larger islands. Large enough to risk lashing the ship to the rocks and disembarking. But then a storm came, the waves so high that the ship smashed to bits against the sharp stones."

Most of Papa's stories were happy tales, funny bits he picked up on his travels. But lately I seemed to only remember the sad ones.

"There was no way to get home, and winter was falling. No new ships would save them, not in the storm. Not before they froze or starved."

"How did they survive?" Grey asked.

I finally met his eyes. "They didn't."

"But—"

"One of the men was able to grab a bit of the boat, a plank that hadn't drifted away yet. It was about as long as his forearm. He took his knife, and he carved his name, and the name of the others, and then he gouged out a sentence in the wood: *We lay down to perish now.*"

Grey's mouth silently repeated the words.

"He threw the board into the sea, never knowing if it would be found. And for a long time it wasn't. The widows and the children walked the shore with candles every night, looking for a trace of their loved ones. A few months later, someone in a nearby village found the board, and it made its way back to the man's widow. She nailed it over the door of their house and read the words every day. And they brought her comfort."

"Comfort?"

"Grey, don't you see?" I shook my head and laughed bitterly. "Mama said that the man hadn't carved the words at all. Someone who loved the widow and couldn't bear to see her walking the shore all winter long, looking for her lost lover, had written the passage for her to find. Because the man—all of the men in the crew—they had died. Of course they had. But it's the not knowing that kills those who are still alive."

I used to think about this story a lot, when I was a girl and enraptured with the romantic ideal of the widow walking by candlelight on the shore. I had believed Papa's version then, that fate had brought the board and the message to the widow, like the last kiss of a ghost.

But I think Mama was right. Some kind person had seen that the widow had no closure, no peace, without *knowing* her husband was gone. So someone else had carved the message, thrown it into the sea, and made sure it was found.

There is peace in knowing.

"But, Nedra," Grey said, still confused. "What does that have to do with—?"

"Why can't you understand?" I interrupted. I grabbed Grey and pulled him over to the railing, ignoring the way he tried to resist. I pointed down. On the steps below, Ronan sat, watching the bay. His father, Dannix, leaned his head against his son's shoulder.

"He knows his son is dead," I said in a low voice. "Of course he does. But if he lets go . . . what will happen to him? Where will Ronan's soul go? That's what he is unsure of. It's the not knowing that kills the heart. That's what I give these people, Grey. I give them certainty."

Grey pulled back, away from the edge, pressing his body against the milky-white face of the clock. "Certainty of what?"

I reached for his hand, gently leading him back inside. "As long as their dead are in front of them, they know where they are," I said. "And that's enough."

Nessie stood where I had left her. My revenants, even now, were fading into hollow shells like my twin. But as long as I had their bodies—as long as I had *her* body, there was still hope for her soul.

EIGHTEEN

Nedra

ONCE WE GOT back inside the clock tower, Grey turned to me, his shoulders slouched in defeat, his eyes downcast. "I'll never be able to convince you to send your revenants back to the grave, will I?"

I shook my head.

"I'll never be able to convince you to run away with me either?" There was still a little hope in his voice.

"Where would I go?" I said. "Anywhere I flee to, it won't matter. I'll still be me. I'll still be a necromancer. And I'll still have my revenants."

He winced.

"Grey." I sighed heavily, all the weariness of the day settling on my shoulders.

Sympathy flooded his gaze. "Sorry. I just—I want to help you." His voice dropped. "I want to be with you."

"Why?" I asked.

He was silent for several long moments.

"Why?" I pressed. "You've made it abundantly clear that you don't approve of necromancy, and I've been equally clear that I won't stop, and nothing you can say or do will change that. So why are you trying to help me? Why are you even here?"

That last question—I had not meant to say it aloud. But I had. And I could not snatch the words back.

I had thought my words would push Grey away, but instead, he took a step closer to me. I could feel the heat radiating from his skin, the cinnamon warmth of his breath. He reached up, touching my paper-white hair, and tucked a strand behind my ear. Without speaking, without warning, his head dropped, his forehead touching mine.

His eyes were closed when he said, "I don't know."

I let that be enough. I let *us* be enough.

"I don't understand what this is between us," Grey said at last, his voice a whisper. "I call it love, but you're right—I don't like necromancy."

I snorted, and Grey laughed.

"Okay, I hate it," he conceded. "But . . ."

His voice trailed off as mine caught in my throat.

"I can't stop thinking about that night."

"Which one?" I asked, pulling away from him and searching his eyes. "There have been many nights."

"The last night, before you changed."

I smiled sadly. I knew he meant the night we ran into each other in Master Ostrum's shattered office, hours before I crossed the threshold and became a necromancer. "But that wasn't the night I changed," I said, shaking my head. It had happened before, when I watched my parents die. When I sawed my sister's hand off. When I burned my home to the ground. My choice was not what had changed me.

"Maybe not," Grey allowed. "I just meant, that night, before . . . after . . . That was my chance, wasn't it? And I ruined it."

I couldn't look into his eyes.

In that moment, if Grey had stopped and listened and tried to help, if he had tried to *understand*, could he have stopped me from becoming what I became?

But then, if he had, I wouldn't have Nessie.

I took another step back from him. If Grey only wanted atonement, I couldn't help him.

He was still too late.

I closed my eyes, letting myself linger on the darkness behind my eyelids, nothing at all like the craving dark power swirling in the base of my crucible.

My hand dropped blindly to the table, and rather than rough-hewn wood, my fingers brushed soft, embossed leather. I picked up my great-grandmother's journal, the little book that had first set me on the path that led, somehow, to this moment. I traced the outline of the emblem stamped on the back, the rising sun with six rays, the symbol of the Allyrian Empire. But this Empire was vast, and surely there were other books to find, other experts beyond Master Ostrum.

Where did Papa get his book on necromancy? I wondered. He traded in books, but it seemed impossible that something like that could've come from some remote village. More likely it came from Hart, maybe from one of the antiques dealers who lived there, like Papa's friend Bunchen, who he traded with often for rare books. And if it hadn't come from Bunchen directly, she would know where it *had* come from. And if she didn't, I could sail across the sea, to Miraband. Surely the largest city in the world would have some sort of information I could use.

I looked up at Grey. "I'll go with you," I said.

Relief and surprise flashed across his face. "Really?"

"Not to run away," I said impatiently. "To learn."

"Who is going to teach you?"

"Books," I said. "As usual."

"Nedra, I won't let—" He stopped short at the look I gave him.

"You didn't help me before," I said. "So help me now."

Grey sucked in a breath as if I'd punched him. It was low, twisting his guilt to suit my needs, but I was thinking only of Nessie.

Grey followed my gaze. "We can't take her," he said. "We can't take any of them."

"Nessie would protect me."

"Nedra . . ."

I scowled. The ships that had come to threaten me had been enough to prove that I was not loved by the citizens of Lunar Island. If I went alone, I could cover my hair, disguise myself so that none would recognize me. But I couldn't hide Nessie. One look, and anyone would recognize her for what she was.

And what would happen then? I let my mind play through the possibilities. If someone tried to harm me, Nessie would attack. I knew she could fight, and fight well. But in the middle of Hart or Miraband, with thousands of people to overtake us . . .

We would lose. And I would hang. And once I died, so, too, would Nessie and every single revenant I had raised.

Besides, it wasn't as if I had no power without my revenants. My fingers clenched involuntarily as I remembered the way I had held Governor Adelaide's soul still. I could protect myself.

And my revenants could protect our home. That was one of the few things in which I had faith.

I shut my eyes, sifting through my connections with my revenants to find the strongest—not in body, but in mind. They were all slowly fading, losing their free will and past memories, but the clearest mind belonged to Ollah, a middle-aged woman who'd been left at the hospital by her husband when the inky black stain of the plague appeared over her heart.

Ollah, I said. *I'm going away.* I did not need to explain further; she was tapped into my mind and understood what wasn't said. *Lead the others; protect the hospital.*

I felt her acceptance of this role. Almost simultaneously, I felt all my revenants start to position themselves at the windows and doors of the hospital, attentive and standing guard. Nessie stepped forward. *Stay in the tower until I return*, I ordered her directly.

"Let me pack a few things," I told Grey. I scooped up my great-grandmother's journal and Master Ostrum's book into my bag, followed by a few articles of clothing and necessities. In moments, I was ready to go, sweeping my cloak over my shoulders.

"Do you need to tell anyone?" Grey asked as I hefted my bag onto my shoulder. He didn't understand my connection to my dead.

"There's no one to tell," I said.

NINETEEN

Nedra

THE CAPTAIN OF Grey's ship was not at all happy when I boarded.

"She's a criminal," he growled at my back as I ignored him, crossing the deck and standing next to the black lacquered railing.

"I'm the representative of the Emperor on this mission," Grey stated.

"Don't care," the captain snapped back. He tugged at his beard. "She should be hanging from a noose, not standing on *my* ship."

I swallowed.

Grey said something else, something I couldn't hear. I could feel the tension building behind me, but I ignored it all, staring up at the quarantine hospital. Doubt twisted my stomach. Would my revenants be able to protect themselves if more intruders came? I scanned the hospital's brick facade, my eyes tracing over the shadowy outlines of my revenants in the windows.

It's not too late for them, I told myself. This was the best possible time for me to go, before they met the same fate as Ernesta. They might be losing some of their memories now, but they could still fight to protect their home. If I waited much longer, it would never be safe for me to leave.

Soon, the ship pushed off from the dock and we were making the short journey north, to the city of Hart. I counted the seconds, measuring the exact moment when I knew my revenants would no longer be able to swim to the ship to protect me. "What did you do to convince him to let me come aboard?"

"Don't worry about it," Grey said.

I reached out and grabbed his wrist. "I *am* worried," I said. "What's to stop him from dumping me in the bay?"

"A hundred allyras," Grey said, flushing. He hated talking about money.

I released his arm. Of course. Why did I always forget how easily things could be fixed with money?

While the captain and crew ignored us, I turned my eyes to the north. I hadn't been to Hart since I rode the ferry with my sister to the hospital, the day they left her locked inside and dragged me, shouting, away from her. The last moment I saw her alive.

"So, do you have any advice for me?" Grey asked.

"Advice?" I could still hear the screams—*my* screams—as I tried to fight my way back to Nessie.

"The north needs to improve its economic standing," Grey said. "If the north could export a product to the mainland, then it might offer more financial security. Right now, the primary source of income is fishing and farms, but all the goods the north produces are sent to Northface Harbor."

"There's no reason to export turnips to the mainland," I pointed out. The mainland was rich in its own right, and besides, any produce sent from our villages across the sea would be bruised and aged by the time it reached Miraband's shores.

"So, any ideas on what else we could send to the mainland to generate income for the north?"

"No," I said simply. Didn't he think that the north would have saved itself already if the answer were that easy? Most people in the north only had the means to labor at their farms. There was no time nor spare money to create art or invent something new or develop unique merchandise. The north was too busy surviving, and barely at that.

Despite the warmth of the day, I adjusted the cloak on my shoulders. The long hood in the back would serve to hide my white hair. My amputated arm wouldn't stand out as unusual in the north, but my hair would.

"Worried you'll be recognized?" Grey asked, concern in his voice.

"Should I be?" I hadn't been north since leaving my parents' burned home. While my army of the undead had marched through the streets of Northface Harbor, did the people of Hart know what had transpired? Did they care? "They don't deliver news sheets to my island," I reminded Grey.

"The official story is that Governor Adelaide was a traitor who'd locked up the Emperor—all true—but I've not actually read anything about you," Grey told me. He looked out over the water as we drew closer to Hart. "The news sheets are pretty vague about *how* the Emperor escaped, mostly just saying 'loyalists' aided him. But everyone knows. Not your face, I don't think. Your name is whispered, and they know you're at the quarantine hospital."

That made sense. People were coming to my little island before I attacked the castle; word spread quickly when it came to necromancy.

"At least, that's how it is in Northface Harbor. If your story has crossed the bay . . ." He shrugged his shoulders to indicate that he wasn't sure.

He opened his mouth to speak, and I knew him well enough to know that he was going to tell me that this was why I needed to go into hiding now, before the truth of my necromancy spread. Fortunately, Grey knew *me* well enough not to bother saying it again.

Instead, Grey gave my arm a comforting squeeze—or he tried to, anyway. He'd forgotten that my left arm was missing, and his fingers grazed the wool of my cloak. He stuttered an apology, flustered, but I ignored him. He would have to get used to the ways I had changed since we first met.

The wind whipped around us as the boat picked up speed over the bay. He looked out over the water, and I wanted to ask him what he thought of it all. Did he remember those first days we went to the quarantine hospital with Master Ostrum and our fellow students? Did he think of some other time, sailing with his parents, perhaps, or with friends like Tomus?

Did he wish he was with them instead of me?

"Do you ever wonder what would have happened if I'd never come to Yūgen?" I asked, my words almost lost in the wind.

Grey's face was somber. For a long time, he didn't answer. He just stared at me.

I wondered what he saw.

"I cannot imagine a life without you," he said finally. "I know I had one, before we met, but it feels . . . like a memory my brain tries to suppress. These past few days . . . I thought you didn't want me anymore."

"Because you didn't want me," I said quickly.

"I *don't* want your revenants," Grey said, emphatic. "But that doesn't mean I don't want you."

I turned my head away, signaling the end of the conversation, but Grey didn't relent.

"This isn't sustainable," he said. He was so close now that his words melted directly into my ear. "You cannot live forever in a clock tower surrounded by corpses."

The wind bit at my eyes, making them water. I touched my crucible, sensing both the power inside it and the souls it linked me to.

"My mother was the practical one," I said. I didn't look at Grey, but I could tell that he was surprised by the sudden shift in conversation, even more so because I so rarely spoke about home to him. "She tried to ground Nessie and me." I laughed. "Nessie walked with her head in the clouds, always, and Mama would be the one reminding us that we had to work to make all those dreams come true."

I heaved a sigh. We were almost to Hart now—I could see the busy dock, even though it was too far to hear.

"Papa, he was the one who believed," I continued. "He believed in us. Believed we could do *anything*."

I turned to Grey now. He studied my face, trying to understand me.

I could go on. I could tell Grey my hope to restore Nessie's soul, my belief that I could do it, if I just had the right knowledge and resources.

But I didn't want to see the doubt in his eyes.

TWENTY

Grey

HART WAS AT once both bigger and smaller than I expected. The docks themselves were narrow, and the Emperor's cruiser had difficulty finding a large port.

But as soon as Nedra and I were past the wooden docks, I realized that this was no provincial town. The streets were made of earth-packed cobblestones, smooth and even. Although the southern part of the city was a mishmash of crisscrossed streets, farther north they settled into a familiar grid pattern. I was reminded that Hart was older than Northface Harbor. It had been the original capital, and Northface Harbor benefitted from the mistakes of the old city. Rather than sprawling chaotically as it grew, Northface Harbor was plotted out with a grid of numbered streets and a dock area large enough to expand as the traffic rose.

"So where are we going?" Nedra asked. She had her cloak pulled up over her white hair, held in place by pins. I had worried she'd look too conspicuous, but several women and a few men wore their hoods pulled low.

"The Emperor's steward arranged for us to have rooms at a local inn." I consulted the little book where I'd written down the information. The inn was called the Eagle & Child, and was located on Lethe Street, but I had no idea how to navigate.

"Us?" Nedra asked, cocking an eyebrow at me.

It took me a moment to understand her. "Well," I said, smiling, "a room for me. But I'm sure we can get another for you." I hoped so, anyway. If worst came to worst, I could sleep on the ship as the soldiers aboard were doing. But it would be noisy, cramped, and uncomfortable.

The ship was going to stock up for the journey across the sea. It should take us eight days total to reach Miraband, the Empire's capital, a few less or more depending on weather. Most of the crew were soldiers who were returning home after their commissioned time abroad was up. The return journey would bring their replacements back to the Emperor as well as, I hoped, a new commission for exports from Lunar Island.

Nedra and I walked along the dock as I explained this all in more detail to her. Rather than be excited by the prospect, though, Nedra frowned.

"Doesn't this all seem a little . . . rushed?" she asked.

I conceded the point. "But the Emperor wants to be able to give people good news at the rally he's holding soon," I said. "He wants to show everyone that he's a different ruler from the tyrant Adelaide painted him to be."

We walked a few more paces along the wooden dock. The boards were weather-worn and splintering, not at all like the smooth planks of Blackdocks.

"Then why you?" Nedra finally asked.

I shook my head, unwilling to answer her question.

"If it's that important to change the north's economy like *that*," she continued, snapping her fingers, "why send you and not a finance expert? Or someone who works with inter-colonial trade?"

I bit my lip. How was I supposed to tell her that I was being sent because I was the only one who'd brought up the north's destitution?

That no one on the council bothered to speak up in support of the idea?

That I wouldn't have cared either, had it not been for Nedra?

We reached the end of the dock, where the streets began, and I looked around. I could see a covered marketplace extending from the docks, though, and a part of me wanted to go straight there, to get started on my task and prove to Ned that I was up for the job.

Nedra slipped her hand around my arm, her fingers gently pulling me back to the here and now. "Let's get to the inn first," she said softly.

I shook my head, clearing it. "Of course." I looked around me. In Northface Harbor, metal-and-enamel street signs were embedded into the sides of buildings at intersections. That was true here, too ... occasionally.

"Where is it?" Nedra asked, a smile playing on her lips. I rattled off the address to her, and in a few moments, she strode confidently down one street and then another.

"How can you tell where we're going?" I said. "This city makes no sense."

Nedra shrugged. "I've been here enough times, I suppose. Here, go this way, it's quicker." Nedra veered off the main street toward a set of stairs that connected to a higher street. My legs pumped as I hurried to keep up with her pace.

I remembered the way I had taken Nedra to the Imperial Gardens in Northface Harbor. She had gotten so turned around that I had to guide her back to Yūgen afterward. She had seemed like such a country girl. But Nedra was in her element now. I realized that back then, she hadn't been overwhelmed by city life; she just hadn't had a chance to get to know *my* city.

"Here," Nedra announced, drawing up short in front of a drab-looking building. The walls were covered in cedar planks, rough-hewn and stained dark, interrupted only by two large windows made of tiny panes filled with blown glass, each little square marred by bubbles and waves. Hanging above the door was a painted wooden sign without words, just a picture of an enormous roc eagle with a naked baby clutched in its talons. The child seemed oddly calm despite its airborne kidnapping.

Nedra noticed me staring. "It's from one of the old myths," she said dismissively, ignoring the sign as she pushed open the door.

I immediately stumbled as I followed her inside; the floor was so old that the entrance dipped in, the wooden planks worn smooth and thin from use. Nedra caught me with her left shoulder, steadying me.

She waited for me to take over; the reservation was in my name. But I saw no serviceman ready to wait on us, and there was no desk. Sighing but still smiling, Nedra nudged me toward the bar.

"Whatchoowan?" the barman said in one breath. I was still trying to discern what he had asked when Nedra spoke for me.

"We have reservations for the night," she said. Before she finished the sentence, more of her country accent had slipped into her speech. The barman grinned at her.

"Oi, yeah, both ya?" he said, nodding to me.

"It's for one room, but could we have two?" Nedra asked. She nudged me again.

"Oh, yes, um," I started, reaching for the slip the travel secretary had given me, a lender paper from the Emperor's funds.

The barman turned to Nedra, ignoring me. "Yeah, w'gotcha. Up and last two left, sav?"

Nedra smiled. "Wonderful, thank you," she said.

She turned and headed toward the set of stairs.

"What about our rooms?" I hissed.

Nedra shot me a look. "We have the last two on the left on the second floor," she said. "Didn't you hear him?"

There were only six guest rooms total, but I suspected we were the only occupants today—the hall was empty and silent. Nedra and I each claimed our room, agreeing to head to supper in a few minutes. When we met in the hall soon after, Nedra leaned against the wall, her cloak slipping off her shock of white hair.

"Here," I said, reaching up and tugging the material down. Her hair was soft and smelled faintly of flowers. She rolled her eyes at me as I tucked a lock back under the dark cloak, checking the pins.

"We're in Hart now; I don't have to be so careful," she said, pushing me away.

The lower floor of the inn served as a tavern. A group of men sat at the bar, steadily drinking mead and rarely talking, but a larger group of people gathered near the big open fireplace, sitting on stuffed leather chairs, plucking meat rolls from the large basket set on the center table.

Nedra led me to a table hidden in the shadows, not that far away from the group by the fire. A lanky boy with a shaved head came by to tell us that supper consisted of two choices: meat rolls or stew with bread. Our drink choices were limited to mead, apple wine, or water. "Though we got some goat milk if you want it?" the boy asked in a cracking voice.

We both chose stew and water. I would see enough of meat rolls on the journey.

Once the steaming bowls were placed in front of us, Nedra took a spoonful and sighed happily. "It's not your fancy food, but it's good, isn't it?" she asked.

I could tell she really cared, so I waited until I'd properly tasted my own supper before grinning at her. "It is," I confirmed.

Nearby, the group by the fire had finished eating and had moved on to mead. The longer they sat together, the louder they got.

And the angrier.

"He's not going!" one woman announced. "We all saw that ship that docked today. He's sent some of his soldiers here."

My eyes widened as I looked at Nedra. They were talking about the Emperor. They were talking about my ship.

"Nah," another man said, touching the woman's arm. "They're just here for a night or two before they head back to Miraband. I heard the captain talking to the dockslip."

"Yeah, but the Emperor's not going, is he?" the woman snarled back. "That ship'll come back with even more soldiers, mark it."

"What's he need soldiers for?" another woman asked. "He can go back to the mainland and leave us be."

I wanted to tell them that they were wrong. The Emperor cared about them all, my mission was to *help* them. Nedra shook her head at me subtly, but I didn't need her warning. I knew better than to speak.

"He needs soldiers to kill the witch," an older man sitting near the fire said. His voice was low, but the entire tavern silenced when he spoke.

Witch? I sucked in a breath, my eyes shooting to Nedra. She ducked her head lower, turning her cloak to they couldn't see her face, let alone her hair. Information of Nedra's necromancy might not have shown up in any of the official news sheets, but I shouldn't be surprised that the story had traveled fast. People talk, and who wouldn't want to talk about this? I found myself wondering how different things would be if the news sheets had just printed the whole truth.

"She may be good. Wellebourne was from here. Wellebourne wanted to lead us to freedom." I couldn't see who spoke, but the words were met with disdain.

"Good? That heretical witch? She should burn for what she did." The old man thumped his leg against the floor, and it thudded heavily; he had a wooden leg to replace one that was likely lost in the plague.

"You read the news sheets," the first one said, swinging her mug of mead toward the old man. "The plague came from Governor Adelaide."

"Can't trust any of 'em," the man snarled back. "Nothing good will come from a witch like that back on our island. *Nothing*," he spat. Most of the others around him nodded in agreement. "We should go to the little rock she's camping out on and kill her ourselves. Throw her head at the Emperor, and maybe then he'd leave us be."

His accent was thick, but it just made the vitriol in his voice that much more evident.

Nedra put her spoon down beside her bowl but otherwise didn't move.

"We don't need any of 'em!" the man said, his voice louder, thunking his wooden foot on the floor for emphasis. "If we want to be true free men of Lunar Island, we can't have a tyrant from the mainland, and we can't have a witch of our own who'll do nothing but turn us into dead flesh puppets."

Nedra flinched.

"Yeah?" A voice from across the fireplace—a woman with short-cropped hair—spoke up, challenging the older man. "And what *do* you want, Rom?"

"Not them," he spat out. "Someone from here. Ain't got a single northerner on the council, do we?"

"That ain't true, Rom," the woman said. I wondered which members of council had been born in the north—certainly none of them spoke with a thick accent like these people. "It's them meetings what's been riling you up. Let the politicians do what they want, at least the plague is over. We can recover on our own."

"If we're to be left on our own, why not let us rule on our own?" Rom looked around for support. I didn't hear anyone clamoring to his side, but he must have been satisfied, because his voice rose in triumph. "We need no ruler to guide us from across the sea; we can rule ourselves!"

"Fine." The woman crossed her arms. "You go start a rebellion against the most powerful man in the world. I'll be busy with the farm, then, and counting my blessings we've no more sick."

A few others muttered their agreement, but the man thumped his foot against the floor again, then slammed his mug on the table.

"Are you that thick, Linna?" Rom gaped at her, as if he couldn't quite believe her words. "That plague, it was from a necromancer. And now you're fine letting another one live in our bay? She could do the same at any moment. Haven't we lost enough?"

He had struck a chord. The woman—Linna—scrunched her face, her eyes welling with rage-filled tears that she swiped away. "Don't you talk to me about what I've lost," she growled.

"There, *that*." The man leaned in closer to her, almost knocking one of the other people out of his way. "That anger? That's what we need now."

"I'm not joining your little cause," Linna said, steeling her spine and turning away from the man.

"There's more of us than you'd think." The man looked around the room. It was clear that, of everyone, he was the political radical, and while most of the people in his crowd avoided his eye contact, there were a few quietly nodding in agreement.

"Besides," Rom said as Linna started to walk away. "I know what your mother would say."

"Don't you dare talk about my mother," Linna said, but the fight was draining from her.

"She was a religious woman, and you know it," Rom said. "She may not have cared about politics, but she wouldn't suffer a witch to live on her island. It's against the gods." He looked around, locking eyes with all of his friends, his gaze thankfully skimming over Nedra and me. "It's against the gods, I say, and they'll only be happy with us if the necromancer burns."

TWENTY-ONE

Nedra

I ALMOST WISHED that there had been no extra rooms at the inn, and that Grey and I had been forced to sleep together. I kept hearing that man's words over and over in my mind, and I wondered what he would do if he knew who I was. Would he have reached into the flames for a torch? Or would he have listened? I didn't want to turn this world into a stage for my undead; I only wanted to be left alone.

In the silent night, I reached out for my revenants.

Ollah?

There was no response for so long that I worried I was too far away from my revenants for us to communicate. But eventually, I felt her—felt the others.

All is quiet, she whispered in my brain. Relief washed over me. There was no threat tonight, at least. Still, anxiety twisted my stomach. I didn't like how far I was from my revenants, how much time it had taken to get such a simple reply.

I woke at dawn. Grey had his work to do, and I saw no point in delaying my own.

My plan was a shot in the dark, and I knew it, but I had mostly resigned myself to the idea of going along with Grey to Miraband. Still, Papa had mostly traded in Hart with one book dealer in particular, so checking her shop first seemed like a logical starting point.

Dressing quickly, I paused before I left, then turned to the small potbelly stove in my room. It was warm enough that I had not lit it last night, but there were ash and coal still inside. I grabbed a chunk of coal and carefully rubbed it against my white hair. It wasn't perfect by any means, but with my cloak pulled and pinned, it was better than before.

I checked my appearance in the grimy mirror by the door. For a moment, walking the streets of Hart beside Grey, I'd felt . . . comfortable.

But that, I knew, was exactly the kind of thinking that would get me—and therefore all my revenants—killed.

Safe did not exist.

Wrapping my cloak tighter and grabbing my knapsack, I slipped from my room and down the stairs, out of the inn, pausing only to ask the barkeep to tell Grey I'd gone to Bunchen's antique shop. I didn't want him to worry, and I wanted to do this alone.

In the cool morning light, traces of fog lingered in the air, but it was rapidly evaporating. The docks were far enough away that I couldn't hear them, but I knew that they would be the busiest place in the whole city now, fresh fish being carted right to the market, ships preparing to cross the bay to the city, journeys beginning or ending. But even the streets uphill from the dock were already bustling with activity.

As I turned a corner, I almost rammed into a mule with a cart lashed against a post. An early delivery to one of the nearby houses, I supposed. The mule was soft grayish-brown, with big warm eyes that reminded me of Jojo, the mule Papa had used for his bookcart. I wished I had an apple or a lump of sugar, but I held my empty palm out anyway. She snuffled my hand.

Her eyes rolled back in fear, and her ears flattened against her head. She let out a wild bray and kicked with her back legs, dislodging her cart. I tried to step forward to calm the animal, but the mule jerked against her stays in her frenzied attempt to get away.

To get away from me.

I was drawing too much attention. I scurried back as the front door of a nearby house opened and a man ran down to the cart. Others crossed the street to help him calm the mule, but I ducked into an alley, my feet pounding over the paving stones. It wasn't until I was several blocks away that I stopped, my heart racing.

I recalled the way the dogs had barked at me when I made my way to the castle with my undead army as I faced Governor Adelaide. Could they sense the dark power I now held? Did I disgust them? I almost didn't mind the way men and women reviled me, but to think that even animals found my presence horrific was too much to consider. The people of the island could label me anything they wanted, believe whatever lies or rumors they'd heard, but if even animals saw me as a monster, what claim to innocence did I have left?

I made my way farther north, climbing up the stairs that connected the alleyways before veering onto Broad Street. Maids swept the stoops of their masters' houses. Milk carts rattled over the cobblestones, followed by the mail carts. Children were already claiming corners from which to sell news sheets.

In many ways, this was still the Hart of my childhood. We hadn't come here often, but I knew the city well enough to have a favorite pastry shop, to remember a few shortcuts, to avoid certain areas. The buildings were unchanged, the streets were still familiar.

But as the morning crept toward noon, I slowly became aware of how the people had changed. There was an edge that hadn't been there before. Hard, cold stares if I lingered near shop windows. Gaunt cheeks on the children at the corner. People crouched in the shadows, drawing away from the growing light, hiding behind tattered coats.

There had been homeless people in Blackdocks. I'd seen them often enough, as I made my way to the factories with Master Ostrum. Anyone who couldn't work—and there were many, thanks to the plague—was turned out. They begged or they stole or they didn't survive.

But I had never seen a homeless person in Hart before.

I paused outside an alleyway. Had it just been the naiveté of childhood that kept me from noticing these men and women, children even, huddled in the shadows?

No. I gritted my teeth together. This was another effect of the plague, of Governor Adelaide's heartlessness.

But I saw the way the people of Hart walked past the homeless, carefully avoiding eye contact, pretending not to hear the plaintive begging, soft as a kitten's mewing. And I remembered Papa's story, about the Boy-Monster.

Fear makes us do horrible things to people, Papa had said. *Apathy makes us allow horrible things to happen to them.*

If I threw off my cloak and held up my iron crucible, I knew I could invoke not just fear but true terror. And the cold horror that would fill the good citizens of Hart at the sight of me would make them strike out. Call the Guard, bring a rope, light the torches.

But right now, it was the people's apathy that seemed far, far worse.

I reached into the pocket of my cloak. I didn't have many coins—what use did I have for money on my little quarantine island?—but I withdrew three large copper pieces and strode into the dark alley, determined to help as much as I could. A man sat at the base of the alley, his body half-hidden by a large trash bin that smelled of old grease and rancid meat. He didn't look up when I approached. His head bent forward, his face hidden behind unwashed locks of stringy dark hair. Part of his torso and his lap were covered with grimy old news sheets, a poor blanket even on mild nights.

I didn't want to wake him, but I pressed the coins into his palm. His fingers responded before the rest of his body awoke, wrapping around the coins. His eyes opened slowly.

I saw it then. Death. This man's soul was tired. I channeled my power, shifting my vision. He had been dying for a while now.

The dark power at the base of my crucible pulsed with longing. I had never sensed it before, but ever since a piece of my soul had touched it, I could not escape my awareness of the starving blackness that swirled inside.

Souls were a type of energy. I had used that small bit of my own soul to energize Ernesta for a few moments. But the body was an imperfect vessel to hold all that energy—at least, a dead body was. This man was too weak to do more than blink at me as I sat back on my heels, watching him die; his soul was rapidly escaping his body, much like steam evaporating from a pot of boiling water.

I held my shadow hand out, and the pale golden light drifted toward me, weaving around my dark fingers like threads made of water.

His eyes were sharper now, but he was still too weak to protest. His soul did, though. As soon as the light touched my shadow hand, I heard his cries of anguish, his longing to just be done with it all and die. And I knew him, as I knew all my revenants. I knew what he'd lost in the plague. Everyone.

But I pushed the sound of his begging voice away, focused only on the energy of his soul. It pooled in the palm of my shadow hand. Already, the man's body was still. His chest did not rise and fall with breath; there was no thrum of life in the bulging vein on his neck.

My shadow fingers wrapped around the man's soul in the same way his fingers had gripped my coins.

Even if the man wanted nothing more than to pass to the afterlife, I could plunge it into my crucible. Rather than raise his dead body, though, I wondered if I could use the raw energy from his soul for my sister. It had seemed to work for a second with the awlspring's life force. If a dead bird could wake my sister up long enough to speak, how much time would I have with one whole, fresh, human soul, bright and burning? Perhaps I could store his energy in my crucible, take a ferry back to the hospital, feed it into her . . .

A voice that sounded like my sister whispered in my mind: *No.*

Here was the line I would not cross.

My shadow fingers unclenched, and the light rose from my palm, fading as the soul dissipated.

Before I left the alley, I took my three copper coins back. He had no use for them now.

I was perhaps fourteen on the last journey I took with Papa to Bunchen's antique shop, maybe fifteen. Nessie had stopped going with Papa a few years before. She liked to stay at home with Mama, slipping away to spend the summer days swimming in the pond outside the village or running about with her friends. We were not just sisters but also the best of friends—regardless, we both relished the weeks we could be free of the other.

So Nessie pushed me to go with Papa while she stayed at home. I preferred it that way, truth be told. I liked the quiet, even thuds of Jojo's hooves on the dirt-packed road, I liked the way Papa's cart swayed, and the heaviness of the books behind us.

And I liked Hart.

Papa was always careful to keep me close to him in the city. It wasn't safe, he said, especially for girls alone. He never let me go by myself down to the docks, and the one time I tried to slip away, when I was eight or so, he'd been so angry at me that I'd cried. I understood now why Papa had been afraid. I'd worked in the poorer section of Blackdocks often enough to recognize the danger to girls alone, lured into the shadows or, worse, swept onto ships against their will.

Papa had been so afraid of this city, the largest in the north, but he never saw what Northface Harbor was like, the factories and the death. Hart seemed laughably small now, and the dangers I'd been warned of seemed distant and easy to avoid.

Bunchen's antique shop was marked with a wooden sign over the door, most of the paint chipped away. Much like the sign at the inn, there were no words, just a painting of a stack of books beside a vase and the bust of a man, probably one of the old Emperors. Not everyone in the north was literate; illustrative signs were common.

I pushed open the heavy wooden door, my fingers coming away grimy. The door scraped on the floor, creating an arc of dirt in the entry as I stepped inside.

"With you in a moment," a voice called from the back. The shelves and tables were so cluttered here that, although the room was small, it was easy to disappear.

The first time I came here with Papa, I had been told to explore while he negotiated with the antiques dealer. Bunchen traded in all kind of goods, but the entire wall along the back was lined with old books, and she was the best at digging up volumes for customers that Papa couldn't find on his own. I'd had enough of books with Papa's cart, though, and I'd lingered on the other side of the shop, where the shelves were cluttered with a myriad of treasures. I closed my eyes, a smile lingering on my lips as I recalled the sense of discovery that had washed over me when I peered inside a dusty, wooden box lined with aged silk. It had contained a plain stone, polished to a shine, and it made me wonder at who had taken the time to so carefully placed the little, insignificant rock against the fine silk.

Bunchen was still not at the front desk, so I wended my way to a glass case containing a line of copper crucibles of varying sizes.

"How can I help you?"

I started at the voice and whirled around. Bunchen was just as she had been when I was younger—very tall, with a wiry frame and stern steel-colored eyes that had intimidated me as a child.

Before I could say anything, her look softened. "Nedra Brysstain."

The corners of my lips twitched up. She recognized me still, despite the cloak and the coal staining my hair. But what was more, her tone of voice was warm and inviting. She greeted me as a friend.

"Hello," I said.

She eyed me for a long moment. "I heard about your village. Your family."

I ducked my head.

"I heard about you."

I met Bunchen's eyes. Papa always said that she was one of the smartest women he knew, and I had no doubt that was true. Bunchen stepped closer to me, and I noticed then that there was a hollow sound to her step. Her skirts covered her legs, but I suspected her left foot had been amputated. No one was untouched by the plague in the north.

Bunchen reached up, and I thought for a moment she was going to caress my face. Instead, she wound her fingers around a lock of my hair that had escaped my pins, pulling it gently over my shoulder. Her fingers came away dusted with coal.

"Nedra Brysstain," Bunchen said again, a small smile on her lips and wonder in her voice. "Your father would be so proud."

TWENTY-TWO

Grey

I SPENT TEN minutes knocking on Nedra's door before the innkeeper peered up the stairs and told me that she'd left at dawn, to a store I hadn't heard of.

"She ya sister?" he asked me as I grabbed a roll from the basket on the table. It took a moment for his thick accent to melt into my ears.

"No," I said, and turned and left before he could further inquire about our relationship. I thought I heard him chuckling as I closed the door behind me.

The market in Hart wasn't hard to find; it was connected to the docks, and we'd passed it on our way into town. The Emperor's steward had told me that I was welcome to take more than just a day perusing the market, but that the ship would leave without me and I'd be forced to wait for the next one, or book my own passage off Lunar Island.

I shouldn't have worried, though. When I reached the market, I knew it would not even take me the full day to examine its offerings.

The building was long, wooden with a thatched roof and no walls, just pillars interspaced between tables. The side closest to the docks was full of fish vendors, but most of them seemed to be closing up for the day.

Beyond fish, farmers from the villages had set up their produce. The largest farms had tables, but people—mostly women and children— pushed wagons or wheelbarrows of vegetables through the crowds, offering cheaper prices but far inferior wares. Every once in a while a merchant with a table shouted down one of the children scalping his business, but, like fleas on a stray dog, when one scampered off, another soon took their place.

I moved quickly through this part of the market—I could sell Miraband neither produce nor fish.

A few stalls were reserved for tinkerers and repairmen. A cobbler nailed a boot heel by a bench; a clock smith offered to repair my watch, even though it wasn't broken. The stalls farthest from the dock were actually little rooms, with a gateway entrance and aisles of wares.

"Can I help you?" a man asked as I picked up a felt hat from the display. I watched as he scanned me, quickly determining that I was from the south and therefore had more money to throw around. "Best hats in the north, in all of Lunar Island," he boasted. "Here, this one's made of orcine." He reached for a hat farther up and handed it to me.

I brushed my fingers along the smooth fur of the hat, soft and sleek as brushed silk. It reminded me of Nedra's story about the widow.

As the hatter wrapped a tape around my head to measure, the enormity of what I was trying to do hit me. I had no idea if there was a market for orcine hats in Miraband. Were there even enough orcines around the northern islands in the Stellar Chain to meet demand, if I could make demand?

"I'll take one," I said finally. I gave the man a coin and ordered the felt hat as well as a bonnet decorated with paper flowers to be sent to the ship at the dock. I did the same with most of the stalls, selecting a sample of leather belts from one, straw dolls from another, wooden engravings from a third.

I'd spent most of the money I'd reserved for today's market trip by the time I reached the end of the market. I wasn't sure which of the items would pique the interest of the trade commission, but surely something would stand out. Perhaps our leather would be tanned more durably, or maybe the homespun cloth would have a nostalgic feel to it that could spark a new fashion trend.

I had to at least try.

"Fancy man!" a young voice called.

I turned—as much as I didn't want the moniker to apply to me, I knew it did. A young woman who looked to be about my age waved at me. "Heard you were the one buying everything in the market," she said coyly as I approached. She had a ring on her finger, and the way her apron gathered over her stomach made me think she might be pregnant.

"I'm looking for authentic wares," I said.

"Authentic wares." She smirked at me. "What sort of *authentic* wares you looking for?"

"Anything," I said. "I have a variety of interests."

She leaned against the post in the market, eyeing me. "You ain't got no clay."

"Clay?"

The woman was subtly leading me away from the main market, but I didn't mind.

"Earthenware," she clarified. "My family makes the best bowls and plates this side of the island." She seemed so proud, I couldn't help but smile as she whistled a little tune. I picked up my pace to keep up with her, bumping into a little girl as we rounded an alleyway.

"Where's your studio?" I asked. It was harder to keep up with her, and the streets were narrow.

"Studio." She laughed gaily. "We just work down by the bay. But here ya are." She stopped in front of a stoop, where a large bowl and a short stack of plates were displayed. She gestured to her wares, and for the first time I noticed that she was missing her right hand.

The clay items were few, and certainly not worthy of the evident pride the woman had for them. When I picked up a plate, red dust clung to my fingertips, and the plate beneath the first was chipped and cracked.

"Best on the island," the woman said again, grinning at me.

Something about this whole exchange felt wrong, but I couldn't place it.

"Ah," I said, trying to think of the right words to politely disengage from her. "Sadly, I don't think these would survive the journey."

She shrugged as if it didn't matter, then sat down on the stoop. "Well, thanks for seeing what I had to offer," she said, clearly ready to dismiss me.

I stood there a moment, struck by the strangeness of the whole situation, then turned and made my way back down the twisting streets toward the market. It wasn't until I rounded the corner that I thought to touch the coin purse on my belt.

Gone.

I remembered the tune the woman had whistled, the little girl who'd bumped into me. Whirling around, I raced back to the stoop, but there was nothing there now but broken bits of red clay pottery.

Rage washed over me. Not at the loss of money—I had taken only a portion of my travel stipend and could afford to lose it. But I felt like a fool not to have seen through such an obvious ruse. Had I been in Northface Harbor, I wouldn't have fallen for the woman's trick, but—my cheeks burned—I hadn't expected the people of Hart to be so ruthless.

Or so clever.

I was so caught up in my own stupidity as I made my way down the streets, back to the market, that I almost missed the woman who'd tried to sell me the earthenware. She'd wrapped a red scarf around her head, making her seem older, and I would have passed her by except that when she saw me, she started like a deer and turned to run. Without thinking about it, I grabbed her hand, yanking her around.

There weren't many people on the street, but the few who were there took one look at me and ducked their heads, disappearing into the alleys.

"All I have to do is shout," I told the girl. "And the Guard will come."

She gaped at me. "You'd have me hung for ten silver?" My grip tightened; she'd just confirmed that she'd worked with the little girl to pick my pockets.

Her surprise at being caught quickly turned to anger. "Fine, then, do as you want," she spat. "Southerners always do."

I wanted to shake the contempt out of her. "Don't you realize I'm trying to *help* you? I'm trying to find exports to help your economy!"

Even though I still gripped her by the wrist and could easily call the authorities on her head for the crime she freely confessed to, the woman looked at me as if I were no more than an annoying pest. "You think you're going to save the north?" she said, her voice dripping with antipathy.

"I—I am." I felt unseated. "I'm bringing a new trade commission from the mainland here."

"How long is that gonna take?" She chatted idly, almost sounding bored.

"A few weeks to go there and back . . ." I started.

"A few weeks and then everything's solved?"

"Well, no," I allowed. "It'll take a while, but—"

"What's going to stop me from starving in the meantime?" she said, the bite back in her voice.

I stuttered at her, no answer rising on my tongue.

My hand slacked, and she wriggled free but didn't try to run away. "Here," she said, reaching into her pocket and spilling my coins on the ground between us. "Go make the world a better place."

"I—I'm sorry," I said, but she was already walking away.

I knelt to pick up the coins. From the shadows of the alley across from me, I saw small eyes staring at me. I stacked the coins up on the sidewalk, a tiny silver tower, then purposefully turned my back and walked in the opposite direction. Scampering feet raced out, coins clinking, and faded back into the silent dark.

TWENTY-THREE

Nedra

"PROUD?" I ASKED, trailing behind Bunchen as she led the way back to the front desk of her antiques shop. There was something about the way she'd looked at me, the way she'd said it that made me think . . .

Bunchen leaned against the counter. "Proud of what you've become," she said finally. She picked up an apple-sized paperweight from the counter, shifting it from one hand to the other as we spoke.

My hand went to my crucible, the cold iron a comfort to me. It was strange to think that the last time I was here, my father had been alive, and now his ashes were mixed with the iron inside.

Bunchen's gaze was sharp. "I had wondered if the rumors were true," she said finally, staring at my crucible. "Truth is always tainted when it comes from other sources."

"What rumors?" I asked.

"That Bardon's girl studied the fourth alchemy."

It had never occurred to me that Papa's fame as a bookseller would mix with my notoriety. I was used to the way everyone in my village had known me. But my identity there was mostly as a twin, a somewhat rare occurrence. And at Yūgen, I was known only as the poor girl. Somehow it hadn't hit me that my identity would be mixed up with my actions as a necromancer. I didn't mind so much being the necromancer, feared by the people of Northface Harbor and left alone with my army of the undead. It felt different, somehow, being known as *Nedra* the necromancer, daughter of Bardon Brysstain, the bookseller.

I could never hide from people who knew my roots. I had believed my greatest protection was first my army of the undead, and then my anonymity. My fading revenants stripped away my first protection; Bunchen had just shown me how flimsy the second was.

But more than that, Bunchen cast doubt on what I'd thought of Papa. "Are you saying my father would have been proud of this?" I asked, touching my crucible. "Of what I have done?" Of what I did do, to him. And Mama.

And Nessie.

I had never thought to speak of Papa with someone who knew him. When I'd left my village, my home nothing but smoldering embers, I had excised the memories of my parents alive from my mind.

Bunchen appraised me, a contemplative look on her face as she weighed her words. "Maybe not what you've done so far," she conceded. "But of what you can do." When I didn't answer, Bunchen put the paperweight she'd been fiddling with into my hand.

It was heavier than I'd anticipated, and it wasn't until I felt the rough metal that I realized it was iron. I rolled it over in my palm, trying to figure out why it was so familiar, but it wasn't until I put the flat end back on the counter that I recognized it. A tiny replica of the remains of the statue of Bennum Wellebourne that stood in the middle of the courtyard at Yūgen Academy, marred by having iron poured over the solid stone in ugly black lumps by the citizens who turned on him when he turned to necromancy.

"Wait," I said. Bunchen seemed to think I was some sort of new Bennum Wellebourne, ready to lead my army of the undead against the Empire. That didn't bother me so much; it was reasonable for her to connect necromancy with rebellion, given our island's history. Bennum Wellebourne had been one of the founding fathers of our colony, the first governor and a leader to our people. But the first years on Lunar Island had been plagued with poor weather, poor crops, and poor health, and when the Emperor of the time hadn't sent aid, Wellebourne had responded with a rebellion, intending to make the island its own nation instead of a lesser colony under the vast Allyrian Empire.

But when his militia had been slaughtered, he'd raised them again, creating an army of the undead that had made it as far as the gates of the castle in Miraband before being defeated.

Wellebourne had been caught and executed for his treason. And I had no intention of following in his footsteps, no matter what Bunchen assumed.

What really disturbed me was Bunchen's other implication. "Are you suggesting Papa supported the rebellion?"

Bunchen looked around the empty shop. "Come with me," she said, leading the way behind the front desk, toward the back room where she and Papa had always negotiated prices while I'd been left to my own devices.

If possible, the back room was even more cluttered than the shop floor, but a small round table was cleared off in the center.

Bunchen settled into a cane chair at the table, while I took the seat across from her. "Your father was no rebel," she said. "Much as I pushed him to be."

"But then—" I started.

"He was sympathetic to our cause," Bunchen clarified. "But he feared for you girls and your mother. He was a careful man. Still," she continued, "Bardon had clear ideas on what was right and what was wrong. He did what he could."

"What did he do?"

"Passed messages, mostly."

That made sense. I imagined it would be easy to hide messages in the books he sold, and no one would suspect him for going from village to village.

I sucked in a breath then, remembering what Nessie had told me about Papa the day before he died. Papa had gotten sick because he'd been traveling from village to village, despite the threat of the plague, determined to pass on books and deliver medicine. I'd thought he was foolish to risk his own life for this, even if he was helping others, but if his books also contained messages for something greater, the fate of our colony, our potential nation . . .

The cold iron of my crucible was so sharp, it felt as if it would burn my skin.

"He spoke of you often," Bunchen said in a gentle tone. "He told me about your studies in the city, how cosmopolitan you were becoming. He never quit talking about you and your sister."

For the first time ever, I was glad Papa couldn't see what I'd become. That he couldn't see what I'd done to Nessie. I didn't think he'd be proud of that.

"I need your help," I told Bunchen.

"I know," she said. "I've got it ready for you. I've been waiting, just as you told me to."

I tried to keep a straight face despite my confusion.

Rather than return to the shop floor, Bunchen shifted boxes out of the way, clearly searching for something in particular. In a moment, she withdrew a copper crucible, about the length of my arm but deep, like a small trough. A leather strap was wrapped around the lip in a sort of sling, making the vessel look like a strange metal purse.

Bunchen set the copper crucible down in front of me, a look of anticipation on her face. Copper crucibles were used for transactions— put the price inside the empty vase, speak the runes, and whatever was hidden inside the depths would appear. Master Ostrum had used a copper crucible to hide Bennum Wellebourne's journal and Bennum Wellebourne's own severed arm. I hoped Bunchen's crucible contained nothing so gruesome.

"It was a risk, sending me this without a note," Bunchen said, a hint of chastisement in her voice. "You'd be surprised at how well this sort of stuff sells, particularly if you can prove it's authentic. At least you had the sense to send it through the right channels."

"Right channels?" I asked, unable to hold back the question.

"Through the rebel network."

I tipped the crucible over, examining it. Most copper crucibles were used to protect valuable items, and the intricate runes on this one indicated that it was highly secure. In fact . . .

There it was. The reason why Bunchen thought that this crucible was meant for me. The runes were clear. Only a necromancer could unlock this crucible.

Or, more accurately, only a necromancer's blood.

At the very base of the copper crucible, two runes were etched inside a circle—*sanga* and *loggia*. The runes for "blood" and "key."

"One day, you must tell me how you found this." Bunchen's voice sounded reverential. "A Bennum Wellebourne original."

"How do you know Wellebourne made this?" I asked.

Bunchen shot me a withering look, and I was reminded that she was the lead antiquities expert in not just Hart but all of Lunar Island, at least according to my father.

"Do you have your silver?" she asked, eyeing my pack, which I'd taken with me this morning. I shook my head, and without another word Bunchen passed me a small silver crucible, about the size of my palm, and then she gave me a knife.

I had read about *sanga loggia* locks before, but never seen one in real life. Still, I understood the principle behind them. Most copper crucibles could be opened with a strand of hair, a drop of saliva, or even just a paper with a secret code written on it. But *sanga loggia* crucibles required a greater price.

I gripped Bunchen's knife between my left arm and chest, a simple task made harder thanks to my amputation, and then slid the forefinger of my right hand along the sharp blade. A blossom of blood bloomed on my fingertip. I held it over the lip of the silver crucible, and when the droplet fell, I whispered, "*Sanga loggia.*"

Rather than a splash, my blood hit the crucible's base with a clatter. When I tipped the crucible toward my palm, a bright red key tumbled into my hand.

"Hurry," Bunchen said. "You have only about five minutes once the blood melts to get whatever you want out, and then you have to do it again."

I carefully placed the key into the center of the copper crucible's base. The blood melted like chocolate on a hot plate, the end of the key sticking straight up.

The seemingly empty crucible was now full to the brim with books, boxes, and various items wrapped in cloth or paper. I sucked in my breath at the sight of half a dozen necromantic texts. Surely the answers I sought would be found here.

"May I?" Bunchen asked, her eyes alight with wonder. I held the unlocked crucible out toward her. She reached inside and withdrew a slender box, as long as a dagger and thick as a book. Bunchen held the box reverently, as if it contained a holy relic. It was made of a smooth, black material—stone or wood, I couldn't tell. She lifted the lid carefully.

"I've only heard rumors of this," she said, turning the box for me to see.

Half the box contained a series of papers scrolled tightly and bound with a hemp cord. The other half of the box housed small, square boxes. I picked up the first box, opening it carefully. Inside was a circular piece of iron the size of a coin and so rusty that it looked on the verge of crumbling.

Bunchen looked at me with eyes wide and lips quirked in surprise. "You don't recognize it?" she asked, a hint of disappointment in her tone.

I examined it more closely. As understanding settled on me, my eyes shot to Bunchen, who nodded grimly. "One of the rings used to seal the graves of the revenants Bennum Wellebourne raised."

Wellebourne had sailed across the Azure Sea, his army of the dead floating behind him. Without the need to breathe, it was easier to drag them like flotsam than afford them a spot on the ship. Wellebourne's necromancy died with him at his execution, and the bodies floated back to the shore, where family and friends gathered them up and reburied the dead, sealing each dirt mound with an iron circle to prevent them from being raised a second time.

"One of the originals," I whispered, my hand hovering over the iron. Some mourner—an ancestor of mine, perhaps—had pressed this metal circle into the fresh grave dirt mounded over their loved one, hoping it would be enough to stop their decaying flesh and bones from pushing through the soil once more.

Governor Adelaide had passed out nails bent into a circle when she'd helped the citizens of Lunar Island celebrate Burial Day last year. I could still smell the wet, red clay of the recent graves as I had pushed my iron into the earth and prayed for my family's safety.

I leaned in closer, turning the iron ring over in my palm. Through the rust, I could see runes.

"Can you read it?" Bunchen asked.

The series of runes engraved in the iron told a story. "This isn't about death," I said, squinting, puzzled. "I see—light and dark . . ."

I shook my head. When used together like this, these runes meant more than light and dark, right and wrong, good and evil. They meant the unclear space between two opposites. The gray area, the murky unknown.

"*Infansik*," I said. A rune without a proper translation in Allyrian, *infansik* meant a circular motion that implied repetition forever. "I think the runes indicate that good and evil, life and death are cyclical," I said. "What an odd choice for a charm meant to seal corpses in their graves."

Bunchen looked thoughtful. "I have seen this kind of thing before," she said. "In the more philosophical necromantic texts. Which I no longer have," she said when she saw my face brighten. "But many of the necromantic philosophies seem to say that our concept of what is right and wrong is not on a linear scale, but on a constantly turning circle."

"I still don't fully understand," I confessed.

"It's just philosophy. The salient point is that this ring was used in Wellebourne's time. It was one of the originals."

I looked at the books, all clearly old, most with lettering so faded I couldn't see their titles on the spines.

"Do you have any other necromantic texts?" I asked. "Even philosophical ones. I can pay," I added when Bunchen shook her head sadly. I didn't have much money, but Grey did.

"It's not a matter of coin," Bunchen said. "Those books are hard to find. What are you looking for?"

"I need something that will help me . . ." I struggled to think of the right words. "Restore a soul," I said finally.

Bunchen raised her eyebrow. "Restore a soul? Yours?"

I shook my head rapidly. "No, no," I said. Then I paused. "Why? Isn't it obvious I still have my own soul?"

Bunchen gave me a somewhat sympathetic smile, but it came out more like a grimace. "I have read of the way a necromancer grows . . . thin about the soul. Manipulating death so much, over time a necromancer's soul will start to weaken. The body, too—you'll age faster, die younger, the more you practice the fourth alchemy," she said. "Necromancers will sometimes steal the souls of others to replenish their own . . ."

"That's not what I want," I said quickly. "It's for—the others."

Bunchen's cold gaze narrowed. "How many do you have?"

"More than fifty," I said.

"A small army," Bunchen said. "But not a force to be ignored. And one that could grow."

Bunchen had given me the copper crucible because she had been instructed to pass it off to a necromancer. She worked with a network of rebels hoping to overthrow the Emperor; it seemed like she wanted me to emulate Wellebourne. I didn't like the idea of deceiving her, but I needed information. "They could be a formidable army," I said. "But they're becoming weaker by the day."

"Their bodies are failing?" she asked. "I've never heard of—"

"Not their bodies." I thought of how strong Nessie had been fighting at the governor's castle. "Their minds."

"Oh." Bunchen looked surprised. "They're not *supposed* to still have their minds, dear. They're dead. They have you to think for them."

So then why were my revenants different? Perhaps it was because they had wanted to come back that they held on to pieces of themselves as they were raised. But that just proved all the more how evil Wellebourne's actions had been. He'd taken his dead and had no problem using them as empty shells to fight his battles for him.

I didn't want to fight. I just wanted to be left alone. With revenants who were more than moving corpses.

As Bunchen turned her focus back to the contents of the box, I picked up the first book in the stack inside the crucible. A piece of paper fluttered out.

In careful black ink were written five small words:

The Collector
Corner Street
Miraband

The words were confusing enough—a partial address, no name—but what struck me was the paper itself. Because unlike everything else in this copper crucible, the paper was new. Crisp and bright white, with the uniform edges of one of the mainland's bookbinders.

"When did you get this box?" I asked.

Bunchen was distracted. "Oh, maybe six or seven months ago. Just when the plague was beginning."

This crucible could only be opened by a necromancer, and this piece of paper was far newer than the antiquities it was packaged with. Someone had recently opened it and had left me that paper.

Another necromancer.

It could have been Governor Adelaide, of course. She had found Bennum Wellebourne's old crucible, after all, and even if it had been cracked, she'd been able to use it to create the plague. But it didn't seem likely she would have worked with a network of rebels.

Master Ostrum? No—he couldn't have opened the crucible, only a necromancer's blood could open the *sanga loggia* lock.

There really must be another necromancer. Someone who had sent this crucible to the shop. Maybe that necromancer intended to return for this—perhaps when the plague hit, that necromancer had recognized what caused it and run away before he or she could be accused of creating the Wasting Death.

Maybe . . . I looked down at the paper, whispering last the word, "Miraband." Finding a skilled, practicing necromancer would be more valuable than finding a book. Someone who could actually teach me.

The bell on the outside door jangled as someone entered the shop. Bunchen's head shot up. In one smooth motion, Bunchen snatched

BID MY SOUL FAREWELL

the book from my hand, dropped it and the other contents back inside the copper crucible, and swiped away the melting remains of the key of blood in the bottom of the crucible. The contents disappeared, leaving nothing but a smear of red at the base.

"Hello?" a voice called.

"A southerner," Bunchen said, rolling her eyes at the accent.

"It's just Grey—he's a friend of mine," I said, already standing up.

"You trust him?" Bunchen asked, gripping my arm so tightly it hurt.

I hesitated. There were moments that lingered in my heart, reminding me of the way I used to fall into Grey's warmth. Nessie always made fun of me for being so slow to show the way I felt. All it ever took was a kiss for her to confess her love. Our entire lives at the village, I never once told someone outside my family that I loved them. That word felt—important. And when Grey and I started to grow close, when I actually did tell him that I loved him, it was more than just romance that swept through my blood. There was trust there, too, and faith in him. In us.

I didn't know what the future held. I only knew that when I'd seen him at the quarantine hospital yesterday morning, I realized that I could not simply turn my emotions off. I could not stop caring for him simply because I wanted to.

"I think I do," I said.

TWENTY-FOUR

Grey

"Hello?" The dusty shelves were labyrinthine. I could hear muted voices near the back, but I wasn't sure how to get to them.

"Back here," Nedra called.

Once I reached her, I sighed in relief. Finally, a friendly face.

I looked curiously at the large copper crucible Nedra carried, but she ignored my questioning eyes. She introduced me to the tall, severe-looking woman she stood beside, and I recognized the name as the owner of the shop. She did not look overly pleased to see me as she led the way to the store's counter.

"I'm Greggori Astor," I said, stepping forward and holding out my hand despite the cool welcome.

Bunchen's eyes widened. "Astor? Related to Linden Astor?"

Something about the way she said it put me on edge. "How do you know my father?"

Bunchen's entire attitude shifted. She no longer seemed wary of me; instead, she seemed almost sympathetic. "Shame about what happened," she said.

"My parents made their choice," I answered evenly.

"As do we all." Bunchen's eyes were sad. "Still, to have to flee like that . . . How can the Emperor issue orders to seize people without trial and not expect citizens to rise up against him?"

"I—er," I stammered. I knew my father's arrest warrant had been issued, and even if it made me sick to think of my father as a traitor, I had been a witness to his violation of the law. Saying he wouldn't get a fair trial was patently untrue, but what did I expect someone in such a remote city as Hart to believe? She likely heard only rumors; of course the Emperor would try the men accused of treachery.

"At least you had a chance to say farewell," Bunchen muttered. "He's a good man."

My head jerked back in shock. I wasn't sure which was more disorientating, that this woman thought I'd said farewell, or that she thought he was good.

"My father left in the dead of night," I said coldly, drawing out the words. "He's halfway to Doisha by now." I shrugged as if it didn't matter.

Bunchen paused. "No," she said, eyeing me warily. Her hand drifted to a small bowl on the counter, filled with iron rings made of horseshoe nails. Nedra's gaze focused on them, her eyes narrowing.

Bunchen selected one of the iron circles and handed it to me. I held it in my palm until she grew impatient, snatching my hand and pulling it over the counter, roughly pushing the ring over my knuckle. "You need to be more observant," she said. Her eyes flicked to a row of antique clocks hanging on the wall over the door to her store. "If you go now, you'll probably see them."

"Go?" I turned to Nedra, lost. She looked quizzically back at me.

"Go!" Bunchen insisted, shooing us toward the door. She stepped around the counter, holding Nedra's arm as she steered us out of her shop. "Check with the *Adamant* first, I think," she told me.

"The *Adamant*?" I repeated.

"The ship. Linden Astor has spent the past several days here in Hart, hiding, but he's scheduled to move this afternoon. I'm not sure which ship—the *Adamant,* probably, but if he's not there, the *Croque* or maybe the *Roc Flyer.* Any ship heading away from the Empire."

"My father's here," I said aloud. "He's here. In Hart." Realization sank into me slowly, and I was overwhelmed with unexpected emotion at the idea. I had spent so much of my life pushing my father away from me that I had thought myself immune to any childish longings for my parents, but I couldn't deny the hope and fear rising in my throat—hope that they would regret leaving me, fear that they would not. And, beneath that, an even deeper fear of regret if I did not seize this chance to say goodbye. "I have to see him!" I exclaimed, my eyes darting between Nedra and Bunchen. "I have to say—"

"Exactly," Bunchen said, letting out a sigh. I turned, looking out at the city, my heart pounding, my feet ready to go.

Nedra started to follow me, but Bunchen grabbed her shoulder, her fingers pressing into Nedra's cloak. Her voice was too low for me to hear, but Nedra's grip on the leather strap of the copper crucible tightened, and she nodded, her jaw set, before Bunchen pushed her toward me.

"Don't forget," Bunchen told Nedra.

"I won't," she promised.

The door shut in our faces.

"Come on," Nedra said, turning to me. She set a fast pace, and when she stumbled on a loose cobblestone, I offered to carry the cumbersome copper crucible she held or the knapsack on her back. Nedra refused.

Going downhill with Nedra as my guide through the old city of Hart was far easier than going uphill on my own, and we reached the docks in less than half an hour. It was far less busy this time of day—mostly ships arrived in the morning, with only a handful of ferries and passenger ships making anchor.

"Oi, Astor!" a voice shouted through the thinning crowd. I whirled around and saw the captain of the Emperor's cruiser ship waving at me.

"What is it?" I asked impatiently.

"We're stocked early, and I've stowed the cargo you purchased and sent to the ship," the captain said. He eyed me curiously. "We can leave ahead of schedule, if you are prepared." He subtly emphasized the word *you*, glancing at Nedra before looking quickly away.

I nodded, distracted. "But first, I have to—"

"Your things at the tavern?" the captain asked. "I can send a man to collect 'em."

"Yes, fine," I said, turning about. I saw a small caravel, with letters painted in black. The *Adamant*. Nedra followed at my heels as I pushed past the captain, racing over to the smaller ship.

A few crew members were loading crates on board—apples, which traveled well for the months-long journey, and barrels of water. "Excuse me," I said, reaching for a crew member, who shook me off. "Can you help me?" I asked, turning to another.

"No," he said gruffly, not even looking up. I whirled on my heel, desperation evident on my face. Nedra grabbed my hand.

"Calm down," she said, rubbing the skin on the back of my hand with her thumb.

My heart was racing. I hadn't been expecting a chance to see my parents. Ever since I'd discovered my home was empty, I'd tried not to think of them at all. They had made their choices.

"Ready?" a voice bellowed from the deck.

"No!" I whirled around. Without thinking of the repercussions of my actions, I jerked free from Nedra and bounded up the wooden gangplank before crew members could pull it up.

"What's the meaning of this?" a woman shouted, striding toward me. Her epaulettes labeled her the captain of the ship.

"Do you have any passengers on board?" I asked. "Please, I'm looking for my parents."

"We're a cargo ship." She spat the words out, glaring at me. "Disembark." Her finger thrust toward the gangplank.

"I—" I stopped, taking a deep, shaking breath.

The captain sucked at her teeth, her eyes on the iron ring around my middle finger. "Come with me," she muttered before turning to one of the crew and shouting, "Hold the stays!"

The captain led me down into the cargo hold, tapping a unique rhythm on the supporting beams as she went. Two figures slowly emerged from behind a row of crates where they had been hiding.

"Mama," I said, my voice barely audible. I hadn't called my mother by that pet name for years, not since I was a little boy, but it was the word that broke free from my throat in that moment.

Mother rushed forward, wrapping her hands around my face and pulling me closer to her. Tears welled in her eyes.

"Son," Father said when Mother released me. I thought for a moment he was going to shake my hand, but instead, he pulled me into a gruff hug, clapping me on the back before letting me go.

"What are you—?" I asked, staring around me with wide eyes.

"We had to go," Mother said. "And I'm sorry—" She turned to Father. "We thought it best . . ."

"You were safe," Father said. His gaze was somewhere just above my eyebrows. He didn't want to look me in the eye, and I wasn't sure why. "My informants said you were there, with the Emperor. No blame would fall on you for my actions. If we left . . ."

"If we didn't tell you," Mother added in a small voice.

". . . you would be safe. You'd inherit everything."

"I'm so glad you found us," Mother said. She reached over and grabbed me again, pulling me closer. "We've been funneling money to Doisha for years, Greggori, you'll like it there."

Mother didn't notice the way I stiffened, but Father did.

"You're not coming with us," Father said.

Mother's eyes grew wide and round, a silent "no" already forming on her lips.

"I found out you were leaving by chance," I said. "I just came to say goodbye. But, Father." I turned to him, unable to bear Mother's heartbroken look any longer. "The Emperor—he's not bent on revenge. Governor Adelaide's death is enough. Come back now, and you'll get a fair trial. You might be sentenced to a fine, but I'm sure he wouldn't . . ." I stopped. Father shook his head, his lips quirked in disappointment.

"There is no going back," Father said. "Not as long as that boy-king claims to be Emperor and rules our colony with an iron fist."

"Emperor Auguste isn't like that," I insisted. "He wants to see change here; he wants to *help* Lunar Island."

Father's jaw clenched, but he didn't speak again, even when I looked away. Heat rose in my cheeks. No matter what I thought of the Emperor, I couldn't be certain of my parents' fate if they stayed. They had acted as traitors. And even if Emperor Auguste had no wish to cut a swath of blood through Lunar Island, he couldn't ignore treason. Just as he couldn't ignore necromancy. Not forever.

Father put his hands behind his back and took a step away from me. "I do not know whether to pray that you never know the truth," he said slowly, "or to hope that, one day, you do."

TWENTY-FIVE

Nedra

AS WE LEFT the *Adamant*, Grey held on to my hand so tightly that it hurt, but I didn't try to pull away even as the strap on the heavy copper crucible slipped on my shoulder uncomfortably. He licked his lips, nervous. "The ironic thing," he said without a trace of irony in his voice, "is that I wanted my parents to stay. Face their trial and then come home. And . . ." He tugged my arm, pulling me closer. His voice was almost a whisper, meant only for me, not the bustling crowd of workers and sailors around us. "And while I wish I could be with you, I want you to go."

"We've discussed this," I started, but Grey cut me off.

"They're right to go!" Grey said so loudly that a few people nearby stopped to stare. He looked over his shoulder as the *Adamant* sailed into the bay. "It's safer."

I squeezed Grey's hand. "I don't care about safe."

I reached out mentally for my revenants. Silence.

I stopped in my tracks. "Nedra?" Grey asked. I shook my head tightly, teeth clenched, eyes shut, concentrating as hard as I could.

Ollah? I screamed silently. *Ronan? Kessel? Anyone?*

Several heartbeats later, images flashed in my mind—different views around the quarantine hospital. My brow creased in worry before I realized what was happening.

My revenants couldn't transmit their words to me any longer, though they could still show me what they were seeing. I choked back a sob. It was worse than I'd thought—they were fading so rapidly. If I didn't act now, soon there would be nothing left of them.

I swallowed down the fear rising within me, straightened, and looked Grey dead in the eye. "I'm going to Miraband," I said. Somewhere out there, there was another necromancer. Someone who might be able to train me, help me restore my revenants fully. Help me save Nessie.

Grey knew better than to argue with me. We headed toward the Emperor's cruiser. I was glad I carried my belongings with me. When I'd gone home after Yūgen closed, I had left behind several things in my dormitory, including the map my father had given me. By the time I returned to campus, there was no time to go back to my room and reclaim the items. I had learned the hard way to carry everything I needed with me wherever I went.

Before we reached the ship, Grey grabbed my shoulder, holding me back. I whirled around to protest, but he silenced me with a look. "The deal was that the captain would take you to Hart, but no farther." I hefted my bag onto my shoulder. "But I think I might know a way around it."

I stood behind a mooring as I watched Grey dart up the gangway, looking for the captain. They talked quickly, heads bowed, then disappeared into the captain's quarters. Enough time passed for me to grow nervous before Grey raced back down the gangway toward me.

"Can you lose the cloak?" he asked me, somewhat breathless.

"My cloak?" I touched the silk cords at my throat. Mama had woven the wool for me, and my sister had sewn it as a present when we found out I'd be attending Yūgen last year. It had taken her a week to embroider the tiny, almost invisible little flowers along the hem.

"It's the only way," Grey said, shooting a look back at the ship. "It won't be cold in Miraband."

"The captain wants my cloak?" I asked.

Grey shook his head. "No, no—you'll see." He held his hand out.

"I suppose," I said, still unsure of whatever plan Grey had come up with.

"Great. Come on." Grey hurried back up to the ship, as if he was nervous the captain would change his mind if we didn't act soon enough. As we strode across the deck, I heard the voices of the crew following us, questioning loudly why I was allowed back on board the cruiser. We went straight to a room on the opposite side of the captain's quarters—spacious for a ship, but still rather small.

I gazed around the room, then nearly gasped in surprise—in the far corner, mostly hidden from view, stood a tall, slender boy I'd never seen before, his wide eyes fixed on me.

"Who—?" I started, but Grey grabbed my arm, squeezing hard.

"Astor!" The captain stood in the doorway, hands on his hips, glowering at Grey.

"But, sir," Grey started, a pleading tone in his voice.

"I told you we weren't taking passengers, least of all a witch!"

"I can pay," Grey started, jangling the coins in his purse, tied to his belt.

"It's not about payment!" the captain's voice rose, and I could see through the doorway that some crew members had stopped what they were doing, watching us. The captain stomped into the room, slamming the door behind him.

"You are under the Emperor's authority!" he shouted at the top of his lungs. But rather than protest, Grey turned to me.

"Quickly," he said, reaching for the silk cords of my cloak. He fumbled with the knot, then whipped the material off my shoulders, crossing the room to where the boy stood.

"And I expect you to fully obey all my orders!" The captain was still shouting, loudly. *So the crew can hear*, I thought as Grey wrapped my cloak over the boy's shoulders. He adjusted the hood, lowering it well over the boy's face.

The boy was half a head taller than me, but he hunched over, keeping the cloak low.

"The Emperor may have saddled me with your dead weight on this journey, but you'd best stay out of our way!" The captain was practically hollering, the wooden walls vibrating with his loud voice. "Just stay in your room and don't bother my men!"

"Ready," Grey said, pushing the boy wrapped up in my cloak toward the captain.

The captain paused, looking over the disguise, and shrugged. "It'll do," he said in a lower voice, one that wouldn't leave this room. He pinned Grey with a pointed look. "And you'll remember the deal?"

"Yes sir. Half now, half when we return."

Half? I wondered, before realizing what Grey meant—he'd paid off the captain. I wondered how many golden allyras had been exchanged for my passage.

"Stay out of our way," the captain added. He started to turn to the door, then looked from Grey to me and back to Grey again. "Well?"

"Yes!" Grey said, jumping to attention. He reached for me and dragged me over to the corner of the room—the one place that no passerby could see without actually coming inside.

The captain swung open the door and shoved the boy wearing my cloak out into the hall. "Get off my boat and curse it with your presence no more!" he shouted.

I could hear the crew jeering at the boy, laughing, tossing slurs at him as he rushed from the deck and back to the dock.

Grey crossed the room and closed the door. "Well," he said, turning to me, "that actually worked. I had to pay the captain from my own finances," Grey continued. "And I had to swear to him that you'd come back—he doesn't think the Emperor would look too kindly on him transporting a criminal, but apparently he also doesn't think the Emperor pays him enough."

I narrowed my eyes. Grey was trusting, but I doubted the captain would so readily risk his own skin to transport me, given my criminal status. Maybe he was secretly sympathetic to Bunchen's rebel network or planned to extort us for some other form of payment. I flexed my fingers. We would deal with that when the time came. Meanwhile, I had to get to Miraband.

I rubbed my shoulder, already missing the feel of the warm cloak resting against my skin.

"Good thing you had a cloak," Grey said. He gestured over his shoulder. "That was Jarron, the captain's nephew. He'll dump the cloak once he's out of sight and then return to his post as cabin boy."

"Oh," I said. I swallowed down the hard lump forming in the back of my throat.

It was just cloth.

"You'll have to stay hidden here for the remainder of the trip though," he said apologetically. "It's only a week, though, and the room is . . . cozy."

"You're right," I said, offering Grey a weak smile. "One week to Miraband."

"Is this okay?" Grey asked. The room was small, with one bed hammered to the floor and a single shelf built into the wall. I set the copper crucible Bunchen had given me onto the bed, noting the thin mattress and thinner blanket that covered it. "I can sleep on the floor," he added.

"It's fine," I said, without elaborating on sleeping arrangements.

This will all be worth it, I told myself. I tried to calculate the odds of someone attacking the quarantine hospital while I was away, then I pushed down the thought. In its place, worry for Ernesta boiled inside. Worry for all my revenants, if I couldn't reverse the way their souls were slowly seeping from their bodies.

While I sat, motionless, on the bed, Grey paced the cabin. I couldn't help but smile, knowing that his only worry was for me. "Peace," I told him, laughing. "This is going to be a long journey if you intend to walk across the ocean."

Grey paused, looking down at his feet. He moved to the bed and collapsed beside me just as the ship pushed away from the dock. His body lurched into mine, but when he righted himself, he didn't shift away. Our knees touched.

"This has all been moving so quickly," he said finally. "Just a few weeks ago, I was having dinner with my parents at their house. I was returning to Yūgen, planning out my last semester. Hoping to see you." His eyes cut to me with a flash of the schoolboy innocence they'd held when I first met him before quickly fading to something darker.

I moved to wrap my arm around him, pull him closer to me. But he sat at my left side, and I realized too late that there was nothing there to drape over his shoulders.

"Yes," I said simply, resting my residual arm against my side.

The ship moved with the rhythm of the waves and my whole body seemed to sway with it. Some people, I knew, got seasick, their stomachs turning with the uneven movement of the sea, but not me. Not us.

"Grey," I said, staring straight ahead. "How do you think this will end?"

It took a long time for him to say, "I don't know."

TWENTY-SIX

Nedra

"AND THIS," GREY said, plopping an orcine hat on his head, "is probably our best bet."

"A hat?"

"An *orcine* hat."

"Yes, I can see that. They don't have orcine hats on the mainland?"

Grey hesitated. "I don't think so," he said. "Orcines like the cold. Miraband is in the south."

I nodded. It was a fair point. Only . . . "You really think this is going to make a difference?"

"If not the hats, then this." He pulled out a set of silver spoons, the handles decorated in a pattern of intertwining vines. When he saw my unimpressed look, however, Grey added, "This may all seem ordinary to you, but the mainland doesn't have the regular wares of Hart. Something will stand out to them, and—"

I waved my hand. I'd heard his argument before, his belief that this scheme of the Emperor's would improve the livelihoods of everyone in the north.

Grey dropped the silver back in the crate and crossed the room to sit beside me on the bed. "Is it that hard to believe that maybe something good will happen? I know you're a pessimist, Ned, but between this and the rally, to say nothing of the new programs Emperor Auguste is implementing—"

"I just don't understand why you trust him," I said.

"What about the new orphanage and hospital he's planning?" Grey asked.

I shrugged. "Ask me again when they're actually completed."

"He's *trying*. I respect that."

Grey scowled when I didn't answer him, but I wasn't looking to pick a fight. Instead, I turned to the contents of the copper crucible Bunchen had given me.

"I've never seen one this large outside of a bank," Grey commented.

"What's inside is more valuable than any gold coins," I said. We spent the rest of the evening skimming through the handful of books, unwrapping the cloth-covered parcels, and opening each of the little boxes. One was full of dirt; the label said it came from a grave in Siber. Hidden in the dry soil were small bones—human finger bones, but far more than could have been taken from a single hand. Another box, marked with several different runes, contained nothing but a small, charred stick crumbling to ash, and several insect exoskeletons.

"What do you think these are?" Grey asked, picking up the hard shell of one of the bugs and examining it.

"Corpse beetle," I said, barely looking up. "Careful, they bite."

"They're dead," he started, but then screeched, dropping the scurrying beetle back into the box.

"Told you. And the captain told us to be quiet."

"It *was* dead!"

"They're called *corpse beetles* for a reason," I said. "They're supposed to look dead. Better close the box."

This time, Grey listened to me, slamming the box shut. "How can it have survived locked up inside here?"

"They eat dead flesh," I said. "Useful for if you need a skeleton. They can go into stasis for centuries after they feast if you set them on fire and store them away from sunlight."

Muffled scratching sounded from within the box. The corpse beetles had awoken. Grey stared at the box, rubbing the place on his finger where the beetle had bitten him.

"Living flesh drives them mad," I added, quickly placing my hand on the box and chanting the runes that sealed it again. "It has a taste for you now."

Grey's eyes grew wide and panicked. "What does that mean?" he asked in a hushed voice.

"That beetle will now hunt you for the rest of its life, until it consumes all the flesh from your bones."

His face paled.

"Kidding," I said, rolling my eyes at him. "They'll eventually go back to sleep if we leave them alone."

Grey pushed the box as far from him as possible, eyeing it distrustfully.

I picked up a different box and passed it to him. Inside was an iron ring, finer than the one Grey wore on his knuckle now. He didn't seem to recognize it. "One of the originals, used to seal the graves of the undead who returned to death after Bennum Wellebourne fell from power," I explained.

Grey dropped the box on the wooden floor of the cabin as if it, too, were full of corpse beetles. I picked it back up, cradling it in my palm with reverence.

"It took a while for me to see its significance," I said, picking the ring up and fingering the fragile iron. "It has runes on it," I told Grey. "Can you see them?"

He peered closer, squinting, then shook his head no.

"They're necromantic runes," I said again.

"Of course they are," Grey said. "Wellebourne—" And he stopped. Because he had realized what I had. Bennum Wellebourne had already been executed—hung for his crimes—when his army of revenants had fallen and been buried. He could not have made the iron rings that ensured they were trapped in their graves. There must have been someone else who at least had enough knowledge of necromancy to create these rings after Wellebourne had hung, someone who wanted to ensure the dead stayed that way.

I wondered how many more necromancers were out there, quietly righting the wrongs of unjust deaths, hiding because of ancient laws that painted us as evil.

"There have been other necromancers throughout history," I said. "And, Grey—some were good, not evil. We've just never heard of them. This ring is proof that a good necromancer helped seal the graves that Wellebourne had emptied. They're not all bad."

By the time I finished speaking, there was a pleading note in my voice, one that I wished I could have hidden but also couldn't deny. Because maybe if Grey could see that not all necromancy was evil . . .

Light danced off the ancient ring, reflecting the oil lamp's warm glow. I gasped, then held the ring closer to the flame. The runes engraved into the metal were small, ruddy, and dim, barely legible. But strands of almost-invisible silver light crisscrossed over the ring. "It looks like a cobweb," I whispered.

"What does?" Grey asked.

My fingers passed through the silver filaments as if they weren't there, but when I reached for them with my shadow hand, pressing the ring against each incorporeal finger, they could not penetrate.

"It's a net," I said. Even centuries old, the alchemy held strong.

Grey started to ask something else, but I shushed him. I put the iron ring on the table, then withdrew my necromancy crucible from the chain around my neck. The crucible was a few centimeters smaller in diameter than the ring, so I placed the iron bead in the center. Using my shadow hand, I tried to lift the ring over my crucible.

The iron bead hung suspended over the hollow center of the ring.

Grey gasped, though he couldn't see what I saw—part of the iron passed through. The net of light tangled with the golden light of my souls. That must have been the true purpose of the ring—to capture any soul that tried to rise from the grave.

But there was more than light in my crucible. There was darkness, too, that inky black in the center that was hungry for the power in my soul. It oozed over the flickering golden lights, down the sides of my iron crucible. The second the black touched the silver net, I could hear in my mind a hissing sound, like scorching. The net caught souls, but it was no match for the darkness.

I hissed in pain as one of the silver filaments broke apart, snapping so violently that I flinched. The darkness ate away at the silver light, poisoning it, burning through it until there was nothing left.

Until the iron ring splintered apart.

TWENTY-SEVEN

Grey

I WOKE WITH a jump, Nedra's face so close to mine that I almost shouted, stilling myself only when I felt the dampness on her cheeks wetting my own skin. The oil lamp had faded, but a flickering flame cast the room in shadows. We were both still dressed; we'd dozed without meaning to fall asleep for the night.

"I can't hear them, Grey," she whispered in my ear.

I turned awkwardly; Nedra's arm was around my neck, and her face was pressed against my shoulder. I couldn't see her, but I could feel her. Her whole body trembled, and her voice quaked as she whispered again, "I can't hear them."

"Who?" I asked, my voice cracking from disuse, sounding far too loud. Ships are silent in ways cities never can be.

"My revenants." Nedra pulled away, her eyes red-rimmed and wide open. "I *always* hear them," she said, touching the side of her temple with her finger. "Every single one that I raise. I hear their thoughts, always. Since I went to Hart without them, it's been . . . quieter. They could still show me what was happening at the hospital, though. But when I just woke up . . ."

"Silence?" I provided for her. She nodded, fresh tears welling in her eyes.

Nedra bit her lip. "What if . . ."

I didn't let her see my frustration. What if the dead were dead again? Good. They *should* be dead again.

But seeing the fear on Nedra's face, I swallowed my words into equal silence.

"I can't fail them," Nedra muttered, falling back against my neck. I wrapped my arms around her, holding tightly.

"I don't know what it's like to lose everyone you love," I said. "But I know it's not your fault."

Nedra made a noise—it could've been a sob or a laugh. "How do you *always* know the exact worst thing to say, Grey?" she muttered. "Besides, you're wrong."

I looked at her curiously, not understanding.

"I haven't lost everything. That's the difference between me and the rebels, the homeless, the other survivors." She took a quavering breath. "I still have something left to lose."

I let her words sink into me slowly. I looked at Nedra's twin and saw only what was gone—her life, her soul, her very self. But Nedra saw something to hold on to.

I held her tighter, pressing her against my skin, wishing that when Nedra measured all she had left, I was listed in her heart. She didn't pull away, instead clinging to me as desperately as I clutched her. She whispered against my chest, "What can I do?"

Gently, I disentangled her arm from around me, pushing her back so I could meet her eyes. "Nedra," I said, forcing as much sincerity and truth into my voice as I could, praying she would believe me. "Why do you always have to *do* something? There are some times when there is simply nothing you *can* do."

Fury flashed in her eyes, and I knew instantly that she'd never agree with me. "I need you to know this," I tried again, my voice low but urgent. "It's okay to let go. That is not failure."

Nedra's lips pressed together in a tight line. I wasn't sure if she wanted to debate or just rage at me, but either way, she swallowed it all back down inside her.

Eventually, without speaking, Nedra settled back on me, her head on my chest, tucked up under my chin. "I don't need you to understand." The bitterness in her voice was palpable. "I just need you to be here, now."

I tried to hold her tighter, but Nedra abruptly sat up. She scooted off me, her absence leaving half my body cold as ice.

Standing, Nedra took off her shirt, revealing only a camisole underneath. "What?" she asked, sticking her tongue out at me when she saw my expression. "I'm not sleeping in my clothes."

"Is that what we're doing?" I asked. "Sleeping?"

"*Yes*," she said, "we're *just* sleeping." She threw her dirty shirt at me, but she was grinning.

We were trapped in this cabin, and just as we were hidden from the rest of the world, the rest of the world was hidden from us. For the first time since she left Yūgen, Nedra seemed like Nedra again, without the ghosts and guilt that seemed to constantly haunt her. It was as if, as long as this ship was crossing the ocean, the entire world had paused for us.

I slid off the bed, standing up so I could more easily remove my belt and my own shirt, tossing the garments into a pile at the foot of the bed. Nedra peeled back the cover on the mattress, then turned to me. I could see the serious expression in the shadows of her face. I thought she wanted to say something, then, but she didn't.

Instead, I reached out, my hand on her shoulder, brushing down her left arm. My fingers grazed the ridged, pale scars that snaked over the place just above where her elbow had been. I wondered—not for the first time—how Nedra had lost her arm. Missing limbs were common on Lunar Island, throwbacks from the plague that had maimed more than a third of our population. But Nedra's amputation had been . . . messy. The scars spoke of the limb being ripped off, not sawn, of the flesh healing strangely.

When I looked up from the scar, I met Nedra's unflinching gaze.

I did not jerk my hand away. Nedra looked at me with a stillness that reminded me both of a frightened doe unable to move and of a mountain cat poised to attack. Without breaking eye contact, I slowly dipped my head down closer. She did not shy away as I leaned in and kissed her.

She sank into my touch, her body melting against mine. My breath caught, and I felt a tightness building in my core. I forced myself to break the kiss and push my want down. Her eyes were closed as I pulled back. Desire squeezed my stomach like a vise.

She looked up at me with warm eyes, her lips slightly parted, heat flushing her skin. She was not unaffected by this either.

As Nedra leaned toward me, the black bead swung out from beneath her camisole.

Her crucible.

Nedra never took it off unless to use it. But despite the fact that it should have been warm with her body's heat, when it brushed my arm, it was so ice-cold that it burned. I hissed and stepped back, and the moment was broken.

Nedra gestured toward the bed, but when she crawled in after me, she didn't lean in close, or lay her head against my chest. I faced the wall, my body pressed against the rocking wooden ship instead of the girl beside me.

TWENTY-EIGHT

Nedra

I DREAMED.

It wasn't a special dream. There was no deeper meaning to it, no guiding voice to tell me what to do. Instead, I was walking with my parents and sister down the path that led to the sakoola blossom trees. Pale golden petals floated through the air, smelling sweetly pure. In the crook of one arm, I carried a basket of sandwiches. My sister toted a bottle of honey wine. My parents walked behind us, their voices low and occasionally infected with giggles.

I looked behind me, then shared a smile with my twin. Our parents were acting like schoolchildren caught in the first blooms of love.

We started to outpace them. "We'll catch up!" Papa called, waving us on. And then we crested a hill, and they were out of sight.

"I'll wait for them," Nessie said, stopping. And for some reason, in the dream I continued on the path.

I paused after a moment and looked behind me.

My family was gone.

And then my brain reminded me that this was a dream.

That they were *really* gone.

And the sorrow was so deep that I awakened in the darkness of a silent night, alone.

Except . . .

I wasn't alone. I rolled over in bed, and there was Grey. His face was illuminated by the pale moonlight streaming through the porthole window. Without waking, Grey reached for me, his arm under the blanket finding my hip, sliding around to my back, pulling me closer. Our faces were so near that I could feel his warm breath on my cheeks.

My eyelids fluttered closed. And when I slept this time, I did not dream at all.

TWENTY-NINE

Grey

WHEN I BROUGHT Nedra her breakfast, she ate voraciously and quickly, and before I'd taken a single sip of my tea, she pushed aside her plate and turned to the stacks of books she'd taken from the copper crucible.

"What are you looking for?" I asked around a biscuit sweetened with honey.

I had half expected her to deflect, but then she lowered the book and looked directly into my eyes.

"Necromancy isn't about restoring life to dead people," she said. "It's about holding on to souls."

I couldn't hide my confusion.

Nedra got up on her knees and crossed the short distance to me. "This," she said, brushing her hand from my chest to my lap. "Your body. It's just a shell to hold your soul. Your body is a house your soul lives in. So when your body dies, your soul can't stay. It has nothing to hold on to."

"Souls . . . hold on to life?" I asked. "What does that say about your role in raising the dead? That the souls hold on to *your* life?"

Nedra nodded gravely. "Through my crucible, yes. That's why I'm connected to my revenants. Why I can hear them, and see their souls."

I tried to push away the image of slimy souls crawling over Nedra, slithering monsters that left trails of muck all over her body.

Nedra frowned. "You don't understand," she said, a statement, not a question. She pulled out her iron crucible and laid it down on her open palm. "What do you see?"

"An iron sphere."

Nedra's gaze intensified. Her focus shifted; her pupils seemed to reflect more light than was natural. Energy crackled between us—no, between Nedra and her crucible.

"There is light here," she said, her voice eerily still. She moved her residual arm, as if there was still a hand at the end of it. "And darkness," she said. "A black, raw sort of power."

When Nedra raised her eyes to me, I could almost see what she meant. There seemed to be a glow about her eyes, almost as if they were reflecting sunlight.

"The light is the souls," Nedra continued. "I can see them. I can touch them." Her eyes darted around, focusing on something I couldn't see, then her gaze shifted to me, sorrow passing over her like a shadow. "All except Nessie's."

I thought of the way Nedra's twin wasn't like the other revenants. If the body was a container for the soul, there was nothing left of Ernesta but the shell. She was an empty house, not even haunted by invisible ghosts.

Nedra stared down into the depths of her crucible.

"I'm not going to pretend to understand," I said. "I don't think I would make the same choices you have. But I've also never had to make them." I opened my hands, palms up, admitting defeat.

Nedra didn't speak for a long time. When she finally did, she didn't meet my gaze. "It scares me sometimes," she said, her voice so low I almost didn't hear her. I didn't speak; I barely breathed, I was so worried of breaking the moment. "The power here," she said, gripping her crucible, "I don't know what it is."

When she didn't say anything else, I spoke. "But it comes from you. Your power is yours alone."

She shook her head, the barest movement. "You have no idea what went into making my crucible." She finally raised her eyes to meet mine. They were—wrong, somehow. The color in her irises was too light, too reflective, but rimmed in black. Her voice didn't sound like hers, either, gravelly and low.

"Nedra?" I said, fear rising in me. "Ned?"

"I can show you, Grey," she said. Her residual arm still moved over her crucible, as if invisible fingers were stroking the iron.

"No, I—" I scooted back, swallowing hard. Nedra drew closer to me, and she seemed to be reaching for me with her residual arm, even though she had no hand with which to restrain me.

Something inside me *moved*. I gasped in shock, but I couldn't breathe. My heartbeat slowed to nothing. My mind faded, black around my thoughts.

Nedra's smile was feral. Hungry.

I looked down at her residual arm, and I could see then, just barely, a ghostlike arm extending from the flesh limb, twining a golden thread between shadow fingers.

"Souls are such little things," Nedra muttered, cocking her head and studying the golden thread of light.

With dawning horror, I realized what was in her hand.

A soul.

My soul.

And I understood—

Ernesta was a shell, separated from her own soul. That's what I was. My body was still, motionless, but my mind screamed with desire to move, to shout, to snatch my soul back from Nedra's grasp. How horrific it must be for Ernesta, for her soul trapped in Nedra's crucible. Ned dipped her ghostly hand down to the crucible, holding it up, my soul dangling near the lip of the iron. And I could see more. I could see the darkness Nedra spoke of. With her shadowy arm touching my soul, I was connected to her and her power. I could see as she did. And I saw the black bubbling over the edge of the iron, the simmering power that almost seemed sentient.

I could feel its hunger.

A longing ache filled me, an echo of the starvation engulfing the black within Nedra's crucible. This was not just a simple matter of light and dark. This darkness—it was alive. It was *voracious*. It wanted to *devour*. The darkness licked at my soul, and I felt the life withering in me.

But it was not I the darkness wanted.

It was her.

My soul was a golden thread of light, connecting my body to hers, and she was connected to her crucible, a linked chain of power. I could feel the darkness in the iron aching to break free from the crucible. Its desire pumped into me as my soul flickered. It wanted to consume Nedra. *Her body?* I thought, but I could tell that wasn't it. There was a glowing essence about her—her *soul*, I realized. The source of her necromantic abilities. It wanted to devour her soul and, therefore, her power.

No, I thought. *Not Nedra. She doesn't belong to the dark.*

She doesn't belong to anything or anyone.

Protectiveness rose inside me, like a swelling wave. It felt strong, but all it resulted in was one weak word emerging from my lips, barely audible: "No."

Nedra's head jerked to me, her eyes wide. I watched as the silver and black left her gaze, replaced with her own eyes, brown and warm and—

Scared.

"Grey," she gasped, and it was her voice, her *real* voice, no power within it, no dark force possessing her. Nedra dropped the crucible, and my soul snapped back into my body, so violently that I fell over, my head cracking on the bedframe I'd been leaning against. Nedra scrambled over to me. "Grey, Grey," she said, emotion making her voice crack. "Are you okay? I don't know what—I didn't mean to, I, I . . ." Her stuttered, frantic voice faded to nothing as I raised my eyes to hers.

"I'm fine," I said. And I was, except for the fact that I couldn't remember the last few minutes of my life. I felt dimly aware that I *hadn't* been fine before, but it was . . . almost like a dream, already fading now that I was awake.

Nedra helped me up.

"What did you mean?" she asked urgently.

I put a hand to my head. "What did I mean by what?" I asked.

"You said, 'No.'" Nedra spoke clearly and slowly. "What did you mean by that?" When I didn't answer, her voice pitched up an octave. "Grey, that's what Nessie told me, before. When I tried to pull her soul from the darkness. She said 'no' as well—just that. Just . . . no. What did you mean? What did you see?"

My heart hammered against my rib cage. I stared at the crucible, resting atop Nedra's tunic. She had held it, hadn't she? But not—not with her hand? I shook my head, and tried to focus on the iron bead. I thought I saw a flicker of light, but . . .

"I don't remember," I said, turning my eyes to Nedra's desperate ones. "I know . . . *something* happened." I paused. "What happened?"

Nedra's eyes were glassy with tears. I felt an overpowering urge to hold her, to protect her.

"I tried to show you the darkness in my crucible," Nedra said. Her gaze focused on me. "There—you flinched. Why?"

I shook my head again. "I flinched?"

"I saw you. When I said 'darkness,' you flinched. Like I was about to strike you."

"No, I didn't."

Nedra moved closer to me, moving her hand to my cheek. "You don't . . ." Her face showed her bitter disappointment. "You don't remember anything?"

"Nedra, what happened?" I asked again.

"I reached for the darkness," she said. "And it reached back for me."

THIRTY

Nedra

I NEVER WANTED power, except to save my sister. But the only time I felt power that seemed strong enough was when I neared the black in my crucible, the echoes of Bennum Wellebourne's own corrupt necromancy. Feeding the light of souls to the dark power made me feel drunk on my own strength.

But what if, I thought, *the only way to save my sister is to sacrifice the lives and souls of others?* I raised my eyes to meet Grey's. *What if saving her means taking him?* I dropped my gaze.

What if, to save her, I have to give up myself, too?

That blackness in my crucible was *starving.* It would have consumed Grey's soul . . . but it had wanted mine.

Books. I had to read more. Every line, every word. There had to be *something.* I would read every day until we got to Miraband, and then . . . I swallowed down the hopelessness welling inside me. *I will find the answers I need,* I swore to myself.

Beams of sunlight poured through the porthole window as the day grew long, dust motes like stars hanging in the air. We read in silence until they faded, the light so dim we could no longer see the printed text. I stretched, the skin on my residual arm pulling almost painfully, my shoulder popping. The events of this morning felt far away. The entire *world* felt far away.

"This is like being back at Yūgen," I said. "Studying all the time. Remember?"

Grey's eyes warmed, matching my smile. "I remember wanting to do more than study," he said.

"I wish I had another book to throw at you."

"There's a whole pile of them over there," he said, pointing.

"They're too precious to risk damaging on your thick skull."

Grey laughed. He let the book he'd been reading drop to the floor, although he was careful to make sure the spine wasn't damaged. "It feels like forever ago," he said. "It's amazing how important I thought all that was."

"All that?"

"Taking the robes, graduating top of the class, getting a high appointment at the Governor's Hospital. Even the people. Trying to impress Master Ostrum." He cut his eyes at me. "Tomus."

I rolled my eyes. I had never understood why Grey liked the childish brute.

"I cared so much about what he thought," Grey mused. "But once I left school, in merely a few days, he just became someone I used to know. There are people in our lives who fill up our whole attention, but they're still only temporary. And there are others who settle into our hearts and minds comfortably and never leave."

Despite the events of this morning, I couldn't help but smile at Grey's words.

"Oh, did you think I meant you?" Grey asked smarmily. "I was absolutely talking about this dog I had when I was a kid, she was a great dog—"

I kissed him to shut him up, tasting his laugh on my tongue.

And then he kissed me back, and there wasn't laughter there anymore. His body shifted, pressing into mine, and everything else fled from my mind past this moment, now, the two of us alone on the sea. In another life, this could be my everything. Not fighting a battle for my sister's soul, but this—just being in love, and laughing, and happy.

But that was not this life.

I pushed Grey away. But rather than step back, he grabbed my hand and held on. "What's wrong?" he asked, his voice husky. "Are we forever going to leave this"—he indicated the small space between us—"unspoken?"

"What *this* do you mean?" I said, wrenching free. "There is no *this*."

If he had tried to hold me down, I would have pulled away. If he had tried to force me into a corner, I would have fought. If he had raised his voice, I would have shouted him down.

But he stood in the center of the room, surrounded by books, and he quietly spoke words that I knew were the truth: "I love you. And you love me. You just won't let yourself admit it."

"You said—"

"We both said a lot of things," Grey countered in that same even tone. "Because neither of us understood the other. But I'm *trying*, Nedra. Why aren't you?"

My fist clenched, my fingernails digging into the palm of my hand. All the fears I had from before rose to the surface, bubbling up, filling the space between us.

"What if I lose control?" I whispered. Grey was wise enough to let me speak without interruption. "This morning, I hadn't meant to . . ." The dark power had possessed me, *it* had been in control as I took Grey's soul, not me.

Power was passion. That hunger—it was desire. A voracious need and longing to consume, to become one. I felt it when the black in my crucible reached for me.

And I felt it when Grey reached for me.

I squeezed my eyes shut, trying to separate my emotions. My crucible's lust for power felt too close to my body's lust for Grey. But when I pushed all that aside, there was another feeling that bloomed, something pure, something I didn't dare give a name.

"I'm so scared," I whispered, my voice cracking. That emotion, at least, I knew was real.

Grey crossed over to me in two strides, wrapping his strong arms around me. "I haven't stopped being scared for you since that night in Master Ostrum's office, when you walked away from me," he said. "I didn't know it then, but you'd already taken my heart. You may as well have my soul, too."

I sob-laughed against his chest. "The worst moments of my life were watching my family die, leaving me behind," I said, too timid to look up at him. It was easier to whisper these words in the shadow between his skin and mine. "But after that, it was the way you let me walk away from you."

His arms tightened around me, as if he couldn't think of letting me go now, but it was too late. The wound was a scar now, marring our love.

"I don't want to be alone," I whispered.

Somehow, Grey heard my muffled words. "You don't have to be."

I pushed away from him, my hand pressing against his chest to ensure that I kept the distance between us. "I think I do," I said. "I'm worried . . ." He waited for me to finish. "I'm afraid I'll hurt you."

"You will," Grey said simply. I was too surprised to answer. "That's what you've taught me, Ned." Grey pushed my hand aside, drawing closer to me. "If you love someone—deeply, in as true a way as you can—you *will* get hurt. People leave us and love falls apart, and when it does, it hurts. It *should* hurt. How can you not hurt when what you love is gone?"

"That's not what I meant," I started.

"I know," Grey said. He sighed heavily. "The deeper we go, the more dangerous it becomes." He searched my eyes. "For what it's worth, I'm sorry. For everything."

"Me too," I said.

He dropped his forehead, resting it against mine. The boat swayed beneath us.

"The other thing you taught me," Grey added, his voice soft, "is that when you love someone, love them as much as you can, while you can."

His gaze met mine. Longing filled me—not just for this life I could never have, but also for Grey. His eyes reflected my desire, and my breath caught in my throat. It would be so easy to sink into the bed, into his arms, into this possibility.

We couldn't have everything, but we could have this moment. If only we dared to take it.

I leaned forward, and it felt as if the whole world tilted, reality taking a step back to allow this one impossibility. When my lips met his again, I could sense the hope he kept held back so often. His tongue slipped forward, tentatively, and I savored the taste of him, rich like honey, hot like whiskey. I shifted my weight, sliding my right arm around him, letting my fingers tangle in his hair. I stumbled back, sinking into the mattress, and Grey followed me, pinning me under him as he deepened the kiss.

I felt him along the length of my body, hard and taut with desire. But when he pulled away from me, panting, his eyes were filled with questions, not longing.

"Ned—" he started, but I leaned up, cutting him off, claiming his lips as mine. He growled, crushing me under him, devouring me in his kiss. But then with a frustrated groan, Grey rolled off me, between my body and the ship's wall. "Ned," he said again, running a hand over his face. "You have no idea . . ."

I scooted over to Grey and ran my fingernails along his spine, watching as shivers rippled over his back. "Grey," I said, my voice low and deep.

He looked over at me.

Without breaking eye contact, I got up on my knees, lifting first my tunic, then the camisole over my head, tossing them to the floor. Grey's eyes raked over my bare skin. "I want this," I said. "I want you."

Grey lunged for me, his arms wrapping around me. My bare skin should have been chilled in the cool evening air, but instead it burned, flames rising under his touch. His mouth moved from my lips to my ear. He nibbled on the flesh of my lobe, his tongue licking along the shell of my ear before his kisses dropped lower, along my jaw, sending ripples of pleasure over my body as his tongue slid down my neck, his teeth nipping at the sensitive skin. I melted into the bed, my body at once languid and tightly coiling with want.

Grey groaned with frustration and desire, but he ripped himself away from me and staggered off the bed. I had barely mustered the energy to lift my head back up when I saw him striding back, contraception in his hand. He stood at the edge of the bed, his eyes wide and lustful, and reclaimed my waiting lips in a kiss so deep it left me panting for air.

"Are you sure?" Grey asked, pulling back, searching my eyes for the truth.

"Mmm," I moaned. He hesitated. I said, loud and clear: "Yes."

Grey groaned as my hands moved down to the waist of his pants. He struggled to open the contraception as I unbuttoned his pants, sliding my hand down, touching the skin that was paler, hidden from the world, smooth and warm. Grey pushed me back, divesting himself of clothes and putting on the contraception quicker than I had thought possible. He bounded onto the bed, the mattress creaking beneath me. A soft gasp escaped my lips, and he seemed nearly undone by the sound.

Grey grabbed my hips, his hands firm but gentle as he pulled my body closer to him. That touch—his thumb pressed into my hipbone, his arms drawing me across the smooth sheets—seemed so much more intimate than the hungry kisses, the daring disrobing. I was deeply aware of my heartbeat thrumming wildly in my chest.

The world seemed vivid but still.

Grey let go of my hips but did not relinquish his touch. His hands slid up, his fingers barely brushing against the skin of my belly, over my ribs, cupping my breasts. His knees nudged my legs wider. Grey dipped his body down, kissing me as gently as he could, but I could feel the muscles in his arms trembling.

I leaned up, uneven on my residual arm.

I love you, I meant to say, a whisper directly in his ear.

Instead, he pulled back. His eyes were heartfelt, his voice loud and clear and without the barest hint of doubt. "I love you," he said as if there was no other truth in this or any world.

And—for that moment at least—I believed him.

THIRTY-ONE

Nedra

IT HAD BEEN the silence of my revenants that changed everything. Without their whispers in my head, I could finally hear the voice of my heart. And it wanted *this*. We spent all our time in the cabin, Grey leaving only to fetch us food. In addition to the books I got from Bunchen, Grey acquired a stack of maps of Miraband, and we charted the courses we would each take on our one day on the mainland. We created an oasis of ourselves, each morning filled with reading, just as we had done as students, each evening filled with each other. It felt like a moment stolen from time, an eternity cast among the waves.

Until the ship docked.

If I had not noticed the ship slowing, the sails lowering, or the gentling of the waves, I would have known we had reached Miraband by the excited yelling of the soldiers returning home from months on Lunar Island. It seemed as if they'd saved every bit of rum for the hour before docking, so raucous were their celebrations.

The Emperor's cruiser would be departing Miraband early the next morning, giving Grey only one day to meet with the trade advisory council and me one day to track down the collector whose address I'd found in the copper crucible. We planned to spend the night aboard the ship together.

Before the ship had finished docking, Grey dropped a purse of gold coins into my hand. "What's this?" I asked.

Instead of answering, Grey said, "This is a short trip for me. I'm returning with the ship so I can be back in Northface Harbor in time for the Emperor's rally."

When I looked again from the bag of money to Grey, he added, "I can't help you, Nedra. I don't know how. I don't have any answers for your revenants. If you have to stay here . . ."

I could see it, then, the defeat and sorrow in Grey's countenance. This was what he had meant by love hurting. He wanted me to stay with him—and give up necromancy—but if I couldn't, he was letting me go.

And this, more than anything else he'd said or done, proved to me that his love was true.

"I'll send a message if I decide to stay," I said. "But otherwise, expect me back here. No matter what, I'm returning home as soon as I can." My revenants needed me.

The ship finally moored. The soldiers clattered down the gang-plank, all eager puppies ready to go home.

"Ready?" Grey asked.

I grabbed Bunchen's copper crucible, which contained not only the relics of necromancy she'd given me, but also my personal belong-ings. Thanks to the alchemical lock, the large basin appeared empty; its contents would only be visible again if I made a key of my own blood. I'd lengthened the strap so that I could comfortably carry the vessel across my body.

A warm breeze blew my white hair over my face as I stepped onto the deck, the last to leave the ship. Miraband was far more southern than Lunar Island, which, even in summer, carried a cold bite on moonless nights. I wondered if this city ever saw snow.

Grey touched my arm, leading me toward the gangplank. Despite the warmth, I felt a chill, and turned to see the captain staring at me, his eyes squinted. Even though I'd spent the entirety of the past week cloistered in the cabin and out of his sight, his tense shoulders didn't relax until Grey and I were off his ship.

The docks at Miraband were easily ten times the size of Blackdocks. Giant ships sliced through the center of the bay while smaller boats darted up and down the connecting estuary. A myriad of languages floated around us, mostly Allyrian, but I caught snatches of Doishan and Choixian, as well as some I didn't recognize.

Grey was fascinated by the boats. "That's an eastern clipper," he said, pointing to one with red sails, "and that's a modified carrack, probably from Siber. Oh, a cog!" He dragged me across the wooden dock, but I couldn't care less about the ships. It was the people streaming around us that captured my attention. One whole crew—the one aboard the cog—had skin so pale I wondered how they didn't burn under the sun. I'd never seen such different colors of hair either—golden brown, yellow, even copper. Lunar Island was a common waypoint on voyages across the Azure Sea, but these pale people must be from Enja, to the west, a part of the mainland that was recently conquered. They had no reason to cross our sea; they'd more likely travel west across the Pan Ocean, visiting the island nations on the other side of the world.

I stared in wonder at everyone around me on the docks. A woman selling rope could have been a cousin of mine, so similar were we in appearance, but she had heavy black tattoos all up and down her arms, over her chest, even a half dozen dots atop each eyebrow. A man wore a fine woman's gown, his face painted with rouge, and he smiled when I returned his curtsy as we passed. I bumped into a tall woman with skin so dark it seemed to have blue undertones. She grinned at me and spoke something in a language I didn't recognize. She shrugged when I just smiled helplessly back, as if to say, *That's the way of it here.*

Gray darted up to a dumpling stall. "Let's get the bean dumplings," he said. "Father always talked about them."

"Bean?" I asked, doubtful such dumplings could be anything other than disgusting. Beans belonged in soup, not mashed up as filling in pastry.

Grey ordered two for us, and the seller quickly plucked a pair of pale brown dumplings from a steam basket, dropping them in a bit of paper before handing them to us. They were so hot they almost burned my hand, but, following Grey's move, I bit into mine.

The paste inside the dumpling was made of something grayish-red, and while it did have the consistency of beans, I was shocked that it was sweet. Not like honey or sugar, but almost like a small cake.

"I didn't expect that," I said, staring down at the dumpling in my hand as steam dissipated in the air. The outer wrapper was chewier and denser than bread from back home, and I liked it just as much as I did the filling.

"Miraband is great," Grey said. He had a look about him like a child who'd gotten every sweet in the shop.

"Oryous is not pleased!" a voice rang out above the crowds. Several people rolled their eyes, and space cleared out near a man who stood on a crate at the end of the dock. "The gods envisioned us as free men, outside the tyranny of an emperor! The Emperor is not our god; we need not obey the laws he puts upon us!"

Grey frowned. I knew he heard the man, but he pretended not to, a trait I'd noticed most of the people from Northface Harbor shared. In the villages, no one could pass by without a greeting, but apparently in the cities, it was best to pretend you could be alone in the crowd. And the more disruptive someone was, the more studiously they were ignored. Grey's pace quickened, heading to the street leading into the city.

I jogged to catch up with him, the copper crucible banging against my back. Three soldiers in red coats—part of the Emperor's personal guard—marched toward the protestor. I turned around just as two of the soldiers dragged the man off his crate, cuffing him as he continued shouting. In moments, they were all gone, taken to a side street I couldn't see, the crowd swallowing them up whole.

But the message was clear. Everyone in Miraband loved the Emperor, because anyone who didn't was silenced.

THIRTY-TWO

Grey

THIS PLACE WAS everything my father told me about and so, so much more. The sounds, the smells, the sights—it was overwhelming in the best possible way.

"Do you think they're happy?" Nedra asked as we passed a Doishan food stall, charging far too much money for drizzled stick meat.

I moved Nedra quickly through the winding streets of the old city, even though many of the shop windows promised exotic wares from around the world, enticing us to stay and look. We passed pockets of areas that seemed to predominantly represent one culture or another—immigrants and refugees, no doubt, who'd turned a little piece of Miraband into the home they'd abandoned.

"Why wouldn't they be?" I asked. The main thoroughfare into the city center was wide, but we shared the road with horses and palanquins, even wheeled carts that drivers operated with pedals to carry small loads.

There seemed to be a vibrant excitement as we neared the enormous doors leading to the wall surrounding the heart of the city. Nearer to the docks, the people in the stores and booths were settled; they had no intention of leaving their boroughs. But here, there was movement. Everyone was focused on farther up, farther in.

The wide stone entrance was slit in the middle, with giant iron doors hidden within the stone walls. But dirt clogged the tracks and rust peeked through the dark metal. It was clear that, while these gates could be shut, protecting the city heart, they had not been for a very long time.

Nedra lingered near the open gates, and I took the moment to recall my instructions. The Emperor's travel secretary had told me to take a trolley to the city center, where a carriage would meet me. I'd been imagining a sort of fancy wagon, designed to carry as many people as possible, but on this side of the wall, where the streets were wider and more evenly spaced, I could see wires hanging over the roads and grooves cut into the stone path.

Ding! Ding! I whirled around, my eyes scanning the bustling crowd, just in time to see a metal, wheeled contraption roll past. A tall pole jutted from the center of the wagon, which had been fitted with bench seats. Atop the pole, a pulley connected the wagon to the wires in the street, sparks flickering as it gained speed. There was no horse or mule—somehow the wires drew the wagon.

"Looking for the trolley?" a woman asked me, tipping a lime-green hat at me. She wore the badge of the city of Miraband, a sun with six pointed rays encircled with a black border, and her eager expression assured me that she wanted to help.

"I'm to go to the trade authority," I said.

"Ah, you'll be wanting the blue trolley," the woman said confidently. She started to lead me to a little stand I'd not noticed before, but I pulled back. "Nedra?"

"Just there," the woman said, pointing to where I needed to go, then she turned to help someone else.

I found Nedra a few moments later, staring up at a street sign that had the name of the road in two different languages—Allyrian and another language, one I didn't recognize. "Ned?" I asked.

"I think the person I'm looking for is close to here," she said. Although we'd both studied the map on our journey, the old district had not been well labeled, and we'd only been able to guess at where her collector was. Nedra's gaze was distant, then she shook herself as another trolley went by. "It's like magic," she marveled.

She wasn't wrong. While the dusty yellow limestone that most of the buildings were made of seemed ancient, there were shiny bits of new technology jutting out in all directions. The lamps along the street weren't stained black with oil; they glittered like crystal, and I wondered if they ran on the same sort of energy that operated the trolleys. A whistle blared distantly, and I recalled the rail lines connecting Miraband to the rest of the mainland. Although it had taken us a week by sea to reach the city, one could cross the same distance across land in a few days thanks to the steam engines that could go faster than any horse and didn't rely upon the wind.

"Why don't we have any of this?" Nedra asked me.

I laughed.

"Lunar Island is a colony of the Allyrian Empire," she insisted. "We don't have . . ." She struggled for the words. "We don't have any of *this*. We should. The Empire should share its wealth, its technology, with all of its colonies. What else does the mainland have that we don't?"

"Blue trolley, departing soon!" a voice called out. I cast my eyes behind me, to the trolley stand. "Lunar Island can't afford any of this," I said, thinking of my meeting with the trade authority. Silently, I promised, *Yet*. First, I needed to secure a strong trade agreement. That would give the north more jobs, which would give the area more security. But a rising tide lifted all boats. As employment increased in the north, prosperity would spread throughout all of Lunar Island. If I was successful today, then later factories would be built, trollies installed, and all the other wonders of Miraband would follow. I swallowed, daunted by the possibilities.

Nedra noticed my distraction. "Go on," she said.

I gave Ned a quick kiss, then darted across the street, paying for a ride in the trolley. I was the last to board, crammed near a woman wearing peridot-green silk, whose hat kept bumping against my ear. The trolley lurched to life, and I could hear the hum of energy as the wires sparked and pulled us up and up into the heart of the largest city in the world.

THIRTY-THREE

Nedra

GREY HAD ALWAYS been good at seeing only what he wanted to see. It was a special kind of blindness, one I almost envied.

He didn't notice the shanties outside the wall. The children swarming in the shadows, some begging, some picking pockets. He had just smiled at the woman with a ripped bodice, not realizing she offered more than coy looks. Oblivious.

Ernesta would have loved that about Grey, how he only saw the light, never the shadow. They were much the same that way.

Thanks to the maps, I knew that the collector I was looking for was near the wall, almost in the old city, not that far from the old municipal building. While the streets were more orderly here than outside the gate, it was still a tangle of dead ends and narrow alleys along the edge. I quickly ducked away from the main thoroughfare, the dinging bells of the trolleys and the bustling noise of the people fading although never quite fully disappearing.

I touched the side of one of the buildings. I imagined the enormous wall that protected the city rising up and encircling just me, trapping me in silence, away from the chaos.

I walked east. I figured the collector's business might be hard to find, but a municipal hall should at least be well labeled. I stopped in front of a stoic-looking rectangular building with wide front steps and high windows carved into the yellow limestone. A placard had been engraved into the stone of this building—*Church hall of Orious,* it claimed, using the old spelling for "Oryous" and giving a date six centuries ago.

I sucked in my breath, staring up at the ancient building. Nothing on Lunar Island was older than two centuries—the colony hadn't existed before that time. But Miraband had been the capital since before there was an Empire. Allyria had originally been just a smaller nation within the larger continent, and it wasn't until the last few centuries that it truly expanded, claiming the outlying city-states first, then, more recently, the nations of Siber and Enja. Then more, past the borders of the mainland. Across the ocean, not just with Lunar Island, but other island nations, reaching deep into the Azure Sea, knocking at the doors of the kingdoms on the other side of the world.

But this plain stone church hall . . . it had been here before the Empire. When Miraband was a city-state, with an Elder instead of an Emperor. When the god Orious had only entered the pantheon, and the people were still choosing who to worship, and how, and why.

"Would you like to come in?" a kind voice asked from the street. An older woman mounted the steps, a ring of keys in her hand. She wore a simple black robe, the only color on her body a bright red pallium embroidered with golden thread that formed runes common in the sacred Oryon texts. The Elders of my village church hall didn't wear palliums outside of important holy days, and I wondered if Miraband's Elders were required to wear formal dress on every visit to the church.

"All are welcome," the woman said again. "You can rest awhile." She nodded to the copper crucible on my shoulder, heavy enough to be a burden even though it appeared empty to her.

"Thank you, Elder," I replied, a hint of a question in my voice. She nodded at me, confirming my suspicion that she was in the holy order, and swept her arm up, inviting me into the church hall.

I didn't have time to visit, but something compelled me to linger there. My hand went unconsciously to my throat. I used to wear a cord with three knots in it, reflective of the three stars in the Oryous constellation and symbolic of his eye watching over the past, present, and future. But I'd replaced it with the chain I wore to hold my iron crucible.

The Elder removed her robe once inside. On her left forearm, right in the middle between her wrist and her elbow, there was a dimple in her flesh, a cavern deep enough that I was certain if I pressed my fingers into it, I would be able to feel her bone.

She noticed me looking.

"A fleshbane spider bite," she said. "They're common in the desert lands, where I did my missionary work."

I nodded, then shifted my shirtsleeve, showing my own scars at the end of my residual limb. The Elder gave me a little smile of shared sympathy.

I moved around the old church hall, but I couldn't stop thinking about the woman's spider bite and the way it had healed. It was an ugly scar. The fleshbane spider's venom caused necrosis, eating away the victim's skin and muscle. I'd seen information about it in my medical texts at Yūgen. The only way to save the person's life was to cut out the flesh, removing an entire chunk of the person's body and hoping it would heal around the hole.

That's what I couldn't make Grey understand. Grief was like a fleshbane spider bite. It caused a wound that tore a chunk out of you. Grey seemed to think that mourning was like healing from a razor slicing through skin—it hurt, but it would heal, leaving nothing but a faint scar. But really, grief left a hole in you, and while you healed around the hole, you never didn't have it. A piece of you was gone. You couldn't heal something that wasn't there. Just as the Elder's arm would never be whole—just as *my* arm would never be whole—neither would the parts inside of me that missed my family. Surviving grief was as simple and difficult as healing around the hole, reshaping your life around what was gone.

I forced myself to take in the architecture of the church hall, driving these thoughts away from my mind. Slit windows were cut into the wall near the roof of the building, sending crisscrossed beams of light into the wide space of the church hall. The Elder's confident steps over the mosaic floor were nearly silent. The only other source of illumination came from the narrow shelves of candles under the large round window set high on the opposite wall. The Oryous eye window had the same diameter of a tree trunk, the stained glass arranged in a myriad of reds, yellows, and oranges with no clear pattern, but it cast sparkling spots of colored light all along the floor.

The frescoes that lined the walls were faded to near invisibility. Squinting in the dim light, I examined the art. The triumphant figure in the foreground was Oryous, and I suspected the sunbeams surrounding him had been gilded with real gold, one of the only parts of the fresco that hadn't faded, although the gilding was tarnished and dull.

"*The Conquering of Death*," the Elder said reverently. "The title," she added when I gaped at her. Death seemed to follow me everywhere.

I turned back to the fresco. I had at first been distracted by the gilded beams of light, but when I looked down, I noticed that Oryous's bare feet were curled over a pair of skulls. In fact, the entire bottom of the painting was cluttered with images of bones.

"Today, Death is his own god," the Elder said. "This scene from the sacred texts is often painted with Oryous fighting a black-robed figure, or some such nonsense."

I thought of the chapel at Yūgen—the billowing robes of Oryous and the strong figure of Death before him.

"But when our religion first formed, there was no god of death." The Elder laughed. "We have to personify everything to understand it, it seems. But no—conquering death meant reaching the afterlife, not a literal battle. Death is not a god. Death is a place."

I bit my tongue. She may have thought Death was not a real god, but I had seen it. Felt it. My hand wrapped around my iron crucible, the icy-hot feel of it burning my skin.

I stared at the fresco, wondering if the gods had truly changed over time, or if I simply had. Oryous would not have wanted me to keep the dead for my own when he would claim them for himself. But perhaps no god had granted me this power; perhaps I had just taken it.

"We still have services here," the Elder said, turning to me. There was an air to her voice I hadn't detected before, a little like desperation and a little like hope. "You're welcome to come and worship whenever you like."

"I'm just visiting."

"Oh." The Elder tried to mask her disappointment. Her eyes dropped to the copper crucible I carried, but she asked no questions.

"Actually," I said, "I'm hoping you can help me. I'm looking for the old municipal building?"

"Oh, are you an art lover?" the Elder said.

"No—I—why?"

"I just assumed," the Elder said. "The old municipal building is far newer than this church hall—only a few centuries old in fact. The mosaic on the wall echoes this fresco," she added when I still looked confused. "Although the material it's made out of . . ."

"Could you tell me where it is?" I asked.

As she rattled off directions, I was relieved to find that I was close. I dropped a handful of Grey's coins into the charity box by the door, and when their clinking sounds made me think the box was otherwise empty, I slipped in a few more—three copper coins from my own pocket. The Elder had advised a shortcut around the back of the church hall, so I did not return to the road by the wall and instead headed into the shadows of the old buildings.

I almost missed the municipal building. In fact, if the Elder hadn't told me about the mosaic, I would have walked right past it.

I had been expecting a mosaic made of tile and glass, glittering in the sun. The mosaic on the municipal building, however, was dull. The faded taupe stone used to make the art was nearly the same color as the heavy blocks of limestone the building was made of; only the gray grout really made the illustration stand out. I wondered if, when the mosaic had been made centuries ago, it had been brightly painted.

I turned my back to the building, scanning the area for a street sign that would point me to the collector's place. The municipal building's front steps spilled out to a wide sidewalk that formed a small square. A park—some mostly bare trees and a pair of weather-worn benches—was in the center. All the streets ended at the square, except two that met in a point that pierced the park with a triangular-shaped building.

An all-too-familiar man caught my attention. A flash of red coat against the dusty green park—the ship's captain. I was instantly suspicious that he'd been following me, but he seemed to have come from a different direction. I froze, my entire body poised to flee, although I had every right to be here.

The captain cut through the square. Even if he wasn't following me, I had no particular desire to be seen now, so I turned my back to him, strolling up the stairs of the municipal building as if that was exactly where I'd intended to go. Too late I realized how foolish this was; it was far more likely that the captain had intended to come here, for official business, rather than to spy on me. Besides, the huge copper crucible I carried was sure to give me away even if he didn't see my face. When I reached the top of the stairs, I dared a glance behind me.

The captain was gone.

I shook myself, almost laughing at the absurdity of running into him in Miraband. I was wound too tightly. I had just not expected to see a familiar face in a city of strangers.

There was a plaque by the door of the municipal building, and I leaned in closer to see it better. All thoughts of the captain fled my mind. Because here, too, was a face I recognized.

THIRTY-FOUR

Nedra

Emperor Aurellious.

I didn't know all the emperors—history wasn't my favorite subject—but every child of Lunar Island knew Aurellious.

This was the emperor against whom Wellebourne had raised an army of the undead. I could not escape his legacy even here.

Emperor Aurellious defeated Wellebourne in the end, although Wellebourne came closer than any other man in history to destroying the Empire. From the date on the plaque, it was still in the glow of Wellebourne's hanging that Aurellious had commissioned this mosaic.

Squinting up at it now, I could make out the rough design carved into the dull material. Whatever these bits of pale stone were, surely colored glass would have been cheaper and prettier.

I was close enough now that I could touch the porous material. I reached for it with my right arm, my fingers bumping along the rough, broken bits. I had been a medical student at Yūgen for a year; I had studied skeletons. I recognized the material in the mosaic.

Bone.

With a calm I didn't know I had, I touched a piece with my left arm, the one made of shadow. It felt . . . familiar. It reminded me of how it felt to touch my revenants, but something was missing. The sense was faint, but undeniable. This was *human* bone.

With new understanding, I gazed up. These bones were old—two centuries old. They had been crushed to bits and carefully arranged on the wall to shape the figure of an emperor who stood in the triumphant pose of a god.

There was no golden light clinging to these old bones—the souls of the dead were long gone, the life bleached out of them like the marrow that had dried up under the sun. But even if the souls were freed, it was still disgusting to see the bones of the dead so disrespected.

And for what? The mosaic was barely recognizable now, just the outline of an emperor, himself long dead.

Remembering the fresco of Oryous and how he stood upon skulls, my eyes drifted down to the ground. Sure enough, I could see the outline of Emperor Aurellious's feet, and, scuffed from years of wear, the rounded outlines of rows of human skulls created a base for the emperor to stand upon.

I knelt down, touching the skulls with my shadow hand. They were varying sizes—one small enough to be a child's. These were *people*, not wall decorations.

It was one thing for a god to stand atop death, triumphant. It was a totally different thing for a man to, even if he was the emperor.

I could see why Wellebourne had wanted to overthrow him. Emperor Auguste seemed, at best, foolishly idealistic, at worst simply inept. But this mosaic was proof of Aurellious's cruel disregard for humanity. Perhaps if Auguste were like this man, I would join Bunchen's rebellion and be the general of an army of the undead.

I wondered if Auguste would make himself out to be lord over death after he hung me. Surely this was the only reason the gods-fearing people of Miraband had allowed this mosaic to be made. The skulls didn't represent death, not like the fresco in the church hall. They represented undeath, and Aurellious's triumph over the necromancer. Apparently it was fine to decorate a building with human remains if you were making a point about defeating someone who had built an army with human remains.

This sort of "art" would never exist in Hart or any of the villages. We still remembered the stories of our grandparents and great-grandparents. We still pressed iron circles over the graves of those we loved.

I turned my back to the mosaic, and to Emperor Aurellious.

From this vantage point, I was better able to see the square and the streets lined up around it. The odd pointed intersection that broke the uniformity of the courtyard held a triangular building, and I noticed a sign hand-painted on the wall identifying it as Corner Street.

The building was four stories high, but all the windows on the third and fourth stories were boarded up, and the second-story windows were empty of glass. One had the ragged remains of a curtain, the wind causing the cloth to billow over the street like a tattered flag.

I headed across the courtyard and pushed open the only door that wasn't barred on the building after no one answered my knock. "Hello?" I called, my voice choking on the dust.

Nothing.

I considered the possibility that I'd come to the wrong location, or that the collector had long since moved on.

The building looked as if it were about to cave in. Crates and cloth-covered boxes lined the walls, each with an inch or more of grime covering them. The wooden floor bowed beneath my feet. "Hello?" I called again, louder, a little desperately.

A man emerged from a small door I'd not noticed before. He was wiping his hands on a piece of cloth that seemed far too dirty for the task. His eyes raked over me, up, down, up again.

When he smiled, I saw that he was missing one of his canines. "About time you got here."

THIRTY-FIVE

Grey

THE PRESENTATION TO the trade authority was not going well at all.

I had expected . . .

I didn't know what I had expected. The city had charmed me immediately, so full of hope and possibility, and the Emperor had so strongly believed in the chance for northern trade with Miraband to put more gold into the pockets of the artisans, farmers, and workers who so desperately needed it. I had been able to push aside the doubts seeded by my father and Nedra. I knew this mission was hasty, but that was out of necessity.

The trolley had dropped me off outside the palace walls. I could see nothing but smooth limestone with onion domes and spires in the distance. Through the bustle and sounds of the city, I caught a few notes of birdsong and smelled the pleasant scent of citrus. I could visualize the lush gardens the Emperor kept protected from the masses beyond the wall. But any hopes I'd had of seeing them for myself were dashed as a short man touched my elbow.

"Greggori Astor of Lunar Island?" he asked.

I nodded, turning to him.

"This way." He led me down the block, then into a small building with walnut floors and shutters on the windows. He opened the door and ushered me inside.

I saw first the crates of goods I'd purchased from the market, delivered by the captain. I'd hoped to have the chance to open them myself, arrange them on tables and present each item in the best light. Instead, three men had already opened the crates and were rummaging through them. Their sour expressions told me I wasn't making a favorable first impression.

"Good sirs!" I said loudly, hoping to draw their attention. I'd practiced this speech with Nedra on the ship, but it sounded hollow now. One of the three men looked up. He nudged another one. "My name is Greggori Astor." I plastered a smile on my face.

"Is this all you have?" the third man asked bluntly. He pulled up the orcine top hat I'd gotten at the market, one of the things I'd considered a frontrunner for trade. His distaste was evident.

"It is made of northern orcine," I said hurriedly. I took it from his hand, smoothing down the fur and showing it to the men. "The villagers of Lunar Island risk their lives on the rough seas amid the icebergs to hunt this rare creature. The result is—"

"The result is not nearly as good as wilver pelts from Jool," the man said, rolling his eyes. "Tell your people to stay at home where it's warmer."

Jool? When did the Allyrian Empire start trading with Jool? I remembered the cog ship in the harbor—the sailors had been Enjan, surely, and now that the nation was folded into the Empire, they must be sailing through the Pan Ocean.

"I appreciate the Emperor's . . . benevolence in arranging this meeting," the man said in a pompous tone clearly meant to mock me. The other two sniggered.

"And your name is?" I asked, hoping I sounded more dignified than I felt.

"Veri Tess."

"Mr. Tess," I started.

"*Lord* Tess."

"Lord Tess," I corrected immediately, inclining my head to him. "The Emperor is indeed generous, and I am grateful for the opportunity he has given me to show you wares from my homeland. As you likely know, our nation has experienced much distress over the past year."

"An earthquake?" one of the other men guessed.

"No, that was Siber," said his friend.

"A plague, good sirs," I supplied.

Their expressions didn't change; if anything, their eyes reflected even more disinterest than before.

"You must understand, Mr. Astra, that all these little colonies—there's always something. A devastating storm, a sickness, crushed insurrections. And yes, we agree with His Imperial Majesty that the best recourse is to have the people help themselves through labor and trade. Trade is what makes the Empire as strong as it is!"

"Hear, hear," one of the men said in a bored voice.

"But," Lord Tess continued, "we cannot give charity. And trying to promote trade with—this." He tossed the hat to the ground, where a small cloud of dust billowed up, marring the shiny surface of the orcine hat. "This would be charity."

"You have not seen the best of what Lunar Island has to offer," I said, unable to hide the desperation rising in my voice. "Our local wares are made by good, honest people—"

"We've heard that before." Lord Tess shrugged. "Every colony in the Empire has good, honest people."

"At least he didn't bring an old woman in one of the crates to show how she tats lace by hand, something every generation has done since Oryous became a god," one of the men said.

"The point is," Lord Tess said, "if you want something to sell, you need to do better than this." He shrugged. "You could set up a market stall outside the wall—see if you can drum up customers with local wares that way. Start a fashion. It's happened before."

I thought of the little buildings and stalls we'd seen outside the docks. I had thought them charming, but there was no way I'd be able to sell goods on my own there, not enough to reshape the economy of my entire colony. And certainly not within enough time to make it to Emperor Auguste's rally.

I changed tactics. "The Emperor himself sent me here—"

"And the Emperor himself appointed us to ensure that the Empire's trade system remains the strongest in the world," Lord Tess snapped back. "He gave you a chance, boy, not a promise."

"There has to be something," I said, turning back to the crates, embarrassed by the way desperation made my voice crack.

"Look, boy," Lord Tess said. My back stiffened. I might be young, but by all the gods, I knew I'd seen more of life and death than he had.

Whatever dismissive words he'd been intending to speak faded to silence as his eyes dropped to my hand. I'd curled it into a fist, but I forced my fingers to relax. His eyes didn't leave my hand, though.

"Lunar Island, you say?" he asked.

I nodded tightly.

The other men were looking at my hand now, too. I held it up, realizing that it was the iron ring on my knuckle that had grabbed their attention.

My mind flew to Bunchen and my father. *Are these men rebels?* I wondered. My heart rate ratcheted up. I was too afraid to be the first to broach the subject, but if they confirmed my suspicion, I had no reluctance in exploiting the connection to help the poor of the north.

Lord Tess held out his hand, palm up. "May I?" he asked.

I slipped the ring from my finger and dropped it into his waiting hand. He inspected it. "An unusual design," he said finally.

"Not on Lunar Island," I said, still hesitant to claim the rebellion.

"No, I imagine not."

One of the other men, the shorter of the two, looked up at me. "Is *this* traditionally made by your good and honest craftsmen?" he said, and although he had sneered at the term before, he seemed genuinely curious now.

"Yes, of course," I said. "It's part of our local legends. There was a necromancer on Lunar Island about two hundred years ago—" I started, but Lord Tess cut me off.

"Wellebourne, we know," he said, nodding. His eyes glittered excitedly. "And rumor has it there's another necromancer on your island now."

She's not on the island, I thought. *She's in this very city.* Cold fear washed over me. But all I gave was a curt "Yes."

"A *real* necromancer?" the short man asked.

"Yes."

Lord Tess grinned warmly at me. "This," he said, a slow, hungry smile spreading over his face. "This we could sell."

THIRTY-SIX

Nedra

"You've been expecting me?" I said, taking one hesitant step closer to him. For the first time since I left the ship, the copper crucible felt painfully heavy. I hitched it higher up onto my shoulder. There was something predatory about the collector that I didn't like.

"We have mutual friends who let me know of your impending arrival," he said, "Nedra."

How did he know my name? Even if Bunchen had been able to get word out, the rebel network couldn't have been faster than the Emperor's cruiser. Thinking of the ship reminded me that I'd seen the captain earlier. *Could he have been the messenger?* I wondered. Perhaps that was why he'd allowed himself to be so easily bribed into taking me here.

"What do you know about me?" I asked, narrowing my eyes.

"Rumors have spread. Those of us who care about the fourth alchemy keep our eyes on Lunar Island. Your colony has a . . . legacy."

"Are there other necromancers that you know of? People in your circle?" I asked.

"Just because we watch doesn't mean we practice," the collector said, drawing closer.

"That doesn't answer my question."

"Just because you asked doesn't mean I have to answer," he countered.

I couldn't shake the immediate and overwhelming distaste I had for the man. He reminded me of an unchecked and older Tomus Abertallin. Not in looks—Tomus was tall and young, handsome to many, while the collector was short and stocky, with grimy hair that stuck out, and patches of stubble on his chin.

But the way they both looked at people—the way they looked at *me*—was the same. As if I were a thing, my value determined not by my humanity, but by my ability to aid them.

The only difference was, Tomus had never wanted me.

And it was clear the collector did.

For the first time since I left my quarantine hospital, I found myself wishing that I had my revenants with me not for their protection, but mine.

"You know my name," I said warily. "But what's yours?"

"I prefer to operate without a name. Collector is fine."

"And you collect things of interest to me?"

His grin broadened to an almost maniacal level. "Indeed." Then, in an instant, his expression sobered, his mouth downturned into a grim line. "But perhaps proof?"

"Proof?"

"Of your . . ." His eyes raked over me again. "Skills."

My right hand was slack, but my shadow hand clenched into a fist. I had no need to prove anything to this man.

But then I thought of Nessie, and how he might have the knowledge I needed to save her. Still, there was something about this strange person in this dirty building on the edge of this vast city that made my toes curl.

"You want proof of my power?" I said, striding forward. For the past week, I had been aboard a ship, severed from my connection to the undead. I still didn't hear them, but I had never once not felt my power. It was mine alone. I threw back my shoulders, raising my shadow arm, clutching my iron crucible at the base. Everything I did—whether I raised the dead or pulled the souls of the living—was done through the cold metal.

I had only rarely used my power against the living. Once to hold Governor Adelaide still while I drove a blade through her heart. Then again, as an experiment with Grey, and later, with the homeless man. It had frightened me each time how easy it had been to do.

This power was far too useful to be frightening now.

Electricity crackled through my paper-white hair, and I felt my vision blur—I saw the Collector as a golden outline of his soul far more than the shape of his flesh. I strode forward, my footsteps echoing off the dusty, wooden floor.

"Yes," the Collector hissed, his voice eager.

If for nothing more than to shut him up, I reached my shadow hand forward, wrapping his soul around my fingers. I *pulled*, and a little breathless "Oh!" escaped his lips.

Golden light dripped from my shadow hand. His soul.

I looked into his eyes, as dead and empty as Ernesta's. Thinking of her renewed the rage within me. All of this—*all* of this—was for her. And I wasn't going to let some little man toy with me while I had business to do.

My shadow fingers clenched, squeezing his soul tighter.

His body didn't flinch, but his soul screamed.

"Satisfied?" I growled. I shoved my hand into his body and let his soul go, seeping life back into him.

A few moments later, he staggered back, blinking. "Oh, *yes*," he said, and he actually smiled. Next time, perhaps, I would keep his ragged soul. It would be worth far more to me than whatever purpose he was using it for, surely.

"If we're quite done," I said, not reining in my voice.

"You want to see my collection."

"Yes." I bit off the word. "And . . ." I took a deep breath. "I need information."

"About what?

"Books, perhaps. Or if you know how I can find other necromancers . . . I know there are more."

"But on what subject?"

"Necromancy," I said.

"Obviously," the Collector said, for the first time displaying impatience. "But what *specific* subject?"

I hesitated. "I'll know it when I see it."

He looked me up and down, a smirk twisting his lips. "A difficult client," he said, as if the prospect pleased him. "Come with me." The Collector turned to the staircase. The steps were uneven, with some missing entirely, and I had a hard time keeping up with the Collector, who knew exactly when to hop over trick steps or broken boards. We went straight past the second floor, open to the elements, past the third and fourth floors, with windows boarded up and furniture covered with sheets of white cloth like ghosts, and to the roof of the triangular building.

I blinked in the sunlight. "Here?" I asked.

"Here." The Collector led me across the roof to a small rectangular shed. "Looks like a cote for messenger pigeons, doesn't it?" he asked. I pitied whatever animals had been kept inside such a hovel. The Collector shifted aside a cover to reveal a lock.

The padlock was made of copper. Rather than reach for a key, though, the Collector pulled a needle from his collar. He pricked his finger until a bubble of blood burst out, bright and red. He turned the lock around—there was no keyhole, just a silver indentation. The Collector pressed his bloody fingertip into the silver, and the copper lock clicked open.

I filed the information away—a lock like this might be useful one day. It wasn't that different from the blood key I'd had to make to access the copper crucible slung over my arm. The Collector noticed the way I shifted it on my shoulder.

"Yes, that's one of mine," he confirmed, smiling. "Sold it to an interested party years ago. How did it wind up in your hands?"

"An interested party?" I said, unable to keep from mocking his voice. "You mean another necromancer."

He made a noncommittal noise in the back of his throat.

The door to the shed creaked open. While the outside had looked like little more than broken planks held together with a few nails and a bit of luck, the inside of the shed was larger than it had appeared. And entirely encased with iron.

Using the same necromantic powers that enabled me to see souls, I could make out the runes etched into the metal. This was not just iron, but iron imbued with alchemy, iron as strong as the cage that had trapped the Emperor in the castle for half a year.

"Who made this?" I asked.

"I don't know." There was a bitter tone to the Collector's voice. "I acquired it not from the source."

I touched the inside of the door. Because the Collector was not himself a necromancer, he couldn't seal it the way Governor Adelaide had sealed in the Emperor, hence the use of the padlock. Grooves scarred the dark metal, at about the same height as my torso. I fit my right hand over a particularly deep set of grooves—my fingers fit into the lines precisely.

"Where did you say it came from?" I asked quietly.

"A seller dug it up from a grave near Siber," the Collector said. He noticed what I was looking at. "I have the skeleton it came with, as well as some of the grave dirt, if you'd like it."

"No, thank you," I said without inflection.

The Collector moved deeper into the shed. There wasn't room for me to follow inside, so I stood in the doorway, careful to not entirely block the sunlight. "Ignore that," the Collector said, sweeping his hand toward one shelf. "Only the best for you." He cast a beaming look back at me, as if he wanted to adorn me with his relics only so that he could keep me in this iron box. My fingers curled around the door, ensuring I was on the safe side.

"Can we narrow down your desire?" the Collector asked. "A weapon? A book?"

"Anything, really," I said slowly, second-guessing how much I should tell him. My ignorance rankled me.

The Collector mused for a moment, then withdrew a single feather from a cup, presenting it to me as if it were a crown.

The shaft of the feather was solid black, but the vanes were white and striped with jade green. The quill had been sharpened to a fine point.

"Any contract signed with blood from this quill must be upheld, even if all the participants die," the Collector said. I made a point to turn the tip away from my skin.

The Collector turned back to the shelf, and I set the feather down. He eagerly shoved a mirror into my hands. There was no glass, but the silver face had been shined as well as any other mirror I'd seen. I looked at him curiously.

"I'm not sure what it does," the Collector said. His lips quirked. "Many of these objects work only for your kind. But legend says that it will show souls rather than flesh in the reflection, to those who see."

"That's rather pointless," I said. I could see souls without the mirror. Idly, I raised the mirror, my wrist straining under the weight of it. Sure enough, I could easily see the golden aura of my own soul. Behind me, I caught a glimpse of the bone mosaic that made up the front of the municipal building. From this high up, it was easier to see the full design and make out the shape of Emperor Aurellious in the bone shards.

But the mirror glowed. While the souls of the victims were long gone, the mirror showed echoes of who had been there. Hundreds of wisping, golden ghosts. They didn't scream or haunt the place, but their presence lingered, a promise that they once had lived, that, even if they had been forgotten, they had been real people with real lives who deserved an honored death.

I turned slowly, looking for more echoes of the past. That was the real value of the mirror—not seeing the living souls, but the ones that were gone. There were traces of death in the square, along the main wall, in the windows of buildings around us. The city was old; more people had died here over the centuries than lived here currently.

The mirror flashed on the iron shed, and I gasped. The ghost that clawed at the door of the iron shed was, like all the others, frozen, merely an echo of the soul that was gone. But this one was vivid, with a grotesque, screaming face, fingers stretched out like claws, body twisted in rage.

"What do you see?" the Collector asked eagerly.

I tried explaining, but words were not adequate to describe the horror. I felt sure that the Collector knew the definition of the word *ghost*, but he probably did not at all grasp how terrible one was.

"Mm, yes." He nodded as if he understood, but of course, he didn't, he couldn't, who could have understood such horrors without seeing them first? "It's an echo of energy," he added at my doubtful expression. "Energy is not like matter. It cannot be destroyed. Even when the matter is gone—the body is gone, so to say, even the soul— energy lingers."

I moved to hand the mirror back to the Collector, his eyes bright and eager. The reflective surface tipped to me, and I saw not my own face, but my iron crucible. I grabbed the mirror back, staring into the silvery depths.

I had thought to see my family there—my parents' ashes were used to forge the iron, and my sister's soul bound them together. And perhaps, somewhere, their ghosts were imprinted in the crucible.

But all I saw when I looked in the mirror was a gaping maw of utter black. It seemed to form a hole that bored inside me, right where my heart should be.

THIRTY-SEVEN

Nedra

SHAKING, I HANDED the mirror back to the Collector. I did not need to see the darkness inside my crucible to know it was there.

"What are these?" I asked, pointing to a shelf that held a collection of cracked bones, splintered blades, shards of metal, and an assortment of other items that looked as if they belonged in the waste bin. Every single thing was broken in varying degrees.

"Reliquaries," the Collector said. "Have you—?" He licked his lips, his eyes gleaming with eagerness. "Have you made one? Can you tell me anything of it? In case the worst happens, it would help me identify it for my collection."

"No, I've not," I said. I frowned at the pile of rubbish.

"But you know of them?"

There was no point lying. I needed information more than I needed his approval. "No."

The Collector made a noise deep in the back of his throat. For the first time, he seemed disappointed in me.

"Tell me," I insisted. There was a limit to what I could do with a soul I didn't take for my own. I knew I could control his body, but I didn't think I could force him to reveal anything hidden in his mind. I could bend a living soul; I had not gone so far as to break one. I didn't even know if I could. Although this slimy man surely tempted me to try.

"People think necromancers command death." The Collector shook his head. "That is false. You command souls. And the greatest control you can have is over your *own* soul." He reached over and plucked a gemstone from the shelf. It was a beautiful emerald green, the size of my thumb, cut to show sparkles, but an enormous crack through the center marred the gem.

"You must select something carefully. This necromancer—the third Duke of Armo—was vain. He chose an object that was too ostentatious, too desirable, an object meant to be looked upon by the eyes of others. Strong, maybe, but not strong enough."

"I don't understand you," I said.

"You can take a piece of your soul and hide it away, protect it from the world. Just be sure to put it in something sturdy; as long as the object you hide your soul in doesn't break, your soul will be safe. Your body can be killed, but you can be resurrected. It is eternal life, in the truest sense. Eternal power." The Collector twisted the gem in his hand, letting the light glint off the enormous crack through it. "But once the object you chose is broken, you can be killed like any man. Or woman," he added, nodding to me.

I took the emerald and examined it, considering. I didn't care about having eternal life for myself. But if having it also meant Nessie could share immortality with me . . .

"So you must be careful," the Collector said. "Choose an object that's hard to destroy, yes." His fingers danced along the shelf, touching stones and metal, bones and marble. "But more than that, hide it well. No one can destroy something they cannot find."

"You have so many reliquaries," I said, looking at the shelf. Dozens of broken objects. Some had dates scratched into them, showing they were centuries old. One was far newer, just a few decades. The reliquaries no longer looked like waste. They looked like defeat.

"Here," the Collector said. "You need this." He put a book into my hands. The runes on the cover had been embossed and gilded, but were so faded now that I could barely read them. I turned to the first few pages, reading painfully slowly through the archaic script.

Breaking my soul apart sounded excruciating. Worse than losing my arm. But not worse than losing my sister.

I quickly used a blood key to unlock my large copper crucible and tucked the book inside.

The Collector seemed happy at my selection. "If you use that," he said, "you'll need this." He turned, taking a step deeper into the shadows, and bent over, lugging something big and heavy up.

"What is it?" I asked. The box was made of silver, embossed with skulls and bones, with a line of copper all around the edge. There was no visible hinge or way to open the box.

"It's a rather recent addition to my collection," he said. "But I've known of its legend for years."

"The box?"

The Collector laughed mirthlessly. "What's inside it."

"So, what's inside the box?" I could feel my impatience mounting.

"Taking apart your soul requires that you be replenished," the Collector said. I felt my nostrils flare, but I didn't think I did anything else to give away my spiked interest. Replenishing souls was *exactly* the sort of thing I was looking for. "You're essentially immortal. Of course, not your *body*, but—"

"What does that mean?" I interrupted. "'*Essentially* immortal'?"

"Your body will die, obviously."

I cocked an eyebrow. "Then how does that make me—"

"Your soul, girl!" The Collector sounded impatient now. "Of course, your soul will have to move to other bodies as yours ages or dies. But that's of no matter. *You* will live on. But after centuries, your soul will grow weak."

Bile rose in my throat. "Are you saying I can't die?" I asked.

The Collector rolled his eyes. "Of course you can. Until you make a reliquary."

I squinted at him in suspicion. "None of my books have even *hinted* at this," I started. "There aren't any legends or superstitions—"

"How many necromantic books have you read, girl?" The Collector sneered at me. "I know where every book on the fourth alchemy exists in the world, at least all the ones that aren't ash or dust. Most of the world thinks necromancers themselves are just legends from the past. Arcane knowledge isn't discussed over tea!"

Sufficiently cowed, I clamped my mouth closed.

"This box contains a replenisher of sorts," the Collector continued. "When a soul fades and grows weak after passing from body to body, this restores it."

"But what is it?" I asked, unable to quell my curiosity, even if he would admonish me for my ignorance. I tried again to find a way to open the box.

The Collector laughed bitterly. "I don't know," he said. "I can't open the box." He looked up at me, his eyes glittering with anticipation. "Only a necromancer can."

I sat down, my back to the scratched iron door, and pulled the silver box onto my lap. The Collector perched on the edge of the shelf, watching me. He knew better than to speak as I inspected the metal.

I could see runes etched all over the surface. Largest, in the center, was *infansik*, the rune to show the cycle of good and evil. But overlaid and repeating around the edge was a pattern of *estro* and *errot*. One meant simply "restore," but the other didn't have a true translation in Allyrian—it meant something similar to being made new over and over again, and it shared a glyph with the rune for "chrysalis."

"Finally the necromancer shows real interest," the Collector said, an eager note in his voice. I ignored him. He had guessed the truth, though he probably thought I wanted it for myself.

My heart hammered in my ears as I turned the box over, looking for a way to open it. The band of copper that encircled the center seemed to be the key. On closer examination, I saw more runes etched into the copper itself—the rune for life, the rune for death, and *infansik* in the middle. A cycle between life and death.

If only a necromancer could open the copper lock, perhaps it was because our blood was the tie between life and death, completing the cycle. I pricked my finger on my brooch and smeared my blood against the band of copper.

"Yes!" the Collector gasped as the copper faded.

"No," I said. Only half the band melted away. After a minute, the other part of the copper returned. I had failed to open the box.

"My blood got me nowhere," the Collector said. "And whatever alchemy made this box is strong—I've not been able to break it open by any means. But you have death and power in your blood. Perhaps you have to form a rune with it?"

I frowned. The fact that I was able to open half the lock meant that I probably had the means to open the rest, and anything this well protected would likely be worth my time. "I'm taking this," I said, putting the box into my copper crucible. I met his eye, expecting a fight. There was lust in his gaze, and sorrow as he looked at the box. "I can pay," I added.

He spared a disdainful glance at me. "You cannot afford it," he said. "It's priceless."

I flexed my shadow hand and considered what lengths I would go to for the box. I didn't think I would feel particularly bad stealing from a man with such selfishly macabre fascinations.

"But . . ." the Collector said wistfully. "It seems I have no choice."

No choice?

"These will likely be of interest to you as well," he continued, handing me three more books, "One's an original." His voice sounded bitter as he handed them over.

I weighed the books in my hand.

"How much?" I asked. "For all of it."

The Collector shut the iron shed, the door closing with a definitive thud, then he locked it again. "Nothing," he told me, not quite meeting my eyes.

"Nothing?"

He shook his head as he led me back to the stairs. "You have a friend," he said finally. He cast a look behind me, but I couldn't read his expression. "A friend who hopes for your help, and will give you anything you need in order to secure it."

"Who?" I demanded.

"Another necromancer."

My heart thudded. "Where can I find this necromancer?"

"It is not my place to say—" he started.

"I don't have time for riddles!" I snarled. Whoever this necromancer was, they'd gone to great lengths to ensure that I would find the information in Bunchen's copper crucible and then this box, halfway across the world.

"I have no answers for you," the Collector said. When I took a threatening step closer, he threw up his hands. "I mean that literally." There was a hint of panic in his voice now, and I was glad my expression conveyed to him just how much he should fear me. "I have gotten only instructions and deliveries. But given the items"—the Collector paused to look at my copper crucible—"I can only assume you are not alone in practicing the fourth alchemy."

I scowled, but there seemed little else I could do. Adjusting the copper crucible on my shoulder, I turned to leave, rushing down the steps.

"What you really should be worrying about," the Collector called behind me, "is whether this other necromancer wants to help you, or use you."

THIRTY-EIGHT

Grey

THE SUN WAS setting by the time the trolley deposited me near the city gates. I made my way back through the old district, heading for the Emperor's cruiser, wondering if Nedra would be waiting for me.

If she ran, disappearing into the busy streets of Miraband, she would be safe.

The Emperor would know I'd aided her, though. The captain would surely tell him of my bribe. *And then what?* I wondered what kind of punishment the captain would face for helping me. I paused, blanching, realizing that surely I would be punished even more than he would. Enabling a necromancer's escape from judgment was surely greater treason than any my father had committed. Would I hang? Then what would happen to the trade commission I'd just earned? Would the entire north suffer because one woman had run for her life?

"Hello." Nedra emerged from an alley near the edge of the dock.

Here she was before me, ready to go home, and even if it cost me my own life, a part of me wished she'd chosen to save herself instead.

"It's almost dark," Nedra added when I didn't speak. The captain had told me the ship would leave as soon as it was able, even if we departed in the night. The docks were flooded with lamplight, and navigating by the stars made it easier to set the course for home.

Nedra touched my elbow, pulling me back to the present. "I still have some of your money, if I need another bribe to board the ship."

Before I could answer, a deep voice spoke from the shadows. "No need." The captain stepped out onto the dock.

Nedra spun around to face him. "Were you following me?"

"Nedra, don't assume—"

"Yes," the captain said. He nodded toward the boat. "The Emperor would not approve of me having taken you here," he said, "but no harm done, as long as I ensure you come back."

Nedra scowled, but, surprisingly, she didn't protest. As the captain led the way back to the ship, she had an inscrutable, contemplative look on her face, as if she were only now seeing the captain for the first time.

The captain didn't speak again until we were in our cabin on the ship. "The same deal still stands," he told me. "My men won't like seeing her aboard, and it's best if as few people as possible know about our transaction."

As soon as he'd shut the door behind him, Nedra dropped the crucible on the bed, pacing the wooden floor much like I had done before we left Lunar Island. "There's something I'm missing," she said. "I feel like I'm always being watched now, like someone already knows what I'm going to do next before I've even decided to do it."

"I . . . take it that you didn't find what you were looking for?"

"Not exactly," she said shortly.

I could tell there was something else wrong, something she was holding back.

"On the bright side," I said, "my mission was a success. I got the trade commission!"

Nedra paused. It seemed to take several moments for my words to sink in, but then she lit up. "Really?" she said. "I know I had my doubts, but—"

"I'm returning home with a production order. And a promise of more orders to come if our exports take off."

Nedra's brow furrowed. "A new export means a new factory," she said.

"One built in the north, with workers treated ethically." If the council were solely in charge, I'd worry that the southern politicians would keep the profits in Northface Harbor. But the Emperor's plans mandated the factories be developed in the north, and that the profits be used for public services in Hart and the villages.

"More jobs, greater income . . ." Nedra continued.

"And more taxes on sales," I added, "which can be used for more schools or structural improvements to villages."

"Grey," Nedra said, her voice ringing with pride. "This really might change everything."

A whistle blared and the ship lurched into motion—the captain was making good on his promise of a fast journey.

"My trip was successful as well," Nedra said. She knelt in front of the large copper crucible, using her blood key to open it. I noticed more books, but also a silver box, about the length of my forearm and banded with copper.

"What is it?" I asked, sitting down opposite Nedra as she withdrew the silver box.

"Locked. But look at the runes."

I peered at the box. I'd been so distracted by the embossed skulls at the corners that I hadn't noticed the intricate, stylized runes that littered the surface. Life and death and the eternal cycle.

"What's inside?" I asked.

"I don't know." There was an odd tone to Nedra's voice, one that sounded reverent to my ear. I sat back on my heels. When I didn't say anything else, Nedra met my eyes. "I've got some new books, too. I'm hoping—" She glanced away, a coquettish look on her face that young ingénues usually reserved for their paramours. "Maybe there really is a way to replenish a soul. There's so much still to learn," she added, touching her iron crucible. Her smile held close-hearted secrets.

"There's a reason for that," I said, my voice flat. "It's because you're not *supposed* to know everything about necromancy. Let alone practice it."

Nedra rolled her eyes.

I heaved out a breath. All the week previous, we'd been able to pretend that Nedra wasn't a necromancer. She hadn't found anything in the books Bunchen had given her, and we'd found other ways to occupy ourselves.

The boat lurched, and I had to put out an arm to brace myself. Nedra carefully picked up the silver box and put it back in the copper crucible. Her fingers lingered over the new books inside, and I could tell she wanted to read them now. But she withdrew her hand and turned to me.

"Tell me more about the trade commission," she said.

I recognized that this was Nedra making an effort to hold on to the way we had been last week, and I couldn't hide my smile. "It went *really* well," I said. "Or, at least, it did after they almost dismissed me. They didn't like anything I brought from the market." I laughed, but Nedra frowned.

"What did they want then?"

"The ring!" I said, still laughing.

"What ring?"

"The iron ring Bunchen gave me."

Her eyes shot to my bare hand.

"I know, I know, it's a symbol of the rebellion," I said dismissively. "But *they* don't know that. They liked it because it's iron and links back to—"

"Wellebourne," Nedra finished for me in a quiet voice.

"Yes, exactly. He's just as legendary in Miraband as he is on Lunar Island. They know the rings aren't actually necromantic, but the fact that the iron comes from Wellebourne's homeland makes them seem more authentic. I gathered that it would be considered fashionable."

"Fashionable."

"Someone has to keep that collector of yours in business, I suppose," I said. "Probably a reason he operates in Miraband. How did Lord Tess put it? A 'dark and morbid fascination.'" I laughed. "But he thinks the rings will sell really well."

"But, Grey," Nedra started.

I cut her off. "And it's partly thanks to you."

Whatever she was going to say fled her mind. "Me?"

"News hasn't fully spread throughout Miraband," I said. "But people *have* heard of the necromancer of the island. It's sparked all this renewed interest in Wellebourne and the rebellion that formed when the colony was new. People want to be a part of it, and they're willing to pay to do so."

Nedra's brows furrowed.

"I know it's a bit odd and not what we were expecting," I started.

"Not what we were expecting?" Nedra threw up her hand. "Grey, the iron bands aren't some sort of trinket to be worn by a lord in the capital who thinks he's fashionable! They're a part of our *religion*."

I blinked in surprise. "We're all Oryan," I said slowly.

"I guess some of us actually believe more than others," Nedra snapped. "Grey, how could you, of all people, think that the iron band was nothing more than an object to sell?"

"Why does it matter?" I said, confused. "Ned, this could help people in the north live somewhere better than the village you were raised in."

"I *loved* my village!" Nedra leapt up, her eyes flashing in fury. "And you would know that if you didn't think value could only be measured with gold coins!"

"Ned—"

"The iron rings are symbolic of the most holy day of our island." The words poured from her lips like boiling water spilling over a pot. "They're meant to be *prayed* over and blessed by the Elders. They're meant to be pushed into the graves of the people we love. They're meant to *mean* something."

"I didn't think you cared about what the gods wanted anymore." My eyes were on her crucible hanging from her neck in the spot where she used to wear a three-knotted cord. She had been the only person I knew who'd ever bothered to wear one; most people were religious only during the holy festival days and then in name only.

"It's complicated!" Nedra shouted.

"Not really." The louder she became, the more my own voice dropped. She was fire, but I was ice. "The gods are against necromancy. Oryous is supposed to conquer death, Nedra, not you." My words sliced into her like a gutting knife, and there was a little piece inside of me that triumphed at the way her words died on her tongue. "It really is that simple. There's right, and there's wrong. You can't expect me to respect a symbol of the gods when you defy them every second of the day."

She stood there, fuming, her hand balled into a fist. But before she could say anything, I continued. "Ned, you can pretend all you want that you've done the right thing. Because I understand, I really do. It was wrong for your family to die. It was wrong for all those people in the plague to die. But just because that was wrong doesn't make what you're doing right. It doesn't solve anything. If you actually cared about what the gods wanted, you'd leave death to them. What you've done, Nedra, what you intend to continue doing—it's monstrous."

Every muscle in Nedra's body was tense. She took a deep breath in. I felt the air around us crackle with electricity, and even though the ship was rocking over rough waves, neither of us moved.

"Get out." She spoke so quietly that if I hadn't expected her to say those words, I don't know if I would have heard them. But I did. Because necromancy was the unspoken line between us, and I had crossed it.

THIRTY-NINE

Nedra

THE NEXT MORNING, at dawn, when the light was still cold and blue, I heard footsteps on the wooden walkway in front of the door. They stopped. I could see a shadow under the door, two feet, so close that all Grey had to do was reach out and knock. I got out of bed and padded silently across the room.

He was on the other side of the door, I knew.

But he didn't knock.

And I didn't open the door.

For the rest of the week, I stayed in the cabin, and he stayed out of it.

It had taken the exact same amount of time to sail to Miraband from Hart, but the voyage to the capital had disappeared in a blink of an eye. And the return had been interminable. I spent every waking moment either reading or trying to reach my revenants. My worry grew as we drew closer to home and their deafening silence persisted.

On the seventh day, I awoke early, pressing my face against the porthole of the cabin, looking for signs of home. I wondered if the Emperor's cruiser would take us directly to Blackdocks and I'd have to find my own passage to my little island. But the ship veered north, looping wide and stopping at the stone steps leading to the quarantine hospital. I wondered if the captain worried that the new recruits would spread word that a white-haired girl got off the boat at the abandoned hospital, or if he no longer feared consequences now that I was back where I belonged.

Everything I needed had been packed since the night before. I shouldered the large copper crucible and headed to the door. I pointedly did not look at any of the new recruits watching me from the deck, instead searching for Grey.

He wasn't there.

Before my foot had touched the second stone step, the gangway was raised. Before I reached the hospital, the ship had already sailed away.

When I reached the large doors of the quarantine hospital, I had to push hard, ramming my shoulder against the mahogany, before they would finally open. Something blocked the door, something heavy but soft. A blackish-red stain smeared a dark rainbow across the white tiles of the floor. I followed the smudged gore to the object that had barred my entry—a dismembered female torso.

The stench of decay filled my nostrils. I gagged, but forced myself to step into the hospital's foyer. The air inside felt heavy and damp. The doors had been closed for too long, entombing the rot inside.

Dozens upon dozens of bloody bits of human remains littered the floor, sticky with blackish-red blood congealing on the tile. I did not flinch at corpses; Death was an old friend of mine. But the sheer gore of these bodies, dismembered flesh strewn around the room, left to decay for the gods knew how long . . . Bile bubbled up my throat. I couldn't stop retching, my eyes streaming as my body heaved long after the contents of my stomach were gone.

I threw myself back to the open doorway, gasping for fresh air. Blearily, I could see Grey's ship as it cut across the bay, back to Blackdocks. I remembered the night I woke Grey up, overwhelmed with the silence in my head. My revenants had slowly quieted over the days, the result,

I'd assumed, of their souls leaking out of their raised bodies. After reading the books from the Collector, I was certain that the silence was from their life energy seeping out, evaporating over time.

I had prepared myself for the worst: coming home to revenants that were all like Nessie, empty inside and hollow shells of who they used to be.

I had been wrong.

That had not been the worst.

I turned back to the interior of the hospital. I had learned long ago there was no point in denying the truth, no matter how gruesome. And the truth was my revenants had *not* been silenced because their souls and energy had slowly dissipated.

The dead cannot die.

But they can be torn apart. Ripped, piece by piece, until they were nothing but bloody chunks and dismembered parts on a dirty, stained floor.

I looked around me at the carnage that stained the walls and littered the floor. Small pieces of the bodies of the people I had given life after it was taken from them too soon—a thigh, a hand, a neck, a jaw.

There had been a battle here.

And my revenants had lost.

I dropped to my knees, ignoring the sticky gore that soaked through the material of my trousers. My eyes darted from body part to body part, trying to piece together who was who. That scalp with long hair—was that Kessel? Oh, gods, that little hand, that had been a child. I recognized the coat that belonged to Dannix. He'd been alive, a defender of my dead—perhaps caught in the crossfire and chopped up . . .

So that I couldn't raise him after.

Who? My heart screamed. I thought we'd scared off the aggressors from Cliffside—had they come back? Or was this the Emperor's doing? Maybe he knew I'd go with Grey, maybe the captain of the ship had betrayed us and told him I'd gone to Miraband. I'd left my revenants with orders—protect the hospital and the people inside. But could they survive a battle without me to direct them? They had already been so weak when I'd left, empty like . . .

Nessie.

I looked around the foyer with blurry eyes, trying to sift through the human remains for a piece of my twin sister, for a face identical to my own. Oh, gods, Nessie. She could more than defend herself, but she wouldn't act without an order from me. Had she just stood there, while the attackers hacked her body apart?

Why did I never fear this? I'd felt in control. Invincible. Confident in my knowledge that no living person could defeat me in battle with my revenants by my side.

But I hadn't been by their side.

My body bent over, and I gasped for breath, the sound harsh and wheezing, too loud in the silence that was only broken by the buzzing of flies. My eyes were wide and stinging, but I couldn't tell if it was sorrow or rage that incapacitated me. When my revenants had needed me the most, I had not been there. Shame burned my cheeks. I had been with Grey, while my revenants had been hacked to pieces.

Whoever had done this had attacked with a plan. My army literally ripped asunder—I could do nothing with necromancy to save handfuls of flesh and the broken ends of splintered bones. This had been done purposefully. Methodically. Nearly all the bits of bodies on the floor were unidentifiable. If I pieced them all together, different parts of a gruesome puzzle, would I be able to reform any one person? Even if I knew which mangled, bloody bits belonged to Nessie in this sea of death, how could I ever hope to put her back together again?

As soon as that thought melted into my wildly beating heart, my entire body sagged. Grief flooded my mind as her loss—finally—overwhelmed my senses. I tried to breathe the heavy, sticky air, too sweet and too metallic. The air in my lungs turned into a choking sob. I had never been so utterly broken and defeated before. There was nothing, *nothing* I could do now. Slowly, my hand stilled. I closed my eyes.

And a new emotion filled me, slowly, like a rising tide drowning out all other feelings.

Relief.

If Nessie was gone, if all my revenants were gone . . .

I was free.

I shouldn't feel this way, I thought dully. *This is wrong.* But I couldn't help it. I had spent every waking moment since becoming a necromancer trying to find a way to get back a small part of the life that the plague had taken from me. If she was past saving, though, if this was it, the end . . .

I felt the tears running down my cheeks, hot as acid. Of course this wasn't the end I wanted, but it was *an* end.

My eyes drifted up. While blood and organs and torn tissue covered the floor of the foyer, the gore did not extend into the halls or up the black stairs leading to the clock tower.

I made my way slowly across the tiled floor, in part so that I wouldn't slip on the congealing blood. I had to wiggle my foot through mounds of chopped flesh, leap over piles of severed limbs. I slipped once, my foot catching in the crook of a dismembered knee, landing face-first in the gore and staining the front of my tunic blackish-red. I struggled to regain my footing, picking pieces of entrails off my face. My hair was stiff with old blood.

My hand slid over something wet and squishy as I tried to push up from the floor, and I fell again. My eyes were on the same level as another brown eye. There was enough left of Lixa's face that I recognized her. Tears blurred my vision; it was easier to see the organs and limbs of humans I couldn't identify. But this was Lixa. I had raised her the first night I'd been a necromancer. She'd been among the last of the plague victims ferried to the hospital before it closed. When I had raised her, all I had felt from her was hope. She had no one to come back for—no family or lover or even close friend who missed her—but she had been so eager to live a life that she had jumped at my offer for a second one.

Most of the top of her skull had been smashed in, and what remained of her warm brown hair was matted in the place where her neck had been.

The attackers had been thorough.

When I mounted the steps to the clock tower, I left behind shining bloody footprints on the black stairs. I gripped the railing, my ascent slow and methodical as I imagined the invaders doing the same.

They called me a monster, all of them. But I never cut someone down. I never hacked away—

My steps stumbled. The worst I'd ever done, I'd done to the one I loved the most. And Nessie had been alive when I'd amputated her arm, unable to do anything but feel me sawing through her bone. At least my revenants had felt no pain when these enemies destroyed them.

When I got to the top of the iron stairs, I looked around, my stomach twisting with dread at what I was sure I would find.

There, in the center of the room, just under the ticking gears of the enormous clock, stood Nessie. Whole, and as alive as I had made her.

She stared blankly at me, and I felt the staggering weight of her death settle on me like an iron mantle around my shoulders. I straightened my spine, my resolution solidifying within me.

It wasn't over yet.

FORTY

Grey

BANNERS AND FLAGS were festooned upon every pole and lamppost in front of Blackdocks—the red and black colors of the Emperor displayed prominently. The cloth made snapping sounds as the wind got stronger. I flicked up the collar of my coat, leaning into the cold. It would storm soon—one of those quick thundershowers that dumped water from the sky in buckets but was completely gone in an hour. I glanced up the hill, wondering if I could make it back to the castle before the downpour.

"News!" a little girl hollered from the corner. "The latest news!"

I dropped a coin in her hand and took one of the news sheets from her stack, reading it immediately. The Emperor had made quite an impression on the people while I'd been away. Last week, he'd attended service at one of the small church halls near Blackdocks, blessing the Elder himself. The plans for the orphanage and a new quarantine hospital had already begun, with notes that the Emperor's coffers would be footing the bill. A splashy headline announced a public festival that would happen in two days' time. I remembered Hamish's reservations about doing so much so soon, but it was clear the Emperor's will would not be denied.

I turned the paper over, and gasped when I saw my face looking up at me. It was a re-creation of the portrait my mother had done before I went to Yūgen, my chin tilted up, my hair a little too long. MEET THE

MAN WHO'S SAVING THE NORTH! the headline beneath my picture proclaimed. The article was brief and was clearly being used to encourage people to come to the upcoming rally in order to hear news of my success. I was deeply grateful I *had* good news to relay.

Beneath the fold was a full article about a group of thirteen rebels who'd been arrested. I scanned the printed black-and-white faces. The images were rough, but I could tell immediately that none of the captured criminals were my family.

A fat raindrop landed on the paper, smearing the ink. I glanced up as the little girl grabbed her remaining stack of news sheets and ran for cover. Holding my own paper above my head as the downpour started, I raced across the street, flagging down a coach. "To the castle," I said as I ducked inside.

Even here, inside a hired coach, evidence of the Emperor's influence persisted. Black-and-red ribbons were stacked in a neat basket on the seat, with a small sign that said TAKE ONE. I did, and I pinned it to my coat. The farther up we climbed, the more bunting I saw draped on the windows of storefronts and even homes. Shiny new flagpoles bore the Allyrian flag, and bunting decorated most of the nicer houses along the streets. I caught sight of street workers huddled in an alley taking shelter from the storm, their bags laden with even more black-and-red cloth.

It'll have to be more than just a cosmetic change, I thought, remembering Hamish's warnings. But I suspected that it already was. This level of change to the face of the city meant that people had to be hired. More jobs meant less homelessness. And with new street decorations came cleaner streets. Stoops had been swept, windows cleaned. No trash piled up in the gutters. Even the rain seemed to be in on the plan, making the city sparkle.

I had thought Miraband to be wondrous, but now I realized how good it was to be home.

The coach brought me to the back of the castle, and I ran inside, doing my best not to get soaking wet. Servants stood near the door, one bending down to wipe my shoes off for me. "Thanks," I muttered, shifting away as soon as possible.

Before I'd even made it to my room, another servant rushed up to me. "Mr. Astor!" he called.

I turned.

"You're wanted in the council room," he said formally.

I was gratified to realize that I mostly knew the way back on my own; he only had to redirect me twice. A herald announced me when I stepped inside.

The Emperor no longer had a cane. Instead, he paced around the council room, looking up as I entered, an inscrutable expression on his face.

"Astor!" he called. "My captain sent word that you have been successful in your mission."

"Ah, yes," I said as every council member turned to look at me. There were new faces among them, people I assumed had been appointed to the council in my absence, though several new empty seats dotted the room.

"Excuse me." A woman I didn't recognize spoke. Several council members fidgeted nervously, and Hamish gave the woman an encouraging nod. "I know Astor's report is important, but we need to talk about the prisoners first," she said.

"Prisoners?" The question slipped past my mouth before I had a chance to bite my tongue.

The Emperor glared at the councilwoman. "We've collected thirteen traitors to the Empire," he said. "Their trial will be soon."

There had clearly been a note of dismissal in his tone, but Hamish ignored it. "'Soon' is a relative term, Your Imperial Majesty. These people are commoners, and whatever role they played in treasonous activity was minimal at best. The prison conditions are atrocious and—"

"There is no such thing as 'minimal' treason, Hamlayton," Emperor Auguste said, his voice brooking no argument. "Treason is treason. They will stand trial soon enough."

"What of the treasonous nobility?" Hamish said, his voice rising. The tension in the room was palpable, but Hamish seemed ignorant of it. "This council has seen time and again that one's personal wealth can buy a faster trial, and with a better outcome—"

"Enough." The Emperor didn't shout; in fact, the word was barely audible. But Hamish's mouth snapped shut, and he slumped down into his chair.

Emperor Auguste turned to me, an easy smile on his face that belied the argument seconds before. "Report, please," he said, waving his hand to indicate that I could continue.

A droplet of rainwater dribbled down my neck, and I shivered. Everyone waited for me to speak. "Er," I started.

"A commission of five thousand units, yes?" the Emperor prompted, smiling at me with a sort of apologetic look; I thought he only just then realized the awkward position he'd placed me in.

"Yes." I nodded, taking a deep breath. Channeling everything my father had ever worked for, I stepped forward, detailing the new trade commission and what it would mean for the north. As soon as I quit speaking, there was a smattering of polite applause from the council. Hamish stood, bowing slightly to me, and a few others followed suit.

"This is truly remarkable," Emperor Auguste said. "I hadn't wanted to scare young Astor, but this sort of negotiating between colonies and homeland can be tricky at best."

Not scaring me was one thing, but a little warning about the process would have been nice. Still, I couldn't help but beam under the Emperor's radiant pride. "I want you to speak at the rally," the

Emperor continued. He turned to one of the new men on the council. "Add him to the schedule," he ordered.

The man looked flustered, but nodded.

"What day will that be?" I asked.

"Tomorrow," the Emperor said.

I swallowed. I knew the Emperor had been planning it for as quickly as possible, but I was intimidated by the suddenness. Still, this was for Nedra. If everyone was focused on all the good that was happening in the north, then they might forget their desire to punish her.

"We've been focused on building national spirit and goodwill among the people," the Emperor continued.

"I noticed," I said.

The Emperor stood, clapping me on the shoulder and then turning me toward the door. Now that my report was done, I was dismissed. "This is how you build a nation," he told me in a voice so low that only I could hear.

"With rallies?"

"With pride."

FORTY-ONE

Nedra

"Nessie." She stood there, emotionless, as I choked out her name, tears streaming down my cheeks. The copper crucible strapped to my back slid and fell onto the metal floor with a loud clang that broke the steady ticking of the enormous clock behind her.

"How did this happen?" I asked, knowing she couldn't answer me.

I had told Nessie to stay here and wait for me. And here she stood, in exactly the same spot I had left her. If I had been gone a year, I had no doubt there would be dust collecting on her shoulders.

But I had ordered all my other revenants to stand watch and protect the hospital. Perhaps the aggressors had thought that the ones who'd converged in the foyer to defend the building were all the revenants I had; perhaps none had thought to climb the hundreds of steps to the clock tower.

I looked up at Nessie, who still stood quiet, motionless. Was her soul aware of what had transpired? Had she stood here, a statue, hearing the wet thwacks of blades against flesh for however many hours it took to decimate my revenants?

The weight of all I had done and all I had failed to do pressed down on my ribs, choking me of breath. I stumbled up, clutching at my chest as I felt my heartbeat ratcheting. Nessie watched me silently as I staggered to my desk, gasping for air. Black spots flickered across my vision. My hand reached for my chair, but it was my left hand, the one that no longer was there, and I stumbled, dropping to the floor.

I couldn't breathe. I couldn't breathe and everything was going wrong and my heart was going to burst, and if I died, so would Nessie. But it didn't matter because she was already dead, and I would be, too, because *I couldn't breathe.*

My right arm curled protectively over my chest as I huddled on the floor, trying to remember what it was like to not be dying.

I gulped for air, sweat stinging my eyes, but I didn't blink away from Nessie's gaze, and she, of course, didn't turn away from mine.

I don't know how many lifetimes passed, but in the end, I got up from the floor. My hair was matted with the drying blood and gore from downstairs, my skin smeared with it, tears tracking down my face. My heart *hurt.* But still, I got up.

There was work to do.

I stabbed at my shaking hand, forming the blood key to open the copper crucible. I didn't know what I was looking for; it was just the last recourse remaining. I shifted the contents carefully, aware of the grime on my skin, trying not to smear congealing blood on the delicate old paper. Even so, my hand brushed against the box the Collector had given me, the one I had been unable to unlock.

One of the copper bands disappeared. The upper band, the one that had refused to open with my blood.

I stopped, my breath catching. The runes spoke of blood that was alive, and blood that was dead. It must have been the gory mess of blood from my ripped-apart revenants that had opened the upper band of the lock. I squeezed a fresh drop of my own, living blood on the box, and let it splash onto the copper. The lower band faded to nothing.

The box was open.

My breath caught in my throat as I carefully lifted the lid. Inside was a single object, long and narrow, wrapped in white silk so aged that it was brittle and yellowing. I peeled the fabric away carefully.

My hand shook as I pulled out a crystal knife.

It was about twenty centimeters long, most of it a thick blade. Clear as glass, but light enough that I thought perhaps the center of the blade was hollow.

"What do you do?" I mused, holding the knife up to the milky-white light streaming through the clockface in the tower.

There was no book inside the box, no helpful instructions. I shifted the knife from my real hand to my shadow hand and felt a jolt of power at the touch.

The blade itself didn't seem that sharp—when I scraped it against my boot leather, it didn't cut at all. But while the entire knife was smooth, I could see embedded inside, glittering as if faceted, runes running all along the hilt.

I squinted, trying to read them. There was one that repeated, almost in a pattern, and while it was familiar, I couldn't quite place where I'd seen it. It took several moments for me to finally remember. I lunged for the copper crucible, pulling out the books the Collector had given me, the ones I'd read over and over again on the long, lonely journey back home. I picked up the oldest book and flipped to a place near the end. "Cadavers," I read aloud, "once raised, store their life energy inside their imperfect bodies. The savvy necromancer can then use his revenants to enhance his own power."

After that, several chapters were ripped from the book. But, in faint pencil and sketched with a shaky hand, someone, perhaps the Collector, had drawn a rune—four lines pointing up, connected by a horizontal line along the bottom. Beneath that was a single word handwritten in the margin: *lich*.

I still didn't know what the word meant, but if the rune in this book matched the one engraved inside the crystal knife, then surely the blade had been made by a necromancer.

Using my shadow hand, I raised the knife up. My shadow hand seemed darker somehow, more corporeal. I gasped and looked down at my crucible. The black energy that swirled in its base, the energy that gave me the power of death over life, was spilling out of the iron bead, pouring over my shadow arm.

Power crackled in my blood. I felt as if electricity was sparking inside me. I felt stronger. Invincible.

I swung the knife through the air. An eerie sort of electricity emanated from the blade.

I wanted to test it. Looking around, I settled on my worktable. I steeled my arms, then threw my full strength behind the crystal knife as I stabbed at the table.

I spun around, off-balance, and fell on my backside. The worktable, despite taking the full brunt of my blow, was unscathed. Not even a scratch.

"What good is a knife that can't cut?" I muttered.

I looked for an answer, which meant, of course, I looked to my sister.

Her eyes were focused on the crystal knife.

I stood slowly, crossing the clock tower. The ticking matched my steps. Nessie's eyes did not leave the clear knife in my hand. But as I drew closer to her, her body started to tremble.

"Nessie?" I said.

Silence.

But I didn't need her words to know that she was more than afraid. She was terrified. Her lip curled over her teeth in a repulsed snarl. This thing, this crystal knife . . . despite the power, I could sense that it was *wrong*.

I stared down at the blade. At the hilt there were glimmers of light, strings of gold that I recognized as my sister's soul.

My body connected my crucible to the blade, and both my sister's soul and the dark power inside my crucible's base bubbled down my arm and around the knife.

I wondered—if I could pull my sister's soul out of the darkness, could I then put it back into her body? Would that be all it took? I couldn't do it on my own. I had reached into my crucible before with my shadow hand, trying to extract Nessie's soul. My power alone wasn't enough.

But perhaps with the crystal knife . . .

I had to test it first, before I risked hurting my sister.

I reached with one finger on my right hand to touch the edge of the clear blade. As soon as my skin brushed against the crystal, I felt indescribable cold, so icy that it burned. I snatched my finger away—there was no mark, no sign of damage, but it took several minutes before feeling returned to my finger.

Meanwhile, a faint golden glow filled the crystal blade.

I looked at Nessie. She looked at the knife. Silent tears streamed down her face.

I shifted the crystal knife to my right hand and lifted my shadow hand toward the edge of the blade, little finger extended. As soon as I touched the crystal, the ghost-finger started to disappear. I jerked away, willing the shadow to reform.

I felt no pain—without flesh, there is no pain—but the shadowy finger did not return. It was gone, eaten by the darkness.

The knife did not cut flesh. It severed souls.

FORTY-TWO

Grey

THE EMPEROR FOUND me in the chapel.

"You did remarkable work," he said. "I wasn't sure if you'd be able to secure a commission, but this bodes well for the future of Lunar Island."

Why can't Nedra see it that way? I thought. Aloud I said, "Thank you."

The Emperor stood beside me, gazing up at the large round Oryous eye window. "Come to thank the gods for your successful journey, Astor?"

At the moment, I disliked religion for the way it had forced Nedra and me to opposite sides. I had only come here for privacy.

As if reading my mind, the Emperor said in a low voice, "You still care about the necromancer, don't you?"

I turned to him.

"My captain sent me a message from Hart, and he gave his final report once he docked at Northface Harbor," the Emperor continued.

A report in Hart . . . "So you know I took Nedra with me to Miraband."

"And brought her back, yes."

I looked him in the eyes. "She doesn't have to hang for necromancy. She's done no evil with it."

"Except for the dozens of dead she raised. And," the Emperor said, as an afterthought, "the dozens of people she killed when she raided this very castle."

I thought about the fierce rage Nedra had shown when she first returned to Yūgen, after her family had died. She had taken all the grief she must surely have been feeling, and she'd pushed it down, down. Instead of taking time to mourn, she took souls.

She took power.

"She used her powers for good, though," I said. "To save *you*." My voice rang out, echoing on the stone walls of the chapel.

The Emperor raised his hand. "Peace. Do you see torches and pitchforks poised to storm her island?"

"I want your word," I said. "I brought you the trade commission. I want a pardon for Nedra in return."

The Emperor gazed at me coolly. I met his eyes defiantly, my jaw set.

"You love her," he said as if only realizing the truth as he spoke it. He tapped his chin. "And yet when you returned from Miraband, my captain says you left her alone on her island and came here."

"Yes," I said, in answer to all his points.

Something in his face softened. "You have my word," he said. "Nedra Brysstain will not hang."

With a nod, the Emperor turned and left the chapel, the door closing almost soundlessly behind him. I was left in the chapel with nothing but his promise and my dark thoughts.

FORTY-THREE

Nedra

I STEPPED OUT of the clock tower and toward the iron staircase, Ernesta following me silently.

From this vantage point, with the crystal knife in my hand, I looked down at the gory remains of my revenants. They deserved a better farewell to this world than this.

Now that the shock had worn off, I saw not the debris of death, but the pale golden glow of life. Even ripped asunder, bits of soul and energy still clung to the chunks of flesh and exposed organs. I didn't want their souls to suffer any longer. I could send my revenants to the afterlife.

Whoever had come to do this—vigilantes or the Emperor's men—had acted in the cruelest way possible. In an attempt to decimate my army of the undead, they had rendered helpless the souls of these people trapped in the decaying remains of their bodies. I held out the crystal knife with my shadow arm and my iron crucible with my right hand, calling the golden light to me.

While before souls had seemed like threads weaving into my crucible, now the dead were so far gone that their souls were little more than a mist. The untethered souls rose slowly, first melting into my iron crucible. But then the power and energy bubbled out, sliding down my shadow arm. I felt each soul pass through me as it moved into the afterlife, impressions of each person, leaving behind nothing but the raw energy of their shorn lives.

This was what I had learned from the Collector's books. When a necromancer raised the dead, the body became merely a container, holding the energy that gave it a second life. This was separate from the soul, which held the essence of the person, the memories and personalities and emotions. The soul could move on to the afterlife, but the energy … it was power for the taking. All life had this energy—the books even hinted that I could manipulate the living with theirs. And it was what made Nessie a shell; her body was animated with this life force, but her soul was trapped inside my crucible.

I said my farewells to my revenants' souls as best I could as they passed into the afterlife. I mourned the loss of time I could have spent with them in death.

Their energy buzzed through my shadow arm, passing through it and into the hilt of the crystal knife. The blade felt like it contained lightning, brimming with possibility. By the time all the flesh on the floor was nothing more than meat, the crystal knife radiated with warm, soft light.

My hand vibrated with the power contained inside the knife. This was what most necromancers wanted from the start. None of them cared about revenants' souls fading; they wanted only the residual energy from their forced lives. Feeding off of this energy would make me even more powerful.

I grazed the tip of the blade over the knuckle of my shadow finger, the one that had evaporated at the knife's touch. It reformed, and my hand was whole again.

And strong. I gripped the blade harder, feeling the power fill me, crackling in my blood. My senses sharpened; my entire body was alert. *I had never felt so alive.* With a wrench, I pulled the tip away from my shadow hand. My muscles were shaking in anticipation; I felt as if I could pull the hospital apart brick by brick and still have the energy to rebuild it again.

But I didn't need this power.

Nessie did.

My shadow hand gripped the glittering hilt. I would not waste this last gift of those I had raised.

I turned to my sister, whose normally passive eyes watched the blade. I wondered at that connection—her soul was wrapped up in the mysterious dark power woven into the iron, and it seemed to react to the crystal blade. Maybe if I gave Nessie more power, she could wrest her soul free from my crucible.

"Hold out your hand." My voice was stronger now.

Nessie offered her left hand, palm up.

I touched the crystal knife to her skin, and I *pushed*. Not the blade—it's tip still rested against her palm. I pushed at the energy inside the blade. My shadow hand shook. The dark power seemed to rage against the loss of the golden energy inside the crystal; it had wanted to consume it. But I fought the black, focusing instead on the light.

The little cloud of golden, sparkling light floated through the crystal knife, down into Nessie's open palm.

My eyes were on my sister's face. I saw the exact instant her body filled with life—just a moment, but impossibly and undeniably *real*. Her eyes snapped to mine, her mouth opened. "Ned," she whispered, and it was *her* voice, real and true.

And then gone again.

I turned the blade over in my hand. The light was gone. There had barely been a wisp of it to start with.

More, I thought. *I need more*.

The clock tower's bell rang out, the sound deafening. I thought I could almost hear the echo of Yūgen's matching clock in Northface Harbor.

And past Yūgen—the Governor's Hospital. A place full of death. If not there, the morgues. The whole city offered possibility. If I drained the energy from a new corpse into the knife's blade, it would likely be much stronger than the wisps of light from my revenants. Maybe enough to give Nessie more than mere snatches of moments. I could go across the bay and find fresh corpses full of potential energy. I would take what I needed.

Time to go to the city.

FORTY-FOUR

Grey

AN ENORMOUS WOODEN platform had been erected in the Imperial Gardens, not too far from the spot where Nedra and I once took a nighttime walk, where I'd told her stories of ghosts in the castle and she'd pretended to be spooked for an excuse to be closer to me. The platform, I thought, was ugly. Rough-hewn wood, with a long, heavy beam extended over the top. A red banner hung from the crossbeam, with the words ORYOUS SAVE THE EMPIRE painted across it in white letters trimmed with black.

"Tables here," a man said, and servants started hauling two long tables up onto the platform, one on either side of the podium in the center. The tables were draped in black linen, and bunting decorated the podium.

It was early yet, but people were already milling about the grounds, watching as the last-minute touches were added to the platform—more bunting along the edge of the railings, enormous vases of fresh flowers in front of the tables, gilded chairs behind them. An entire orchestra set up beneath the stage, the sounds of tuning instruments drifting through the boards.

Hamish appeared at my side. He frowned at the platform and the decorations. "It's not enough," he muttered.

"What isn't?" I asked.

"This." Hamish waved his hand, but didn't really seem to indicate anything specific. When I didn't answer, Hamish elaborated. "The rally. All the 'goodwill' stuff the Emperor is doing."

"You don't think the orphanage is a good idea?" I asked, thinking of the newspaper clipping.

Hamish's scowl deepened. "Of course we needed one. We need half a dozen now, thanks to the plague. It's just . . . showy."

"Showy?"

"All the news articles on it, the speeches, this." Hamish gestured again to the platform, then turned to face me. "You."

"Me?"

"Your mission. The Emperor has been talking about it for weeks. You're the face of change for the north, Astor." I thought of the article I'd seen in the news sheet. I'd assumed it was the first, but perhaps more had run while I had been away.

Behind me, the crowd was growing. Food vendors pushed small carts full of honey buns and stick meat, calling out their wares. Cheerful volunteers passed out tiny replicas of the Allyrian flag. Children ran by, laughing.

It felt odd, being called "the face of change." But by being some-thing of a public figure, I could draw attention to the problems of the north and garner support.

"Maybe being showy is the point," I said, looking at the crowd and not Hamish. "The Emperor is trying to build up national pride."

Hamish mumbled something I didn't hear.

"What?" I asked.

"We're *not* a nation, though," he spat. "He's building *colonial* pride." He looked at me the same way my father had, the last time we spoke. "There's a difference."

Before I had a chance to answer, Hamish withdrew a pocket watch. "We're starting in an hour," he said. "You're to meet behind the platform with the others." Hamish pointed the way, and I left.

A large tent had been set up behind the main platform. The orchestra was louder here, as were the people. A man with a leather portfolio kept checking his paper and shouting directions at people. His eyes skimmed over me, then settled on my face. "Ah," he said, "Astor. You're after the awards."

I'd never met this man before, but I guessed he recognized my face from the news sheets. I followed him to the section of the tent where he pointed. Half a dozen people stood around, sipping sparkling wine. They were mostly common people—I recognized a factory owner named Berrywine, and the others introduced themselves as a merchant, a city worker, a potion maker, a forester, and a butcher. The merchant and the forester were from the north; the others were all from Northface Harbor.

"I must say, I am deeply honored," Berrywine told me. It was clear he thought the others were beneath him; while they talked among themselves, Berrywine maneuvered me into a corner of the tent, away from the workers.

"To think the Emperor chose me, of all the elite businessmen of the city, to be recognized in this way . . ." He droned on, but I was able to glean from his blustering talk that the Emperor was granting special citizenship awards today.

"Places!" a woman shouted.

A servant rushed forward, herding us into a line. "Astor?" the servant asked. When I nodded, he pulled me in front of the award winners.

The orchestra started playing the Allyrian anthem, and I could hear singing from the crowd of people in front of the platform. Before I could wrap my head around what was happening, we were pushed forward, up the stairs, and onto the platform.

I squinted out at the crowd. Several hundred people were here, staring up at us in eager anticipation. I was seated directly to the left of the podium, Berrywine beside me. The orchestra shifted from the Allyrian anthem into trumpet-heavy fanfare. The crowd erupted in screams and cheers, and I looked around just as Emperor Auguste mounted the stairs. He waved at the mob of people with an elegant twist of his wrist as he made his way to the podium. Just before he took his position in the center of the platform, he clapped a hand against my back and gave my shoulder a comforting squeeze. I felt Berrywine shift his seat closer to mine.

"Oryous save the Empire!" the Emperor shouted as he stood behind the podium. The crowd roared the words back up at him, cheering until he put out both his hands to silence them.

"Today, we want to honor those citizens who have helped Lunar Island during one of her most trying times," the Emperor said. He proceeded to call forth all the people I'd shared the tent with, singling them out and describing how they went above and beyond the call of duty to help save others during the plague. As each individual was called forth, I noticed that certain parts of the crowd cheered louder. The Emperor had wisely selected a person from each borough of the city, giving each district their own moment of glory through one of their citizens.

"And let us also praise the council for the progress they have made these past weeks," Emperor Auguste announced after giving Berrywine his medal of honor.

The council was seated to the Emperor's right, and each member stood and gave a brief report, focusing on the improvements, planned or recently finished. "Here to help revitalize the north after its devastation is Greggori Astor," the Emperor said finally, gesturing to me.

I stood, swallowing. I didn't know how the people in the back of the crowd could hear me, but I shouted out the plan for new mercantile trade with Miraband, keeping my report as short as possible. I detailed the plans for a new factory in Hart that would create many new jobs, with the promise of more if the sales were effective. I added that the tariffs from the new trade would be funneled back into the north, in a new library, schools, and public buildings—all of which would provide even more opportunities for employment for northern folk. I didn't realize how badly I was shaking until I finished, collapsing back into my chair with a clatter I hoped most of the crowd didn't hear.

"Good man, good man," Berrywine whispered to me, clapping me on the back. His medal glinted in the sunlight, blinding me for a moment.

A ripple moved through the crowd, then a shout.

"What about the thirteen?"

A ring formed around the man who had yelled as people stepped back, not wishing to be associated with the person who'd disrupted the rally. "Make them pay!" the man shouted.

"The thirteen?" I asked under my breath.

I hadn't expected an answer, but Berrywine heard me. "Those street rats they arrested," he said. "Hickory and the lot."

I remembered then what Hamish had said in the council meeting, about a group of commoners awaiting trial for conspiracy against the Empire. I had seen the whispers of treachery among the people, and the article in the news sheet. Lord Anton and his ilk had led the fledgling revolution. Men like my father. I hadn't heard of any commoners who had done anything that could have been half as damaging as what the nobility had plotted, the men with power and means to actually disrupt the system.

I squinted at the crowd. The man who'd shouted about the thirteen traitors first was now leading a chant—"Hang the traitors! Hang the traitors!" Since no Imperial Guard came to stop the man, the people nearby were emboldened to join in. The crowd quickly picked up the chant, turning it into a demand as they faced the Emperor.

I glanced up at Emperor Auguste. His face looked grim.

The crowd had lifted the shouting man on their shoulders, and they bounced him high above the rest of the mob as the chant spread throughout.

I sucked in a breath.

I *knew* him. That was Finip Brundl, one of the men on the council. He wasn't dressed as a lord, though—he wore tan pants and a navy shirt, clothing common among dock workers. The people on the grounds looked to be embracing him as one of their own, unwittingly raising a lord above their shoulders as a champion of the common people.

My eyes shot to the Emperor.

Red-suited guards rushed onto the platform, swarming around the Emperor. The award winners were rushed offstage, but Emperor Auguste refused his guards, raising his hands above the crowd. They didn't quite silence, but the chanting grew softer, soft enough for the Emperor to shout out, "I have heard you, my people!" before allowing himself to be escorted to his carriage and whisked away.

The remaining council members onstage followed him off. Coaches awaited us, a barrier of the Emperor's Guard keeping the mob at a safe distance. Their chant of "Hang the traitors!" was just as loud as ever, drowning out the orchestra as they tried to shift the attention to another rendition of the Allyrian anthem.

I headed to one of the waiting coaches, but felt a tug at my sleeve. "This one," Hamish said, pulling me into a different coach. A few council members were already seated, but they turned to Hamish respectfully as he shut the door and the coach rumbled up to the castle.

"That was Finip Brundl," I said. "Did you notice? He started the chanting."

Hamish stared darkly at me. "Of course he did."

"He's on the council." Why did no one else think it odd that a council member broke up the Emperor's rally with a mob demanding blood?

The woman opposite Hamish snorted. She was Prinna, another member of council—or at least she had been. I recalled how her spot at the council table had been empty since I returned from Miraband. Hamish shook his head subtly at her. "Don't you see, Greggori?"

"The point of the rally was to instill pride among the people," I said slowly. "Make them remember what's good about Lunar Island so they forget about the tragedy of the plague."

"The *point*," Prinna said, "was to find a scapegoat."

"Since you've been gone, the Emperor has been trying to boost morale with public visits among the people and plans for city improvements, but it's not been enough."

"Cheap awards and a single orphanage don't make up for thousands of dead and thousands more still adjusting to amputations," Prinna muttered.

My focus bounced between them.

"The only thing that's going to make the people happy," Hamish said bluntly, "is a hanging."

I shook my head violently. The Emperor had given me his word. He wouldn't hang Nedra. *But he never said he wouldn't hang the others.* I was reminded of my father's words, his fear of a death sentence without a trial.

At my reaction, one of the other people in the carriage, a stocky man with a deep voice, asked, "Can we trust this boy?"

Hamish looked me up and down. "I'm choosing to," he said finally. "And if you run to the Emperor and give him all our names, Greggori, you'll have to try to find a way to sleep at night, knowing it was you who put the noose around our necks."

"Why are you telling me this?" I asked, looking around with wide eyes. "What's going on?"

"We want you to help us," Prinna said, leaning forward.

"I may not have been important enough to be invited to your father's rebellion," Hamish said, a trace of bitterness in his voice. "But I've seen the way the Emperor works. He is a master manipulator, and we're just hanging from his puppet strings."

"He needs to be the hero," Prinna added.

"The Emperor," Hamish clarified. "Do you think the common people care about treason? They just want to live their lives, or what's left of them after the plague. It's the nobles—the ones who weren't as affected by the Wasting Death—who are still angry about the taxes and politics of it all. They're the ones who want to secede. But if the common people don't want to rebel, then the nobles will have no support in their fight against the Emperor."

"The 'good works' were a start," Prinna jumped in, her tone dismissing the Emperor's attempts at charity. "But in the end, people still wake up every day without an arm or a leg, or without a husband or a child."

"It's their rage, Greggori, that they *will* turn against the Emperor if he doesn't find a way to appease it," Hamish added, speaking slowly as if I were a child who didn't understand the lessons of the day. He rubbed a spot on his hand where, I suspected, he longed to wear a ring made of iron like the ones Bunchen gave to the rebel network.

"So he sets up a group of people for the commoners to focus their rage on," Prinna said. "Perhaps, if Adelaide hadn't been killed, she could have hung in their place."

That made me pause.

"Why these thirteen commoners, though?" I asked. "Shouldn't he try to hang the nobility inciting the rebellion?"

"People like your father, you mean?" Prinna said. The carriage lurched in the opposite direction of my stomach.

"Yes," I answered bluntly.

"There's rebellion boiling on all fronts," Prinna said. "The nobility might be appeased with tax reform. But some, like us . . ." She looked around at the others in the carriage, most of whom had been silently watching me. "We actually care. We want change, *real* change, that will help all of our citizens. The thirteen are just a symbol. A message from the Emperor, telling us that if we don't stop, more of the people we want to save will die. And the more innocents that die, the more the Emperor will manipulate the common folk into blaming us and chanting for *our* deaths. All he has to do is twitch his fingers."

"Greggori, you really don't understand politics at all," Hamish said, a little mournfully. "This is about controlling the masses. This is about telling the people what they want, and then giving them exactly that."

"Has the Emperor told you anything?" Prinna asked, leaning forward. "He confides in no one, but we know he's sought you out a few times. He trusted you with the trade commission. We can see only bits and pieces of his plan as they fall into place. It's hard to counteract someone who's pulling all the strings."

I shook my head. "I don't really know his plans. He only said . . ."

"Yes?" Hamish prompted when I didn't complete my thought.

"The Emperor swore to me," I said. "He's not going to go after Nedra."

Hamish looked at me pityingly. "And you believed him?"

FORTY-FIVE

Nedra

I HAD TO take one of the emergency skiffs the hospital kept in storage to reach Northface Harbor. Nessie rowed for me; it was fortunate she never tired. We left before dawn, when the night sky was just turning pale blue and there was less chance of being seen.

Blackdocks was surprisingly empty. There were, of course, still dock workers around, but they moved with the determined focus of men and women who were doing more than just their own job. While a few people noticed me as I disembarked with Nessie, taking in my white hair and mumbling near-silent curses as they backed away, most people were so intent that they barely spared me a passing glance. I pulled the hood of the cloak I'd gotten from the hospital over my white hair and made sure Nessie was similarly covered, then strode through the factory district undisturbed.

My stomach unclenched—I had expected to have to fight my way into the city. My nerves were on edge, but my body didn't know what to do with passivity.

During the plague, the Whitesides hospital had been full to the brim with victims near death. I had seen the carts of infected people dropped off at the overflowing hospital, and I had witnessed the corpse cart that left just as full.

But the plague was over. The hospital was still operating, but I could not go into the rooms of the sick without being detected. The building wasn't overrun or understaffed, not like it had been a month ago.

I cursed. I needed people who were freshly dead, with more vibrant energy I could channel into my sister. But short of going on a murder spree . . .

Someone bumped into me, almost knocking me down.

"Sorry, miss," the man said. He tipped his hat at me, not even really looking my way before turning and rushing down the street.

I frowned. It was a workday, but the streets were almost entirely empty.

Where was everyone?

"Excuse me!" I shouted, running to catch up with the man. He slowed but did not stop. "Where are you going?" I asked.

He laughed. "To the Imperial Gardens, of course," he said.

"Of course," I repeated slowly.

He hurried on, and I followed, remembering the way to the Imperial Gardens thanks to Grey.

The closer I got, the more people appeared. Some moved quicker than others, but all headed in the general direction of the vast public park bestowed upon Northface Harbor by Emperor Aurellious.

I wrapped my hand in Nessie's, determined not to lose her in the growing crowd. All around me were people of all different social classes. Gowned women walked beside factory workers. Orphans with amputations from the plague played with schoolboys and schoolgirls dressed in uniforms from the elite private academies. Everyone seemed . . . happy. Food vendors called out wares, clusters of people sang cheery folk tunes, and a man nearby tuned his fiddle as another invited any passing person, male or female, to dance a jig with him.

The energy reminded me of the docks at Miraband, except more joyful.

But there was no holy day today. No festival or memorial. I opened my mouth, ready to stop someone nearby and ask what the cause of the celebration was, when I saw it.

At the far end of the gardens, a large, long gallows stood, holding thirteen empty nooses.

I stopped in my tracks. Lunar Island hadn't had a public execution since Bennum Wellebourne.

But then another thought seized me. "Come on," I whispered to Nessie, pulling her along faster behind me.

I had no idea who was going to be hung today, but I knew I wasn't likely to find thirteen fresher souls to take than these.

FORTY-SIX

Grey

BEFORE I'D GONE to bed last night, two messages were delivered to my suite. One was from the Emperor—an order given to everyone in the castle that our presence at the public execution was mandatory. The other was an iron ring made from a horseshoe nail. From Hamish, I was certain of it. I hid it in my trunk.

I was just about to leave for the Imperial Gardens when I received a summons to the throne room.

The last time I had been here, Master Ostrum had been a revenant, controlled by Governor Adelaide. Together, they had tried to convince me to lure Nedra to the castle, where Governor Adelaide had planned a trap to steal Nedra's necromancy crucible.

I had not known then to be wary. I had blindly trusted all I had been told.

As I entered the throne room now, my stomach tightened in trepidation.

The enormous, life-size painting of the Emperor hung over the throne as a reminder of his power over every colony in the Empire. But as ostentatious as the portrait was, it was not nearly as commanding as Emperor Auguste himself.

He draped himself over the throne, the picture of ease and relaxation. All traces of the weakened boy Governor Adelaide had locked away were entirely gone. Most of the council was there, milling about the edges of the room, clinging to the shadows. The people standing closer to the Emperor held notepads, their eyes flitting around, absorbing every detail. *Reporters*, I realized.

When Emperor Auguste saw me, his face lit up. He straightened in the throne and motioned for me to approach. The room silenced as I crossed the tile floor; I felt the attention shift to me, and I tried to pretend not to notice.

A flash of anger washed through me. The Emperor was making a habit of summoning me without warning. I never knew what I would find—the Emperor's private chambers, a council room where I was expected to give a report I had not prepared, or a throne room full of reporters. Emperor Auguste's easy, bright smile lit up his face as I neared him. The more uncomfortable I was, the more calm and in control he appeared.

"Astor!" the Emperor said loudly. Not as a greeting, although it appeared to be that. But the flurry of movement and whispers from the reporters made me realize that he spoke for their benefit, not mine.

Emperor Auguste leapt down from the throne and took my arm. "A turn around the room," he said, leading me in a casual stroll away from the group of people who'd gathered near.

"What is this?" I asked in a low voice.

"A little intrigue gets them excited." The Emperor flicked his gaze at the reporters, who were watching us raptly.

Emperor Auguste squeezed my elbow, then relaxed his hand in the crook of my arm. "It's fine," he assured me.

"What are they all doing here?" I asked.

The Emperor frowned. "Vultures, that's what reporters are. But feeding them keeps them at bay." When I didn't respond, the Emperor added, "You're young."

"So are you," I shot back.

The Emperor stopped short. It was only in the ringing silence of the room that I realized how my comeback came across. How I had insulted the most powerful man in the world.

But Emperor Auguste barked out a laugh.

"I cannot stay on Lunar Island forever," he said as we turned the corner of the throne room. We were close to Hamish now, his eyes narrow slits as he watched us from the shadows. "And I will need new leadership—leadership I can trust—in place here before I go."

A new sort of tension coiled around my insides. Was he offering me the governorship of Lunar Island? Technically, the position should be chosen through an election, but as the Emperor reminded us all when Governor Adelaide had been appointed, the Emperor's choice trumped any vote.

"But before I make any decisions," Emperor Auguste continued, seemingly oblivious to the chaos his words had created in my mind, "I need to know that whoever I appoint to the role will be able to make the hard decisions that this colony needs."

He waited for me to respond. I felt foolish, but all I could say was, "I don't understand."

"The plague has left so many people angry. And rightly so; it was a true tragedy. They want someone to blame." His voice was so low it was nearly a whisper. I couldn't help but think that if this conversation needed to be so private, then we probably shouldn't have been having it in front of a room full of observers.

"The execution of the thirteen traitors," I said. I bit the words off. The Emperor said the people demanded it, but it had been one of his own council members who had started the rallying cry for a hanging.

The Emperor nodded at me tightly, then flicked his gaze to the reporters still crowded around the throne. "They are going to have to hang," the Emperor said. "You understand. *Someone* has to hang."

And I didn't want it to be Nedra.

"And," Emperor Auguste continued, his voice a little louder now, "they *are* guilty. I'm not plucking innocents from the streets, Astor. They've committed the crimes they will pay for."

I didn't turn to see Hamish, but I felt keenly aware of his presence. Because others had committed crimes, too. They simply had the means to pay for them in a way that didn't involve a noose. Not people like my father; he'd gone too far and would never see a fair trial, of that I was now certain. But others, who had been less vocal and less powerful, could make the law turn a blind eye with coins.

"Everyone pays for their crimes," I mused, "either with their life or their gold." It was how the rich stayed rich and the poor stayed poor. After their indiscretions, the rich could recover, and even earn more money. But the poor—unless aided by Nedra—could not earn another life.

I had ignored Father's rants at the supper table, about how Lunar Island wasn't progressing the way it should, how our colony was under the thumb of the Empire. Hadn't I seen this for myself in Miraband? The capital city, the home of the Empire, had electricity and trolleys, advanced city planning and networks of established trade. The Emperor was here on Lunar Island now, and he'd made plans to build us orphanages and hospitals, but hadn't mentioned developing a railroad or trolley system for public transportation. Hamish worked as city planner, and he'd been tasked with reorganizing the city blocks, but no allowance had been made for future advancements. Even our factories were outdated and unsafe, but the Emperor didn't seem to have a plan to address them.

I burned with shame. I had thought the Emperor would save us, that he was good and helping. He was only giving us scraps from a table set with a feast only he partook of, and he expected our everlasting adoration for it.

The Emperor paused. We were near the middle of the room, opposite the throne. The reporters stood on one side of us, the council members along the wall on the other. We were as isolated as we could be in this room.

"Is that what you truly think, that some can escape punishment?" the Emperor asked me, his tone still light. "I can name at least one person who has yet to answer for her crimes."

There it was—the threat against Nedra, should I not play the Emperor's game. I wondered if he kept Nedra alive just to use me, or if I was a convenient pawn, easiest to move across the board in this round of his game.

"What we're doing today—it cannot come from me, Greggori," Emperor Auguste said. He turned to face me, his eyes sincere. "I don't have a governor appointed—not *yet*," he added, subtly leaning into the word. "The people don't trust the council; too many members were corrupt and have fled, and they're seen as an . . ." The Emperor waved his hand, searching for the right word. "Elite," he concluded.

When I didn't answer, the Emperor added, "You are a man of the people. A homegrown boy, a hero who worked to fight the plague and free the Emperor. Me."

Over his shoulder, I could see the reporters all watching us, eyes wide, waiting eagerly.

"What do you need me to do?" I asked. A dread I couldn't explain filled my gut.

"I need you to be my representative," Emperor Auguste said. "Can you stand beside me?"

I swallowed. "At the hanging," I said, even though I already knew that's what he meant.

The Emperor nodded gravely. "At the hanging of thirteen traitors," he said in a voice so low I almost couldn't hear it. "Not of your Nedra."

"I—" I hesitated. I had never—*never*—wanted this. I had wanted to help the north by traveling to Miraband, but this was something else entirely.

The entire room watched me.

"Governor Adelaide saw only the power and glory. But you—you see the responsibility, don't you? The work?"

"Yes," I said. The Emperor's face lit up, and I knew he thought I'd accepted the role.

As soon as I spoke, the Emperor whirled around, facing the reporters. "I present to you the Lunar Island Colonial Representative!" he announced. The council members behind me clapped politely, and the reporters rushed forward.

Emperor Auguste took something from a servant and then turned to offer it ceremoniously to me. A sheathed sword. "Defender of your people," the Emperor said at my confused look. He inclined his head to me. When I didn't move, Emperor Auguste himself crossed over to me and affixed the sheath to my belt. The sword felt heavy at my side, but also strangely comfortable.

A group of servants rushed toward me as soon as the Emperor stood back. Two footmen carried a table, and another brought a chair. "Sit," the Emperor told me, and before I had a chance to agree, I felt the seat of the chair bumping against the backs of my knees. I sat, and the servant pushed the seat under the table.

A council member—Finip Brundl—stepped forward with a scroll as a different servant arranged a desk set on the table, a leather writing pad before me, with an ornate ink bottle and quill on one corner, and a lit candle with a wax burner suspended over it on the other.

"Of course," the Emperor said, twinkling at the reporters, "we all know the pen is mightier than the sword."

Finip unrolled the linen parchment in front of me. Across the top, in elegant calligraphy, were the words *Execution Orders*.

My eyes grew round, and I tried to find the Emperor. But he'd walked behind me, standing with one hand draped over the high back of my seat.

"How does it feel to represent Lunar Island?" a reporter asked me, stepping forward.

"Um—an honor," I said, unsure of myself.

"You're young, but you've already completed major tasks at the direct behest of His Imperial Majesty," another said. She waited for me to respond, even though she hadn't really asked a question.

"Er, yes," I said. "I went to Miraband to secure a trade commission to aid commerce in the north."

"Successfully," Emperor Auguste said, beaming at me as he dropped a hand on my shoulder. I jumped under his touch, and felt more than heard the low rumble of his chuckle.

My eyes kept falling to the open scroll in front of me. It listed the names of the thirteen conspirators, along with the command that they be hung by the neck until dead.

There was a blank line at the bottom.

"We are eagerly awaiting news of who the next governor will be," the first reporter said, eyeing me.

"And you'll continue waiting," the Emperor said. It was hard to see him from my angle. "For now, we have grave business to attend to."

The mood of the room shifted perceptibly, all eagerness replaced with solemnity.

"It is with no small measure of grief that we find ourselves faced with the heaviest responsibility of the crown," the Emperor continued. I wasn't sure if he meant the royal "we," or if he included me in the statement. "But the people have spoken. They will not see unjust criminals go unpunished. And the people"—Emperor Auguste squeezed my shoulder—"have been answered."

Every eye turned to me.

I stared down at the execution orders. This was far more than standing beside the Emperor at the hanging today. The blank line at the bottom of the scroll stared up at me. The hot wax bubbled in the burner, the heavy metal seal of Lunar Island lying beside it, waiting for me, just as every person in the room waited for me.

The pressure of the Emperor's hand on my shoulder tightened. I remembered his unspoken threat—them or Nedra. And these men would hang anyway. This hanging would happen, regardless of whether I signed my name. But if I didn't, so, too, would Ned.

My hand shook as I picked up the quill and dipped it in the black ink.

I couldn't look up. Not at the people watching me. Not at the words at the top of the parchment. I focused on the blank line until it was blank no more. My signature scrawled across the bottom, small but undeniably there.

A servant picked up the metal burner and poured a measure of hot red wax in a circle beside my name. I lifted the heavy seal and dropped it onto the parchment. A tiny droplet splattered up, burning my skin. I did not wipe it away.

FORTY-SEVEN

Nedra

MOST OF THE crowd pushed to the front of the platform, jostling to get as close as possible. I kept to the edge, on the lane, behind the food vendors. Children had tied ribbons of red and black, the Allyrian colors, on their wrists, and they screamed with joy as they wove in and out of the trees, their parents only half-heartedly calling for them to stay nearby.

Ten or so meters from the platform was another, smaller raised box. A banner painted with the words ORYOUS SAVE THE EMPIRE hung around the box, and I could see a large, gilded chair in the center, with a smaller chair beside it.

The Emperor's private box for the best view of the execution.

I kept well away from the box—and the circle of guards that surrounded it. It was easier to move on the perimeter of the crowd anyway.

"A flag, miss?" A woman held out a little patch of cloth with the Allyrian flag on it, the material so stiff with paint that the flag stuck out without the need of a breeze to lift it.

"I don't have any money," I said, already walking away.

"It's free." She grabbed my shoulder—my left shoulder, where the arm gave way to nothing. "Oh, I'm so sorry," she said, still awkwardly holding on to my residual limb. I looked down at her hand. "It's free," she said again, lamely, taking her hand away and holding the painted cloth to me. "The Emperor himself commissioned the Sewing Society to make them."

"Thank you," I said, taking the little flag and pinning it to my cloak, because it seemed apparent that she wouldn't leave me be if I didn't.

"And one for your"—she peered up at Nessie, to see if this was a relative or a spouse—"sister?"

I took the second flag and turned to attach it to Ernesta's cloak myself. I could feel the woman's eyes on us.

"The plague?" she said in a near whisper. Rather than help me, she watched as I held the cloth steady with my residual arm and used my right hand to slide the pin through Nessie's cloak.

"Obviously," I snapped. I cast my eyes at her. The Sewing Society, she had said. Women and men whose parents, spouses, or inheritances supported them enough that they could sew for fun rather than necessity. What must it be like to turn labor into a hobby? That was the definition of luxury—not only to be able to buy what you needed, but to have the time to create things that no one did.

"Yes, well," the woman said, unsure of how to politely disengage. I didn't bother to respond to her; I just walked away, my sister following mutely behind me.

As I suspected, the prisoners had not yet arrived, but there was a space blocked off behind the platform, surrounded by guards. Members of the council milled about under a large tent. Servants poured glasses of wine for the esteemed guests. A table with charcuterie had been laid out, thinly sliced meats on plates nestled over glass, garlic-stuffed olives sprinkled between blocks of cheese.

The Emperor wasn't there—surely he'd be seated at the box later—but the gathering under and around the tent was large enough that I felt like I could at least be ignored if I drew closer.

"Excuse me," the guard closest to me said as I approached. Under my cloak, I had the crystal blade strapped to my waist. My hand went not to it, though, but to the iron crucible hanging from my neck. The book on philosophy from the Collector had hinted that, while I could not control a mind, I could use a soul to help . . . distract it. I hadn't had a chance to practice this in person, but desperate times called for drastic measures. I brushed the golden light of his soul, tugging his attention past Nessie and me.

His eyes grew distant, and he focused on a spot well over my shoulders.

We walked right past him, into the private circle of the elite.

I kept to the edges, in the shadow of the tent. I didn't want to draw attention to myself, nor did I want to be mistaken for a servant, which would draw a different sort of attention. Instead, I turned to Nessie, as if engaging her in a fascinating conversation, both of our shoulders turned to the bulk of the crowd.

It wasn't long until a large prisoners' carriage drove through the trees from the northern side of the Imperial Gardens. A contingent of guards on horseback flanked the large wooden box on wheels, pulled by two draft horses.

The carriage was hidden by the platform, and there was no fanfare announcing its arrival. There would be a grand entrance for the crowd on the other side of the platform soon enough.

I used necromancy to see the vibrant golden light radiating from the wagon. Thirteen people were cramped inside. Without meaning to, I'd drawn closer, Nessie following dutifully. A few of the other elite guests had also lingered nearby, so we didn't stand out, just two more cloaked girls among a group of other morbidly curious folks.

I could hear crying from inside the wagon. Cursing. Praying.

My blood felt alight. I should mourn these deaths, I knew I should, but I could not stop their hanging. What I could do was siphon some of the energy from their already stolen lives and give it to my sister.

And then, through it all—through the noise of the people around me and the ever-growing crowd on the other side of the platform, through the horses huffing and the cries of the prisoners inside the wagon, the shouts of the guards to not get too close, through it all, I heard a voice I recognized.

Grey was here.

FORTY-EIGHT

Nedra

I WHIRLED AROUND, drawing Nessie closer to me, lingering at the back of the crowd. I didn't want Grey to see me now. I felt like a vulture, waiting for the prisoners to die, and even if I was doing nothing wrong, I still didn't want him to see me. I could not forget the last word he'd spoken to me at the end of our fight on the ship, the label he slapped upon me, as if he had not witnessed the very reason why I'd become what I had.

Grey was talking to another man, probably around forty years old or so, plump in the middle. "I don't need this," Grey said, and he moved as if to walk away from the man.

The man blocked him. "You should at least be aware of what you did." He swept his arm toward the prisoners' wagon.

I frowned.

"I didn't write the order," Grey grumbled. The fingers on his left hand tapped the pommel of a sword strapped to his waist. *Where did Grey get a sword?*

"No, but you signed it."

I was so close to Nessie that I could feel the coolness of her skin. I reached out, grabbing her hand, intertwining her icy fingers in mine.

Grey mumbled something, but whatever it was seemed to make the other man angrier. "Don't you see?" he said, his voice so loud that Grey tried to shush him. "These men don't deserve death." He snorted derisively. "They're not even all men. That boy—he's younger than you. And all he did was carry messages."

My breath caught in my throat as I remembered what Bunchen had told me about my father. *He* had carried messages for the rebellion. Would he have hung, too?

"Mr. Astor?" a servant said, approaching Grey. "Your presence has been requested by His Imperial Majesty."

Grey turned without bidding farewell to the man he'd been speaking to. But the man stepped forward, blocking Grey from following the servant. "You heard him yourself," the man said. "You know he's seeking an underdog, a scapegoat for the plague. You think people will be satisfied by one hanging? Thirteen dead don't make up for thousands. And once they're gone, he'll need another scapegoat."

Grey's brow furrowed in true worry.

"Make sure it's not you," the man said.

"That's not what concerns me," Grey answered, knocking past the man and following the servant away.

The man stared at Grey as he strode around the platform. I did, too. And so when the man finally turned around, his eyes met mine directly.

And he recognized me.

I could see it in the slight widening of his eyes, followed by the palpable fear that washed over him.

I didn't hesitate. I walked straight toward him. My fingers were already twining around his soul, ready to force him into silence. But the man didn't flinch as I drew near.

"Hello," he said.

"You know who I am."

His eyes slid over to Ernesta, and I knew he recognized her, too. "I was there that night," he said. "In the castle."

I inclined my head but did not speak.

"My name is Hamish Hamlayton," he added. I didn't bother telling him my name. He already knew it. "Did you want me to get Greggori?" he asked, looking over his shoulder.

I shook my head. "What did you mean?" I asked. "How is Grey to blame for . . . ?" I gestured to the prisoners' wagon.

Hamish's face was inscrutable. "He signed the execution orders for the prisoners' deaths," he said after only a moment's hesitation.

"Grey wouldn't do that," I said immediately.

"The Emperor chose him to be the colony's representative," Hamish said. "Didn't you see the sword he wore? 'Defender of the people.'" I didn't know what such a title entailed, but Hamish seemed to think that was enough of an explanation.

Behind us, the guards called out an order. Servants appeared, pushing the onlookers back as the prisoners' wagon rolled into motion.

"Come this way," Hamish said, leading me to the right as all the elite guests followed servants to the left. While the others went to a roped-off and guarded section to observe the execution, Hamish led me to the other side. There were more trees on this side of the platform, and no food vendors. People hung around—several schoolboys and schoolgirls had climbed the trees for better viewing—but it was relatively secluded, and no one spared us a second glance.

When we stopped, Hamish turned to me. Before he could speak, I said, "You know who I am and what I've done," I said. "But you're not afraid?"

"I'm not an idiot," he said. "I'm terrified."

I cocked my head.

"You do things no person should ever do," Hamish said. "But you're not a monster."

"Am I not?" I asked, unable to keep my lips from twisting into a sardonic smile.

Hamish saw nothing funny about what he'd said. "You're honest about what you do and who you are. Nothing true can be monstrous." He turned, but he wasn't looking at me. He was looking at the Emperor, seated on the gilded chair in his viewing box, high above the crowd gathered to see the hanging. The Emperor drank wine from a goblet, as if this were a cocktail party, not an execution.

But my eyes were on Grey, seated beside him.

"Grey told me about his mission from the Emperor, but I did not know that they were so close," I said. My words were drowned out by the chorus of "Oryous Bless the Empire" the crowd had started singing.

I tasted bile on the back of my tongue. Grey looked nervous, sitting in the small chair beside the Emperor's ornate one.

The prisoners' wagon cut through the crowd, and the people cheered wildly, as if they were greeting war heroes, not condemned prisoners. Soon enough, people started picking up rocks from the ground and hurtling them against the wagon's wooden sides, the cracking thuds loud enough to carry over the rest of the noise.

I flinched and reached for Nessie's hand. Hamish noticed, but he didn't say anything.

The prisoners, weighted down by shackles and chains, staggered from the cramped wagon out into the open, blinking in the bright sunlight. They were herded toward the stairs leading up to the stage, and for a moment, they were out of my sight on the opposite side of the platform.

"This isn't right," Hamish muttered. "They only *talked*." I was surprised to hear him so openly contradicting the Emperor's decree. It was the same sort of talk that had led to the prisoners' death sentences. "There's lots of grumbling against the Empire. People want change. They want fair representation in their own government. But the Emperor needs something from them."

Hamish looked out over the crowd. I couldn't see an end to the sea of people on the far side of the gardens. There had to be hundreds, maybe thousands here.

But then I thought about the mass graves in the center of Lunar Island, the forest cleared away to accommodate all the dead. Because despite how many living people stood in this crowd, I was still certain the mass graves held more.

Once every prisoner was lined up in front of a rope noose, the Emperor stood up. The crowd watched him.

"We can grant mercy," the Emperor called loudly.

Hamish snorted. "He only says that because he knows no one will back down now," he said in a low undertone, meant for my ears alone. "This is all his way of manipulating the crowd. Let him appear merciful, so that, later, when everyone's in bed tonight, and they can't get the idea of swinging bodies out of their heads, they'll feel as if they only have themselves to blame."

"Let 'em swing!" a voice shouted, clear and distinct from the crowd, which roared in agreement.

The Emperor touched Grey's forearm lightly.

Hamish followed my gaze. "It's very purposeful," Hamish said, still in that low voice. The executioner, shrouded in a black hood, started to mask the prisoners and loop the nooses around their necks.

"Young Mr. Astor doesn't even see it," Hamish continued. "The way the Emperor is using him. Puppets never feel their own strings."

"What do you mean?" I asked.

Hamish gave me a sidelong glance. "I suppose you don't get news sheets on your island."

"No."

"Nearly every day Astor was abroad, some article or another mentioned him and his mission. Some of the Elders in the church led a prayer day for him. The Emperor has ensured that praise was heaped upon that young man before he even did anything praiseworthy. If he hadn't been successful in getting a trade commission, I wonder if someone else would be hanging instead."

My eyes shot up to the prisoners.

"Plans for an event this day have been in place since we started organizing the rally yesterday. Why do you think the stage was designed to hang not just banners but also people? The Emperor's idea has always been to both celebrate his people and remind them of his power."

My eyes widened. "Are you suggesting they would have hung Grey if he hadn't succeeded?"

Hamish shook his head. "No. They would have hung *you*. Or maybe the news sheets would have changed the story, touting Grey's association with you, shifting the blame to him until he was poisoned in the people's eyes. It doesn't matter, not in the end. This is the Emperor's game. A constant push and pull of the people's emotions." Hamish watched the executioner walk behind the prisoners on the gallows. "The people are happy now, and they'll remember the Emperor was the one who created a whole day of celebration. But later, when they're unhappy, when they're reminded of why others have spoken against the Empire, and the cost behind such words, the person they're going to remember is Greggori Astor. The person they're going to *blame* is him."

I stared up at Grey's face. He was too far away for me to really see him, but I imagined him looking proud, sitting beside the Emperor, oblivious to the role he had played.

"The Emperor was always going to kill these people," I said. "Whether or not Grey signed the papers."

Hamish nodded, his jaw tight. Then he said, "But he still didn't have to."

"I know," I whispered. And I agreed.

I had truly thought Grey was different after Yūgen. He may have started school to raise his rank in society and be one of the elite at the Governor's Hospital, but he had worked in the quarantine hospital with me, he had seen the amputations, he had held the hands of victims alongside me. I had thought he cared.

But maybe he wasn't who I thought he was. Because the Grey I loved would not sit idly by, watching an execution that he was responsible for.

Before I could say anything else, the first man was pushed from the platform, his body swinging wide, then jerking back as the noose tightened.

Grey watched them die.

I watched Grey.

And when the last of the thirteen dangled lifelessly from their ropes, I squared my shoulders and pulled out my iron crucible.

"What are you going to do?" Hamish asked, fear creeping into his voice.

"One of those things no person should ever do," I said.

FORTY-NINE

Nedra

My ATTENTION WAS focused on the dead hanging from their nooses as Hamish scampered off. The golden threads of their souls wafted through the air.

I clutched the crystal knife in my shadow hand. I did not need to raise it to feel the power washing over me. I called to the souls.

And they answered.

The golden threads flew from the corpses and into my waiting crucible. No one but Nessie could see the light pooling into the hollow black bead I wore around my neck. No one but she could see the black darkness spilling out, down my shadow arm, pure dark power that gave me the strength to do exactly as I willed.

Open your eyes, I ordered silently.

The thirteen corpses hanging from the ropes opened their eyes.

I lifted my arm. And they lifted theirs. Dimly, I was aware of screams erupting from the crowd. But I kept my eyes—*their* eyes—trained on Grey. He was so angry for what I had done, the path necromancy had taken me on. But I only raised the dead after their breath was gone. I did not sign my name to their kill orders.

I could not fix the bodies of the dead—their throats were crushed by the ropes, and they could no longer speak. But I had their mouths form one word, one I knew Grey would recognize.

Monstrous.

I let the dead live again just long enough to turn the crowd of watchers into a terrified mob. The screams grew louder. People started running—stampeding. I felt a thud beside me, and it broke my concentration enough for me to notice one of the kids who'd climbed the nearby trees had seen me and realized who I was and what I was doing.

Time to go.

Twisting the crystal knife, I severed the golden threads of light emanating from the dead prisoners. Their bodies hung limply in their nooses once more, but the damage was done, the panic had spread.

The energy from the dead raised again filled the crystal blade, making it shine in sparkling light, so brilliant that it was a marvel to me that no one else could see it. The dim light from the broken bodies of my revenants had been nothing compared to this radiant energy from corpses newly killed.

I backed into the trees. The children had fled, and the shadows were growing long. With our dark cloaks and the panic as the crowd ran away from the Imperial Gardens, it was easy to fade into the forest.

The brightest light by far was the one I held in my hand, and no one could see it but Nessie and me. The crystal knife shone like a tiny star, but it cast no shadows among the trees that loomed over us.

Come closer, I ordered my twin, and she did . . . although perhaps a bit slower than normal, her eyes downcast. I moved the crystal knife in my shadow hand, and her eyes followed the glowing blade.

Did she sense the power within it? Did she realize that it was going to save her? I raised the blade between us, our eyes even.

But then I saw my hand, solid black now, so black that it didn't seem real, so black that it seemed to eat the light around it, making everything dimmer in comparison. I gaped at the smooth obsidian of my ghost arm, strong and powerful. Part of me wanted to run from the forest, find a human who wasn't a necromancer, and demand to know if they could see what I saw.

My eyes trailed from the black wrist to the elbow, up to the point where my flesh still existed. The skin there was stained black, too. I sucked in a breath as an icy cold washed over me. Inky black stains snaked up into my shoulder. I looked under my shirt. Black shadows crept under my skin, swirling over my heart.

It looked *exactly* like the plague.

I took a few steadying breaths. There was no plague anymore. It had died with Governor Adelaide. But the plague that had existed had been necromantic in origin. And this, too, this power, it was necromantic as well.

I looked up at Nessie. She had put more distance between us.

Come closer, I ordered her again.

Slowly, slowly she did.

When I severed the threads of golden light that were the souls of the revenants, their souls went to the afterlife and their lingering energy filled the crystal blade. This energy was a life force. Exactly what Nessie needed.

I poised the crystal blade over her chest, then I plunged the energy into her heart.

The golden light poured from the crystal blade, filling my sister. I watched first as the blade turned clear, emptying of energy, and then I shifted my gaze to Ernesta's eyes, watching as they filled once more with life.

"Nessie?" I whispered, barely daring to hope.

She blinked.

"Can you hear me?" I asked, a little louder now.

Her lips parted. "Yes," she said.

My entire body sagged with relief at the same moment my heart filled with joy. "Nessie!" I shouted, throwing my arms around her. Tears sprang to my eyes.

I felt her arms move—awkwardly at first, as if she'd forgotten how it was to live inside her own body—and then she wrapped me in a hug that was warm even if her body was still cold.

"Ned," she whispered against my ear, and it was *her* voice, truly hers.

Her arms slipped from around me. Her body shifted, straightened.

I pulled back. Already, I could see the life fading from her, like a candle flickering at the end of its wick. "Nessie?" I asked, my voice cracking in desperation. "Nessie!"

Her blinks slowed.

"How do I save you?" I screamed at her.

I could see it now—the golden glow of life evaporating off her, a smoggy mist that twinkled and faded to nothing. *A burning house with all the doors and windows open*, I thought dimly, then panic seized me. I grabbed her shoulder with my right hand. "Nessie!" I shouted, forcing every bit of power I had within me into the command. "Tell me how to save you!"

She met my eyes, and I could still see a tiny spark of life. And when she spoke, I knew—because she was my twin, because she was the person I loved most in all the world—I *knew* she believed what she said:

"You don't."

FIFTY

Grey

I HAD NEVER seen a crowd turn into a mob, or a mob turn into a riot. That is, until Nedra raised the dead in front of most of Northface Harbor.

When the dead first opened their eyes and pointed to me, I could not rip my gaze away from theirs. While I doubted many people were able to discern the word their silent lips mouthed, I did.

When the corpses hung limp once more, I turned to the Emperor.

His face was filled with an expression I could not name. Not fear, not exactly.

I'm sure he thinks they were pointing at him, I thought. But I knew: The shame of these people's deaths was on me and me alone.

And I wished, more than anything else in that moment, that Nedra didn't know the role I had played in the hanging. My father had once told me that executioners always shrouded their faces under a black hood so that they could hide from the death they were inflicting. But it wasn't true. They hid from the living, the ones who saw what they were doing.

How foolish of me to assume I could hide behind a scroll of parchment with the words *Execution Order* written across the top.

The captain of the Emperor's Guard rushed up the steps of the viewing box. "Your Imperial Majesty," she said breathlessly. She threw one arm over the Emperor's shoulder, half leading, half pushing him to the steps. I raced after them, tripping on the Emperor's gilded chair as I ran. The sword the Emperor had given me jabbed painfully at my thigh.

The Guard swarmed around us as we touched the ground. Ropes had been arranged to partition the crowd, giving the invited guests a special viewing area. Now everyone ran wildly, pushing and shoving in an effort to get somewhere, anywhere else. Just *away*.

But the Guard, trained from the best soldiers Miraband had to offer, was too well disciplined for that. They easily formed a triangular shape with their bodies, moving as one like a spear through the crowd. The Emperor was placed in the center of the formation, and he latched on to my wrist, dragging me with him into the protective barrier of his soldiers. Behind the red-coated Guard, I could hear people screaming and running, the noise of their feet thunderous.

The gardens will be ruined, I thought, then shook my head. Flowers and trees could be replanted. What about the people who'd been plague victims, walking with the aid of crutches or wooden legs? What about the orphans, with no one to guide them to safety?

While everyone else streamed away from the gallows, the Guard led us directly beneath the hanging dead. I looked up at their feet dangling over me. And beyond them, to the bright blue sky with powdery clouds swirling through the air.

Past the platform, there were fewer people—everyone here had already fled. The Guard broke their formation, but only after the mounted patrol had encircled them.

"No," the Emperor said.

"It's safest—" the captain started, but she was cut off by a withering stare from Emperor Auguste. The Guard wanted us to travel back to the castle using the prisoners' carriage, now empty. But I could see why the Emperor didn't want to get inside. It might be protected with thick walls, but there were also iron bars and locks. And the lingering memory of the fate of the last occupants.

"You there." Emperor Auguste pointed to one of the mounted patrol. The soldier broke away from the protective circle that surrounded us, dismounting as soon as he was in front of the Emperor. He held the reins of his black gelding in one hand, artfully bowing. It was all so formal and practiced, as if the chaos outside the circle wasn't happening at all.

The Emperor took the reins out of the soldier's hand. He turned to me. "You ride?" he asked.

"I can, yes."

The Emperor pointed at another mounted soldier. "You." He pointed, and in moments that soldier's horse's reins were in my hand.

"Your Imperial Majesty," the captain of the Emperor's Guard said. "You will be exposed if you ride. My soldiers will have a more difficult time protecting—"

The Emperor cut her off. "Your soldiers aren't coming with us."

"Sire?" the captain said, her brow furrowing.

"You men," the Emperor said, waving a hand at the mounted patrol still astride their horses. "Head east, in formation. The Guard will head south. Astor and I are riding north."

"We don't know where the necromancer is," the captain said. "You could be riding straight into a trap."

"Nedra's not a threat," I said, but everyone ignored me.

And I wasn't sure I even believed myself at this point. I had understood why she raised her sister, and even why she'd raised the dead at the hospital. But she seemed to have turned the prisoners into revenants out of spite.

"I gave a command," the Emperor said coldly. "Not a request for your input."

The captain squared her shoulders. As the Emperor and I mounted our horses, she called out orders to the Guard and the mounted patrol, directing them exactly as the Emperor had commanded.

The Emperor dug his heels into the side of the black gelding, racing north. Gravel sprayed out around us. I allowed myself one last look at the Imperial Gardens—the trampled grass, the emptying grounds, the thirteen dead bodies—before my horse galloped after him.

FIFTY-ONE

Nedra

I PACED THE forest.

A part of me knew it was dangerous. Most of the mob had fled, running to cower in their homes, comforting their children. Young ones didn't belong at public executions, and it shouldn't have taken necromancy to remind their guardians of that.

The Emperor's Guard had disappeared—presumably whisking His Imperial Majesty off to safety. I looked up to the Emperor's viewing box. Both he and Grey were gone, the ornate gilded chair tipped over. Two dozen soldiers—most on foot, some on horseback— patrolled the area.

And there were workers, too. Everyone always forgot about the poor souls who had to clean up after the dead.

I watched from the forest that lined the gardens as workers mounted the platform. A slender woman stretched out over the edge of the stage with a long pole that had a hook at the end. She grabbed each rope noose and pulled it—and the body that hung from it— closer to her, while another worker hacked at the rope with a machete. The bodies fell, one by one, onto the ground below them. Once all thirteen lay, limbs akimbo, in a heap on the ground, a soldier dragged an Elder closer.

The Elder trembled as he stood over the corpses. He moved his lips in prayer and his hands in a circle, the blessing for the dead to remain dead.

As soon as he was done, he scampered off. More workers appeared, loading the thirteen bodies into the same boxy wagon that had carted the prisoners to the Imperial Gardens while they still lived.

Follow me, Nessie, I ordered in my mind. What little life I had been able to give her was gone now, along with the black energy that had turned my ghost arm obsidian. But there were still inky shadows of black under my skin, swirling over my heart.

"Hurry it up," the wagon driver called. "Got a long road, don't I? Want to be back before dark."

A long road . . .

There were plenty of crematoriums in Northface Harbor, all no more than an hour's drive away.

But the superstitious people of the city wouldn't want revenants burned here. They would want distance.

The pauper's grave. They were going to bury the thirteen traitors in the pauper's grave in the cleared-away forest in the center of Lunar Island. Nearly all the plague victims had been buried there. I had gone there with Grey, pressing an iron ring into the mounded earth for Burial Day.

There were thousands of dead buried in the earth there. And while I had gotten just a wisp of energy from the dead at the quarantine hospital, if I multiplied that with *all* the dead buried in the pauper's grave . . .

I tried to tamp down the hope rising in me. They'd been dead for weeks, though in Miraband I'd seen the echoes of life, the impressions of the dead that had been gone for centuries. But perhaps, with that many dead in one place, there would be enough energy to give Nessie more than a few moments of real life. I was buying time I knew couldn't last, but I had gotten this far on nothing but books and instinct. I would steal what moments I could with Nessie until I found a way to truly restore her.

I refused to believe it was impossible. What was impossible, any-way? I had already defied the world once when I raised the dead. I could do it again.

As long as she stood before me, there was still hope.

Without giving myself a moment to doubt, I left the forest, head-ing to the prisoners' wagon. The driver was already atop it, pulling his gloves on and picking up the whip. The last worker was loading the final body inside—a slender boy about my age. I walked past the worker, stepping inside the wagon, and then turned to help her haul the body inside.

"Thanks," she said, wiping her brow.

Nessie strode past her and climbed inside the wagon after me.

I could see the worker piecing together what was happening. Without thinking, I reached out and grabbed the threads of her soul with my shadow hand, freezing her in place. I raised my right hand up, pressing my forefinger to my lips.

"Shhh," I instructed.

Eyes wide and terror-filled, the girl nodded the second I released her soul and backed away. The doors to the wagon slammed shut, the latch falling into place. A moment later, the wagon lurched into motion, the driver clicking his tongue at the draft horses.

I settled into a corner of the wagon, my back against the wall. Thirteen dead bodies bumped along the uneven road with me. I glanced at Nessie. Fourteen dead, I supposed. It didn't matter. I was used to death.

FIFTY-TWO

Grey

I HAD THOUGHT the Emperor was taking us on a roundabout route back to the castle. But once we left the residential district and headed northeast, I kicked my horse harder to catch up with him.

"Where are we going?" I asked. My hand drifted to the sword at my hip. When the Emperor had strapped it to me earlier today, I'd thought of it as only decoration. Now, though, I was glad to have a weapon.

The Emperor didn't stop, but he did allow his horse to slow. "Somewhere safe," he said. He didn't look at me.

"Safe? Where?"

The Emperor didn't answer my question, instead yanking on his reins, guiding his horse off the cobblestone road and down a dirt path that was rutted with wagon-wheel tracks.

I followed him off the road and pulled my horse up beside him. When I got closer to the Emperor, I saw that his face looked pale and ashen, and he had dark circles under his eyes. "Your Imperial Majesty?" I asked. "Are you well?"

"No," Emperor Auguste said. He cast a sideways glance at me. "I haven't been for a long while."

He had seemed to me to have improved so much since his imprisonment by Governor Adelaide, but then, I had only seen him over the last week in flashes and moments—at a council meeting, during the rally, before I signed the execution order. He had been able to maintain the appearance of strength and health, but it must have been a facade. After all, he was the one who insisted that the people needed to see strength. They needed to feel pride in their Emperor, not sympathy or fear.

I tried to hold my horse back, but Emperor Auguste maintained a steady pace, outdistancing me. "Come on," he called over his shoulder.

I nudged my horse back up.

"It's been so long since I've ridden," the Emperor muttered, mostly to himself. "Not since Enja, really. We use rail more often on the mainland."

"Perhaps we could get a rail system here," I said. "One reason why the north seems so cut off from the south is because the quickest way to get there is to cross the water. Ships in the bay are not as fast as a train could be."

"Hmm," the Emperor said. "Perhaps." But it was clear his mind was elsewhere.

"This is an old road, did you know that, Astor?" the Emperor continued, deftly changing the subject. "One of the first roads on Lunar Island."

I looked past my horse's neck, at the worn grooves of the dirt path.

"Wellebourne's army took this path," the Emperor added.

"You know your Lunar Island history well," I commented.

"I know more about the colonies than the mainland," Emperor Auguste said. "And Lunar Island more than most other colonies. It was Emperor Aurellious whom Wellebourne marched against. He came closer than the history books say."

"I didn't know that," I said.

The Emperor laughed once, a bitter sound. "Because Aurellious wrote the history books. Or rather, he had them written. The victor always writes history. So the books say Wellebourne was betrayed and caught and hung. But they don't say how far Wellebourne actually

BETH REVIS

got. He had Aurellious's soul in his hands before he was caught. The Empire knew what to make public and what to hide. All the history books leave that out. Only the heirs are taught that part of history. To remind us how close we came to losing the Empire."

For a long while, there was only the sound of the horses' hooves on the dirt road.

"That's why I've had my eye on your necromancer," the Emperor said finally. "I've read about necromancy," he continued. "I know what she could do—to me, to the Empire." His back was very straight, but his shoulders were hunched, almost in defeat. "I was raised to fear necromancers. All heirs are."

I frowned. Necromancy was almost unheard of in this day and age. Nedra was the exception, not the rule.

Seeing my look, Emperor Auguste smiled bitterly. "Necromancy is about more than raising the dead," he said. "It's about control, and it's about power. What greater power is there than that over life and death?"

He seemed to want me to answer, so I said, "I don't know."

"Nothing. A necromancer in the right position would be more powerful even than me. The Empire doesn't need to fall for a rebellion to take place. Simply shift hands."

"Nedra wouldn't—"

"I'm not talking about Nedra," the Emperor said. He spurred his horse on, outpacing me.

In a few hours, we reached the place the Emperor had told me would be safer than the castle. I stared out at the mounds of earth, now with patches of grass covering the raw marks of red clay. "The pauper's grave?" I asked.

The Emperor looked around, his eyes scanning the trees that lined the massive gravesite. "We need to hide," he said. He dismounted and led his horse by foot toward the remains of the forest.

"But—"

He silenced me with a look, and I followed him without another word, my hand gripping my sheathed sword.

"What are we doing?" I asked once we were in the shadows of the trees. It would be twilight soon.

The Emperor didn't look at me as he stared over the long lines of scarred earth. "Waiting," he answered.

FIFTY-THREE

Nedra

THE WAGON FINALLY rolled to a stop. Through the iron bars on the window, I could see the last rays of sunlight dip below the bay.

I heard the wagoner hop off his seat in the front, pausing to pet the horses. I stood and faced the door, so that when he opened it, he saw not the pile of jostled dead bodies, but me.

I lowered my cloak's hood as he gaped at me. My white tresses tumbled out onto the black cloth.

He stuttered unintelligibly, scrambling back and tripping on a stone. I hopped out of the back of the wagon, with Nessie trailing behind. The wagoner's eyes looked from me to her, and he blanched even more.

"Go," I said.

He launched himself back up to the front of the wagon and whipped the already-tired horses into a frenzy. I was barely aware of the clatter of his departure. Dusk had settled over the graveyard, but I hardly noticed that either. Because now that I was here, I realized I didn't need the sun to see what had been waiting for me all along.

The earth itself radiated light, a golden glow that was warm and inviting.

And *powerful.*

"What is this?" I muttered, awed by what was before me. The corpses buried here had all been dead for at least a month, some for half a year. Their souls should have long since disappeared, but they were *here*. Thousands of souls, hidden under only a few feet of earth.

My ghost hand reached blindly for the crystal knife. I wasn't even sure if it could hold this much pure, raw energy. But I was damn sure going to try. A fraction of this energy had given Nessie back to me for a moment. What if this could buy her months, a year?

I licked my lips, my mouth unintentionally salivating at the power so readily available to me.

Nessie followed me as I walked through the center of the graves, the long mounds extending all the way to the dark forest on the far end. How could this be? I dropped to my knees, inspecting the grave dirt.

The entire field was lit up in gold, veins of light weaving through the dirt, pooling over the mounded trenches. I could feel each body buried in the field as if I were connected to them by a long string. I knew some of them. Carso, Dilada's brother, far more rotted than she had been. Kava, the girl my sister had a crush on, whose leg had been amputated before she died anyway. People I'd met only once or twice, as I siphoned their pain away in the hospital or the mills. And the ones I didn't know, I knew now as my power sank into their illuminated bones. Glimpses of their histories, their lives, their wants, their regrets—everything of everyone, seeping into my mind.

But how? I thought. Their souls should have left their bodies.

I dug out a fistful of the rich red clay, and my fingers wrapped around something hard and round. I wiped the dirt away from a rusted iron ring, then laid the circle in my open palm. I shifted it to my shadow hand. Little strings of light formed a net inside the ring.

When Grey and I had boarded the ferry and placed the iron over the graves on Burial Day, I was not a necromancer. I was just a girl, and I was scared—for my life, for my family's lives. And when Governor

Adelaide had distributed the iron rings, a gift from her to the people of her colony, I had thought she was being generous.

Horror caught in my throat, choking me. I scrambled to another mound of dirt, clawing at the earth until I found a second ring. It had been altered by necromancy as well. I flung myself at a third grave, digging out another ring. Each one was like the ancient ring Bunchen had given me—a tiny necromantic net designed to trap the soul in the earth. I gagged, thinking of the tortured people within, imprisoned in their graves.

Governor Adelaide had developed the plague in order to kill as many people as possible, intending to raise them into an army of the undead. But she must have known what I did not—that souls fade over time, evaporating into nothing as they move on into the realm of Death. She could have easily learned of the rings that had sealed the revenants of Bennum Wellebourne after his failed rebellion. But rather than trap the dead in their graves, Adelaide had twisted the rings' original purpose, using them to ensure that both the life force and the souls of the dead remained in their graves, waiting for the day she could raise an army of her own.

I felt bile rising in my throat as I remembered the sincere prayer I had whispered to Oryous on Burial Day. The way I had pressed an iron ring into the fresh upturned earth. I had been sealing the dead in their graves, trapping them there, *torturing* them, without even realizing it. How could I have so easily and unwittingly done Governor Adelaide's bidding?

I stood, renewed determination giving me strength as I gripped the crystal blade in my shadow hand. If I cut out this golden light, absorbing it into my blade, it would free these trapped souls. Their souls would move on, and I could pass the energy on to Nessie.

A momentary panic seized my heart as I remembered how *good* it felt for the power to flow through me, pooling into my shadow arm.

But I knew, no matter how tempting the power was, that I would be the crucible for it, transferring it into the one who needed it most—my sister. And I would be saving the thousands dead here from a fate far worse even than the plague that stole their lives.

My power could save them all.

FIFTY-FOUR

Grey

"NEDRA?" MY VOICE was almost a whisper, and I was certain that, standing in the middle of the graves, she wouldn't be able to hear me. But I thought for a moment that her twin sister looked my way.

The Emperor gripped my shoulders, spinning me around to face him. "It is as I feared," he said. "She's going to raise all of the dead that were laid to rest here."

I shook my head. "She would never."

The Emperor's hold on me tightened. "Quit seeing what you want to see and look at what's actually happening." He forced me to turn and look out at the graves again. Nedra's right hand was buried deep in grave dirt, a look of spasming joy crossing her face.

I didn't recognize her in that moment. Drunk with power, she looked manic.

The Emperor reached for the reins of his horse. "I—I did not expect it, not like this."

"What did you think would happen when you brought us here?" I demanded.

He shook his head again. "Not . . . not this." He looked at the horses. They were tired from a full day of riding—first patrolling the Imperial Gardens, then taking us halfway across the island.

My mind flashed back to the night Nedra used her revenants to attack the castle and free the Emperor. Her undead *never* tired. They would overtake the horses.

"Let me talk to her," I said.

The Emperor raised his eyebrow.

"She's *not* evil," I insisted. "Let me talk to her. Perhaps I can—" I didn't finish the sentence, because I didn't know how to. I had no idea what I would do. I just knew I needed to try *something*.

"Go," the Emperor said after a moment. "Let us hope that words will be enough." His hand moved from the reins to the sword at his belt, the one I had always thought was merely decorative. Although in that moment, he did not even look strong enough to pull the blade from the sheath.

I turned immediately, running from the forest out to the graves. "Nedra!" I called. My voice broke her concentration. Her entire body shifted, and her hand relaxed.

Her head whipped around, shock plain on her face even from a distance. I rushed to her. "Ned," I said again, breathless.

"Grey? What are you doing here?"

I shook my head, my heart and my breath both riotous. "Ned, don't raise these dead."

"You don't know what you're talking about."

"I know you're not evil," I said. "Everyone else on the island, in the whole Empire, thinks that all you want is power. But I know . . ." I hoped I knew. ". . . that you aren't a monster."

"Of course I'm not." She gave me a blank stare.

"So don't do this."

Nedra scoffed. "You have no idea what I'm doing."

"Raising a thousand dead?" I countered.

A cold mask washed over her features. "I may raise the dead, but at least I didn't kill them."

Her words sliced into me. I remembered the way the traitors had hung, their necks broken inside the nooses, their hands slowly raising to point at me, their mouths forming an accusation I could not deny. "They would have hung anyway," I said, angry at the petulant tone I couldn't keep from my voice. "They broke the law."

"So do I, Grey," Nedra said softly. "Would you sign my death orders?"

"No, I—"

My words died in my throat as she cocked an eyebrow at me. "You're just like all the rest," she said. "A hypocrite. I remember what you told me, that night. 'I will not follow you into that darkness.' And you didn't. You were in a darkness all of your own making."

"Nedra, I—"

"Did you come all the way here just to lecture me on morality?" Nedra asked. "How could you—?"

"Nedra, what are *you* doing here?" I interrupted.

The question seemed to stop her short. Then she turned away from me. "I'm giving my sister her life back," she said. "That's all I've ever wanted to do. Now get out of my way."

I stumbled back. The events of the day whirled in my mind, a chaos I couldn't sort through. I had woken up in the castle, without a single thought in my head that I would end the day *here*. I looked behind me, trying to see through the shadows to the Emperor.

Nedra, meanwhile, knelt again, red clay staining her skirt at the knees. Veins popped at her neck. Her hair raised in wisps, as if blown by the wind, but the air was still.

When she opened her eyes, there was nothing but white. The dark, warm brown was gone. Her pupils were gone.

Her humanity was gone.

FIFTY-FIVE

Nedra

I COULD FEEL the thousands of dead beneath the cold dirt. They called to me, sensing my power. They begged to be released from the ground.

I squeezed the red clay in my fist, the raw earth seeping between my fingers. I wasn't sure I could harness enough power for this. But I was still going to try.

I turned to my sister, reminding myself of what I struggled for.

Behind her was the forest. Movement caught my eye, near the edge of the tree line. I wouldn't have noticed if the entire Emperor's Guard was marching toward me, but this—this was different. Clods of earth dropped from my hand as I fell back, gaping at the man who strolled casually over the graves toward us. Grey said something, but it was muffled by the blood pounding in my ears.

Dimly, I was aware that this man was the Emperor. But with the power of the dead beneath the ground rising up inside me, I could better see past the Emperor's body and into his soul.

So I knew the man drawing closer to me was *not* the Emperor.

My hand tightened around the hilt of the crystal knife as I stood up. Every time I'd been before Emperor Auguste previously, I had hardly looked at him. When I met him the first time, I'd been focused on defeating Governor Adelaide. At the execution, my attention had been on Grey. But I *saw* him now. It was the same body, the same outward shell of a man I'd met before.

But the soul . . . the soul wasn't right. I was used to seeing at least a faint glimmer of gold around people, even around myself. But this . . . this looked like the same light-eating black I saw at the base of my crucible, the black that currently crept over my own heart.

He was in front of me now.

"Who are you?" I whispered.

"It's the Emperor," Grey said.

"Who *are* you?" My voice was choked. Something was very, very wrong.

The man who looked like the Emperor smiled. "You know who I am," he said.

I stared—using all the power within and without me—at him. The body of the Emperor was not dead. He wasn't a revenant like Nessie. But the soul did not match the body. The soul was . . . old. So old.

Centuries old.

My breath caught in my throat.

"Nedra?" Grey asked, moving to stand beside me. The Emperor—whoever he was—stood in front of us, an easy smile on his face, like a cat about to pounce on a wounded bird.

"And to think," the not-Emperor said, "I had been worried before that you wouldn't be strong enough to become what I needed you to be."

"What's going on?" Grey asked.

"The technical term is a *lich*," the not-Emperor said.

I gripped the crystal knife. I had seen that rune twice before—once in the Collector's books and once etched inside this very blade—but I didn't understand what it meant.

"I made sure all the texts about liches were destroyed." The not-Emperor tilted his head, thinking. "That was early on, about one hundred and ninety-four years ago. I purged the libraries of any book, scroll, or parchment that even mentioned the word *lich*."

Grey shifted beside me. I thought he wanted to take my hand, but I pulled away, reaching for my crucible instead. The not-Emperor took a step closer to me. The crystal blade was in my shadow hand. I still did not understand, exactly, what a lich was, but I knew that I did not want whoever—whatever—this man was to get any closer.

With the crystal blade, I was strong enough to touch his corrupt soul. When I had commanded Governor Adelaide's soul to stop, she had been still as a statue while I drove the sword into her heart.

This man was not Governor Adelaide.

His soul fought back.

FIFTY-SIX

Nedra

THE WORLD AROUND me melted into nothing.

This man's soul didn't just touch mine—it *overwhelmed* it. His soul moved like mercury, oozing more than glowing. It touched my skin, then sank past it, into my flesh, into *me*.

I felt him—everywhere.

It was a violation beyond any I could imagine. I could not move. There was nowhere to run. I could not escape him.

He was inside me.

My mind screamed and *screamed*. I tipped my head back, my throat still gagging, my stomach churning, trying to vomit him out, but this was not something I could control.

I was no longer something I could control.

My right hand rose. I did not will the movement. *He* did. I felt his thoughts—not in words, but the intention. I tried to jerk my face away, but I couldn't so much as flinch as he raised my hand, stroked my cheek.

I felt his amusement inside me. His laughter.

I felt him *settle* into me, growing comfortable and at ease with this violation. With me as nothing but a vehicle. I felt his satisfaction. His pleasure.

Like a cat with a bowl of cream, my mother would have said.

I felt him reach out at that, my memory of my mother.

No! my mind screamed. I could not control my body, but my memory, my heart, they still belonged to me.

He pried deeper. I felt him there, looking through my soul, sorting out my feelings. *Knowing* me in a way I did not even know myself.

Mine, mine, mine, I thought. I felt warm tears trailing down my cheeks, leaving cold streaks behind. *Mine.*

I pushed back—hard. And it was then I realized that when he forced my mind to open, he left his mind vulnerable to me. I felt his memories. It was more than images. Traces of scent, feelings, sounds and whispers half-heard. It was not like being told what a moment felt like, or seeing a painting of a scene. It was as if he was giving me his memories, depositing them into my own brain. It was as if I had lived the life he showed me.

And it was then that I finally knew him.

"Bennum Wellebourne."

The name escaped my lips before he realized how deep into his own soul I'd pushed. He pulled back so abruptly that for a moment, my body felt bereft. I crashed to my knees, not registering the pain as I fell prone among the disturbed graves. Grey cried out and swooped to help me stand.

"Ned?" he whispered, his hands warm and firm on my trembling arm as I staggered up.

"It's him," I struggled to say. "It's Wellebourne."

Grey's eyes darted from me to the man before us, the man we'd both thought was Emperor Auguste.

I had barely skimmed his black soul, but the memories lived in my head as if I had experienced his life as well. Born in Miraband, sent by Emperor Aurellious to help settle the new colony on Lunar Island. I hoped and feared during the voyage, then had different hopes and stronger fears as the land proved difficult to conquer. I felt myself fall in love with Wellebourne's wife. I married her, and I built a home, and we lived together.

And I felt the oppression of the Empire, and the desire—unquenchable as a house fire—for freedom. As my colony, *my* people suffered under terrible weather and sickness, as they died from lack of support from the Empire that had sent them, my desperation grew. I studied—not to be a necromancer, but to save my—*his*—people. I felt the echoing laughter, because the reason he became who he became was so similar to my own.

The desperation. The power.

The hunger.

I felt it all. I *lived* it all. And without being told, I knew. I understood. I even agreed with all Bennum Wellebourne had done.

I felt the bone saw and the blood splatter as I took my wife's hand to form my first crucible. I raised the dead. I rebelled against the Empire.

And I lost.

"When you were finally defeated," I said, twisting the last word like a knife, because I knew it would hurt him like one, "you sawed off your own hand."

"What?" Grey asked, confusion dripping from his voice.

The Emperor—Bennum Wellebourne—smiled. "It worked rather well," he said. "Centuries of protection."

I didn't take my eyes off Wellebourne as I filled Grey in. "Wellebourne was caught, and put in the iron prison at the castle."

"Ironic, that," Wellebourne said idly, "getting trapped there again, in this body."

I ignored him. "Wellebourne sawed off his own hand. Everyone assumed he was trying to make another crucible, using his hand as the base. But that's not what he made."

"What did he make?" Grey asked.

"A reliquary," Wellebourne answered. "It's when a necromancer takes a piece of his soul and hides it in an object."

"As long as the object isn't broken," I add, "the necromancer can't die."

I thought of all the shattered gems and cracked metal I'd seen on the Collector's shelf. The necromancers who'd made those reliquaries had given their souls precious, showy homes. But there was genius behind Wellebourne's reliquary.

It was protected there, safe. A crucible cage was hard to destroy; a crucible almost impossible. Destroying Governor Adelaide's crucible had taken all my strength, turned my hair white, and left me weak and trembling, and that crucible had been cracked and old and almost lost to time anyway.

Wellebourne had left the crucible cage with his family, along with instructions for his descendants to protect it, giving them the task that, almost two centuries later, Master Ostrum would uphold. As long as that crucible cage existed, Bennum Wellebourne could never truly die.

It did not matter to him at all when they hung his body, when they burned his corpse.

His soul was *free*.

"How many?" I asked. I felt Grey shift beside me, so I added for his benefit, "How many bodies have you lived in?"

Wellebourne rolled his hand dismissively. "I've lost track. Emperor Aurellious was the first, of course."

Of course he had—how had I been such a fool not to realize sooner? Hadn't I seen the municipal building in Miraband, the one where Aurellious conquered death? That hadn't been Emperor Aurellious at all. That had been Wellebourne. And he had been right. He *had* conquered death.

He had originally wanted Lunar Island to be free from the Empire, but once *he* ruled the Empire, his goals changed.

"I've been several emperors, and quite a few empresses," Wellebourne said, a note of pride in his voice. "But politics grow tedious."

Grey's brow was furrowed. "That's why the Empire is always expanding. You fight wars when you get bored," he said.

Wellebourne smiled as if pleased Grey understood. "Exactly," he said. "Sometimes I bounce between the sides, general to general. It's more fun that way."

My mind battled with my memories and his; touching his black soul had stained my own. I remembered, as Wellebourne, flitting between bodies. Sometimes a woman, sometimes a man. Gender didn't matter to him; flesh was flesh. He took lovers. He married. He had children—those he sired, and those he bore.

And when he was done with that life, that experience, he disposed of the body and took another.

He learned. Languages, art, music.

War.

"That's why you're a war hero," Grey snarled. "It's easy to risk everything and charge into battle, knowing you cannot truly die."

He can't die, I thought. *But like my revenants, he's fading.* He had more power than them, more control, but a soul was meant for one body alone, and once that body was gone—or once that soul was in someone else—it was an imperfect fit. The soul grew tired. It's what Bunchen and the Collector had both warned me about. The trade-off of the immortality a reliquary provided was a soul that would grow weaker over time.

I could see it all in my mind's eye. As time wore on, Wellebourne's soul had grown thin. He pored over the books in his private library. His reliquary was safe—he even checked on it occasionally, ensuring that his descendants took seriously the responsibility of protecting the crucible cage that contained his soul. Even so, his soul was weakening, and with it, his power.

He needed replenishing.

Wellebourne cocked his head. "I tried, at first, to take younger bodies, even though that was foolish. No matter how young the body, my soul is old."

I looked at the body he was in now, Emperor Auguste's. So much about him made sense now. A celebrated strategist and war hero against some of the rebellious tribes—he was hailed as a prodigy by everyone who didn't know he'd already had centuries of practice at war.

"How young was Auguste when you took him?" Grey asked, his voice tight with anger.

"A few years," Wellebourne said. "Childhood is tiresome, but it can be entertaining. No one ever suspects the innocent toddler of sabotaging his playmates."

I wondered then at what horrors his nursemaids had seen, and how they had to hold their tongues. Their young charge was richer and more powerful than they ever would be. The child they bathed could put them to death.

I felt Grey tense beside me. "You have everything. You're the Emperor, for Oryous's sake! And immortal. What more could you possibly want?"

My hand gripped the crystal knife.

Wellebourne saw.

"Yes, exactly," he answered me.

"He needs power," I said aloud for Grey.

"Especially after all my plans with Adelaide fell apart," Wellebourne said. "I was . . . disappointed by the way she went rogue. But of course, I had learned long ago to never put *all* my hopes in one person."

I recalled, as if it were my own memory, getting a letter from a poor book merchant who lived in a remote village in the northern part of Lunar Island. Papa's letter, the one he'd written about me, begging for a chance to send me to Yūgen Alchemical Academy. Bennum saw the potential in me even if my father didn't. No. He saw the *desperation*. Because that was what he had been when he became a necromancer. Desperate.

What struck me the most was that I wasn't the first. There were others—a boy in Siber, a teenager in Enja, a rebel leader on the mainland near Roc Wynt. They had all shown my same potential. They had all been tested.

And so had I. The alchemists who came through the village with their golden crucibles and entertained my curiosity had been sent by the Emperor. One of the village Elders was interviewed and paid for his assessment of me.

And I had been found lacking.

Bennum had focused on Adelaide. He'd given *her* everything she needed to become a necromancer. My stomach twisted with rage. *She* had not had to sacrifice anything, anything at all. Knowledge, guidance—even a crucible had simply been handed to her.

"The plague," I gasped.

"Of course," he said.

I looked around me, at the graves sprinkled with iron rings, forcing the souls of the dead to lie waiting beneath the earth. All those iron rings—they had been Wellebourne's idea, not Governor Adelaide's.

All those trapped souls were for *him*.

FIFTY-SEVEN

Grey

"AND NOW, IT'S time for the end," the Emperor who was really Bennum Wellebourne said, in a booming, theatrical voice. He gave a little bow to Nedra, one that I wasn't sure was mocking or sincere. "You've risen above my expectations, certainly. I gambled poorly with Adelaide. I had to scramble to ensure you could adequately replace her."

"Replace her?" Nedra said. Her entire body was tense. Wellebourne watched her the way an awlspring watches a baby mouse.

"I need that knife," he said. He coughed lightly, and in the growing twilight, the shadows under his eyes seemed darker, his cheeks hollower.

Nedra raised her hand—not her right hand, but her left one. I gaped at it. Where her limb should have ended from amputation was now a black obsidian arm and hand gripping a knife made of what appeared to be crystal. Her cloak fell away, exposing the dark veins of inky black that ran over her shoulder, across her clavicle, and down her chest where her shirt blocked my view. *It looks like the plague*, I thought, my stomach dropping.

"This is not for you," Nedra said, twisting her wrist so the facets of the blade caught the last rays of the sun.

"What is that?" I asked in a low voice.

Wellebourne heard me. "A lich blade," he answered.

"It will restore Nessie's life." Nedra reached out for her sister with her right hand. The silent twin's eyes moved, as if hypnotized, watching the glittering blade.

"It won't work." Wellebourne spoke in a bored tone.

"It has before," Nedra hissed at him.

"For a few minutes at most, yes?"

"I'll have a thousand souls," Nedra said fiercely.

"Yes," Wellebourne allowed, drawling out the word. "But even with thousands of souls, you'll only give her a week, maybe. That sort of energy doesn't help revenants. Burns right through them. The dead aren't meant to live like you and me, little girl."

"A year," Nedra insisted.

Wellebourne raised his eyes. "Do you really think you can negotiate with Death?" He chuckled, the sound raising Nedra's ire even more. "I don't make the rules."

He took a step closer to Nedra. "Stay back!" she screamed, brandishing the knife. My hand went directly to the sword at my waist, whipping it from the sheath and stepping between Nedra and Wellebourne before I had a chance to think twice.

Wellebourne reached out to me, pushing the edge of my blade away, swatting at it as if I were a bothersome fly.

"Do you really think I would have given you a weapon that could hurt me?" he asked.

I whirled around, raising the sword again, but he wasn't talking to me. He was talking to Nedra.

She looked down at the knife in her hand. "You didn't give this to me."

"Didn't I?" he asked, smiling at her in a way that made my blood boil.

She looked up at him, her eyes wide. "You're the other necromancer."

"Obviously."

Ned's brow furrowed, her nose scrunched in the same way she'd looked when she was studying at Yūgen. Her mind was piecing together a puzzle, and the final image it created made the blood drain from her face.

She opened her mouth to speak, but Wellebourne cut her off. "I made sure the copper crucible was prepared for—well, I'd originally prepared it for Adelaide, but she didn't follow the path I'd built for her. Fortunately, you did. I paid the Collector handsomely to ensure no one but the necromancer I sent him would get the box that contained that blade."

How could he have been so sure of his plan? I wondered. But then the answer came to me. *The captain of the ship . . .* I cursed under my breath. I had known that the captain had been following Nedra—he'd admitted it flatly—and the Emperor had told me that the captain had reported to him. But what if the captain had gone first to the Collector, to warn him of Nedra's impending arrival? No wonder he had been so easy to bribe at the start of the journey.

And no wonder the Emperor had chosen me for the mission to Miraband. I had been grossly unqualified for the position, but I'd allowed myself to believe I was the right man for the job. Instead, I had been selected because the Emperor knew I would use the opportunity to try to save Nedra. Hadn't he steered our initial conversation back to her and the potential execution she faced? I had been a pawn from the very start.

Nedra took a step back, bumping into her sister. "Why didn't you just get it yourself? You live in Miraband."

For the first time, Wellebourne looked angry. His teeth bared as he snarled, "Can't you *see*, little girl?"

Nedra's pupils flashed silver as she focused on Wellebourne. "Your soul is black."

"My soul is *weak*."

Nedra shuddered. "You can't raise the dead." She paused. "And if you can't raise the dead, you can't open the box."

"I can barely keep myself alive," Wellebourne growled. "And besides, even if I could have opened the box and taken the knife, I couldn't have used it without you."

Confusion flashed over Nedra's face. She took another step back, pushing into her sister.

"I grow bored," Wellebourne said. "These plans have been in place longer than you know, little girl. Let's just get on with it. I will use you to take the energy from the knife and replenish my soul, and you will become nothing more than a scary story the children of Lunar Island hear at bedtime."

Nedra dropped to her knees. She was a supplicant at the Emperor's feet, her head bowed, defeated. He smiled down on her beneficently.

The ends of her paper-white hair started to rise, wafting around her like a halo. When she looked up at him, her pupils were silvery, her grin triumphant.

FIFTY-EIGHT

Nedra

I *PULLED*.

And from the earth arose the dead.

They clawed their way out of the ground, their fingers broken stumps by the time they emerged from the red clay. They could not walk; they shambled. Their jaws were slack, their tongues fat and lolling, some eaten away by worms. I turned in circles, and I saw more and more, each of them drawn to me, to my power.

The wards Adelaide had placed on the graves—the iron rings—slowed the decomposition process, but the inevitable could not be put off forever. They were rotting. They were broken.

But they were standing.

And moving closer.

Hundreds—a thousand or more.

More, more, my blood sang.

The skin drooped under their eyes, sagging low, exposing the underside of their dull, red-rimmed eyeballs. Their faces were like melting wax. The one closest to me twitched its lips, spasming over the yellowed, dirt-encrusted teeth and white-pink gums. It made a grunting-moaning sound, nothing at all human or even animal-like, the sound akin to air being forced out of a bellows.

They waited. For my command.

Black, raw energy poured from my crucible. A spiderweb of black crept from my heart, down my shoulder, then spilled over my ghostly arm, forging an obsidian limb that felt more powerful than any muscle of flesh in my weak corporeal body.

"Ned?" Grey's voice quaked. His fear was primal, based on the living's anathema to death. The dead were nothing to fear. Flesh and bone were nothing.

Nothing at all next to my rage.

The dead all turned, as one, to face Bennum Wellebourne.

"Nedra," he called, his voice high-pitched. "You don't want to do this."

I licked my lips. "Oh," I breathed, my voice crackling with power. "But I do."

I thought of my revenants, my beloved friends, who had been ripped apart, their flesh shredded, their bones splintered, their skulls fractured. My nostrils flared, remembering the sickly sweet and coppery smell of rotting meat that had once been a person. *He* had done that, I was sure of it now. He needed undead blood to open the box that held the crystal knife, and there had been gallons of it congealing on the black-and-white tiled floor.

It was this image that I pushed into the minds of the thousand dead plague victims. It was this idea.

They descended upon the Emperor's body with cold, methodical glee.

His screams were quickly drowned out by the sound of flesh being torn from his bones with teeth and hands crooked like claws. My new revenants pulled at his arms and legs until they burst from the sockets. They rended his flesh. They trampled his rib cage, mangling the twisted heart, squishing the soft organs. They dug at his body like a dog digs in the sand, clawing through the gore, blood spattering in arcs through the air.

It was done all too quickly. But it was done.

I breathed out a sigh, tilting my head back up to the darkening sky. "It's over," I said aloud.

And then I turned to Grey.

His head was cocked oddly, his eyes alight, a teeth-baring grin spread across his face. "You silly little girl," Grey said in a voice that wasn't entirely his own. "You think I can be killed? My soul is immortal. All I need is a body. Any body. And this one will do just fine."

FIFTY-NINE

Grey

NEDRA STARED AT me in horror.

My mouth opened. "You don't like me inside the boy, do you?"

Get out, get out, get out. My soul pleaded with this alien presence inside of me, but I might as well have been speaking to a wall. I felt— an absence. That was the only way to describe it. I had been whole, but now I wasn't.

Now my soul was pushed to the side.

But two souls cannot occupy one body without knowledge passing between them. I *felt* Wellebourne's intent. Nedra had never been anything more than a possible source of power for him, nothing more, nothing less. He was a spider, and she was one of many flies. Wellebourne looked through my eyes at Nedra, and he saw nothing worthwhile.

You're wrong. My quivering, cowering, fading soul could see Nedra, too, and it saw something different.

We had fought—often and bitterly—over what she had become. I didn't need a field of dead bodies to remind me that what she had done was wrong. But I still loved her. Love didn't have to make sense. It didn't have to agree with everything. It just had to exist, and, when my entire life was spread before me, I knew, I *knew*, that our love was the only thing I truly believed in.

Be quiet! Wellebourne's soul raged at mine. In response, my soul flared up, trying to wrest control of my body back from Wellebourne.

But my anger wasn't strong enough. I could do nothing as Wellebourne forced me to stride toward Nedra, shoulders back, sneering down at her.

I felt my soul growing smaller, weaker. I knew, through Wellebourne's triumph, that he had done this before. He'd expelled dozens of souls from dozens of people, claiming their bodies and using them up.

You can't win, he taunted me.

I don't have to.

My body's steps faltered.

I didn't have to win. I just had to hold out long enough for Nedra to defeat him. Wellebourne might control my body, but I still controlled my heart.

I love her. And I would do everything in my soul's power to help her triumph now.

Wellebourne sent me feelings, images, flashes of the torture he would put my soul through for daring to fight back. I knew—I *knew*—I would never have my body again. This was a sort of death I had never envisioned before, but it would be as sure as the one Nedra's twin suffered.

I would do it anyway.

I could see now that I had let myself become the monster she had accused me of being. I had let myself fall into the spider's trap, just as she had. All her life, Nedra had never been in a position to win. Raised by poor villagers in a poor village, she had no hope of rising above her station.

She had done it anyway.

She had been faced with an unstoppable plague that no medicine could ever cure.

She found a cure anyway.

Her whole family had been taken from her, her beloved sister dead despite all her best efforts.

She had brought her back anyway.

Nedra never had a chance. She took one anyway.

I couldn't let rage rule me. I focused my heart with the calm determination that Nedra walked through life with. The only thing my soul knew, the only thing Wellebourne couldn't touch, the only thing that kept me real was my love for her.

Nothing had ever stopped her. Nothing would stop me now.

SIXTY

Nedra

I COULD STILL see, flickering and pale, the golden wisp of Grey's soul.

I still had a chance.

The thousand dead plague victim revenants turned to me. I could still see the reddish-black gore staining their hands and feet and mouths. Dirt clung to their too-soft skin, maggots squirmed inside their flesh, occasionally wiggling out of gaping wounds.

I sensed their longing to be free from this world. *Go, then*, I thought. When I'd severed the souls of the thirteen hanging traitors, I had not needed to be beside them. The same was true now. I swirled my ghost hand in a circle, not unlike the circle the Elder had made when he blessed the corpses. The golden threads of souls all around me snapped. They seemed to breathe a sigh of relief as they faded into the afterlife. And the lingering energy of the lives they had lived all poured into the blade. The clear crystal burned a bright gold, full of pulsing, vivid energy, more power than I had ever dreamed possible.

Before, breaking Governor Adelaide's old crucible had nearly destroyed me. But now, the dark power from my crucible and the sheer might of the crystal knife made my body burn with their combined energy.

A house on fire.

The roar of power, thundering through my head. Something warm dribbled down my chin. I licked my lips, tasting copper. Tasting blood. My snarling, feral grin curled over my teeth. My soul was hungry.

The dead fell back into the earth, truly empty, their souls free. The crystal blade pulsed with power.

I turned to my sister.

"Wait!" Grey screamed at me, but it was not him who spoke the word. Still, my hand stayed, the crystal knife poised over my sister's heart.

"The crystal blade is designed for a lich to regain power," Wellebourne said through Grey. "Stab your little lover, and my soul will be strong enough to take a different body. I'll give him back to you, and take someone else."

Grey's soul flared.

"You're lying to me," I said.

"I'm not. I'll leave this body."

I squinted. Grey's soul couldn't speak, but it was trying to communicate with me. The pulsing light burned bright, as if it were trying to warn me of Wellebourne's lies.

I squeezed the knife in my shadow hand, black and corporeal now. *Something isn't right.* Wellebourne could easily use Grey's body to physically fight me and wrest the crystal knife from my grip. I narrowed my eyes as he watched me with a smug smile. I didn't have time for his game, though. My first priority was Nessie, and then I'd figure out a way to save Grey.

Grey's face twisted with cruel mockery as I turned to Nessie's still body and poised the blade over her heart.

My hand shook. Grey's chuckle sounded out over the decimated field of corpses. I threw all my weight behind the blade, but I could not pierce my sister's heart. All the energy and power whirled within me, but there was something else, something *stronger*, that stayed my hand.

Nessie stared straight ahead.

Wellebourne moved Grey's body closer, right beside my sister.

My grip tightened around the hilt and I put all my weight behind my arm. But it still wouldn't move.

Power pulsed through me—starting in my heart, all the way down the black arm. No . . . it didn't start in my heart.

It started in my crucible.

The energy that was Bennum's soul had been staining my skin black, just like a plague victim's. His dark soul had infected me. And now it could control me—or, at least, my shadow arm.

I did not have the power to resist him, because I had invited him inside. Hadn't I asked for the power? Hadn't I offered anything for it?

My body shifted, the crystal blade aiming for Grey's heart, for Wellebourne's soul. Not Nessie's. I was going to kill Grey and strengthen Wellebourne enough for him to kill me, and I could not do a thing to stop it.

I looked into Grey's eyes, and I saw nothing left of him. Just Wellebourne. *Hungry*. Hungry for power. For me. Cold terror washed over me as my hand, gripping the crystal knife brimming with energy, plunged down.

A force stronger than I could have imagined slammed into me, throwing my body aside. I landed with a teeth-cracking slam on the ground, amid the dead and rotting bodies of the plague victims.

"Call your dog off, girl!" Grey's voice snarled.

Nessie stood in front of Grey's body, passive as she always was. But when Wellebourne took a step forward, she sprang into action, blocking him, before standing empty before him again.

She always protects me.

My right hand clutched my iron crucible, finally, *finally* realizing the truth. I yanked the tiny iron bead off the chain, holding it in my palm. Bennum's soul was inside my crucible. The evil inside it should have overwhelmed me, but it never had. I had spent so long agonizing over the way I'd trapped my sister's soul inside my crucible, but that's not what had happened at all.

Nessie's soul had never been trapped.

She *chose* to leave her soul inside the crucible.

She *chose* to fight the darkness. For me. She fought it with her soul inside my crucible, and she was fighting it now, with her shell of a body, protecting me.

The more I learned about the darkness inside my crucible, the more convinced I'd become that Nessie was a prisoner, and that I had imprisoned her. It was that darkness that my revenants had feared. Pure, concentrated evil, at the heart of my own crucible.

And my twin sister had been wrapped up in it. She had never been its prisoner.

It had been hers.

I had never been able to look at my crucible without feeling guilt, both for Nessie's death and her failed second life. That guilt drove deep inside me, a screw twisting into my own soul, making it impossible for me to see the truth.

It was not my fault that she had died. It was not my fault that I had lived.

It was that realization, more than anything else, that made me understand the push and pull between the darkness in my crucible and Nessie's soul made of golden light. From the very start, Nessie's soul had seen the darkness and blocked it out. She'd protected my revenants, my crucible, *me*. She'd held back the dark all by herself, sacrificing the false life I'd offered her in order to contain it.

Wellebourne was using Grey's body to fight against Nessie, but she kept driving him back, away from me.

Giving me time.

"No," I whispered. I knew what I had to do. My eyes grew bleary with unshed tears.

I knew what it would cost.

I had thought raising Nessie from the dead would save her. But it was only now I understood that in that moment—and every moment after—she'd never stopped trying to save *me*. And the only thing I could do to help her now would be to let her go.

With a shaking hand, I placed my iron crucible onto a nearby gore-splattered rock. Crouching over it, I aimed the tip of the crystal blade, charged with the energy of every wronged soul victimized by the plague, over the top of the iron bead.

Wellebourne saw me. He tried to break past Nessie, but my sister blocked him again, throwing him to the ground. He struggled up, and Nessie grabbed his ankles, dragging him back.

"I'll kill him!" Wellebourne screamed. "You think you can stop me? I'm inside his body, little girl, I will *eat* his soul!"

I blinked at him. "You cannot negotiate with Death," I said. I plunged the crystal blade into the heart of my iron crucible.

"No—" Wellebourne started to say, the word turning to a strangled scream.

Nessie's soul was severed first. That little string of light, the only part of her she could spare to be with me while she fought the darkness inside my crucible, snapped. Her body fell gracefully, like a petal. She was truly dead now.

But not entirely gone.

Before the thread of my sister's soul left me for the afterlife, it wrapped around me. I felt all the things she wished she could say but could not put into words.

I felt her love.

And her trust, too. She had been fighting the darkness since I'd formed my crucible.

I was ready to fight now.

I pushed the tip of the crystal blade deeper into my crucible.

Wellebourne now had no one to hold him back—Nessie's body could no longer repulse him. He staggered up and lurched toward me, but his feet stilled. Light flashed around the darkness within his body. Grey was fighting him from within, soul against soul.

"Stop!" Wellebourne screamed. "You'll break it!"

"That's the point," I said, power laced through my voice.

I drove the blade into the iron. I felt it cracking, splintering like glass, the reverberations of its destruction thundering all the way up my shadow arm, threatening to shatter my bones.

Wellebourne shouted in pure rage and lunged at me once more, but there was Grey, blocking him again.

Wellebourne's immortality was linked to the darkness. There was a reason why he'd hidden his soul inside his mummified hand. Why he had been so smug that it had been turned into a crucible. It had taken almost two hundred years of degradation and nearly all my power to break Wellebourne's original crucible.

I could never remove the dark from my own. It was melted into the iron, irrevocable.

I pushed harder against the crystal blade. It was designed to suck in the energy of life, of souls. It did not matter if that energy was light, like the pure love of my sister, or dark, like the evil in Wellebourne's broken soul.

"You'll lose everything!" Wellebourne roared. "You destroy it, you destroy all your power! It is no easy thing to crack a crucible. It will *kill* you, girl, it'll consume all your power and leave you with nothing!"

I cocked my head. "I know," I said simply. I had read the same books he had. I knew that to destroy a necromancer's crucible, it would take everything I had.

Little lightning bolts of black crackled up my shadow arm. Pain seared through me. The crystal knife was cracking, the crucible was cracking, my shadow arm was cracking, my whole entire *being* was cracking apart, splintering, shattering. I tipped my head back and *screamed*.

But I did not let go.

Even as my shadow fingers faded into nothing, I pressed against the hilt of the crystal blade with all my strength and power. My arm evaporated, leaving nothing but the raw pink skin covered in scars. I pressed the end against the crystal blade's hilt, not caring as the crystal finally cracked through, splintering into sharp ends. I still pressed down, blood pouring from my residual limb as the razor edges of the crystal pierced my skin and flesh.

The metal of my crucible vibrated, flaking away as if it were made of old paper.

Wellebourne screamed as my crucible—the iron bead made of my parents' ashes and my sister's soul and tainted with Wellebourne's evil machinations—broke apart.

Black oozed out of the two pieces, the earth below sizzling. The darkness was gone, leaving only the broken pieces of iron. I picked the shards up with my right hand, and as soon as they touched my skin, they turned back into ash. My whole body hunched over the last remains of my parents and sister.

I always asked before I raised the dead. Always. Except when it mattered. Because I knew what the answer would be, and I didn't want to hear it. I didn't ask Papa and Mama if they'd want to come back. I didn't ask Nessie. I pretended I knew the answer.

I wasn't ready to let go then, so I'd told myself I did it for her, not me. I let myself believe the lie.

I pressed the ash against my chest harder, ignoring the way it burned my skin and seared into my flesh. I chanted the rune for *ending* over and over again. My hair lifted, a cloud of white, as the souls of my family faded.

And—for the very last time—I felt their love. And I felt their farewell.

SIXTY-ONE

Nedra

I OPENED MY hand. Ash and dust fell out.

I felt the power draining from my body, but when I looked at Grey, I could still see the souls—Grey's flickering golden light and Wellebourne's dark void.

Wellebourne reached out to me, begging. Even as I watched, I could see Grey's soul growing stronger. I'd destroyed pieces of Wellebourne—the part that made him immortal, and a part of his soul. Now he was inside a body that wasn't his, partial and weak.

I walked over the broken bodies of the dead until I was directly across from him. When I looked into Grey's eyes, I could still see the flickering soul of Wellebourne inside.

"I don't want to die," Wellebourne whispered.

I leaned in closer. "Do it anyway."

EPILOGUE

With no Emperor to guide the Empire, chaos ruled instead.

Many of the colonies, Lunar Island included, used the resulting turmoil to formally secede from the Empire. Civil war ravaged the mainland for a few years, and by the time a new Emperor was crowned—a distant niece of Auguste—the Empire was much smaller than it had been before.

Lunar Island, however, escaped mostly unscathed. An unimposing man who cared for the island from the sewers to the towers rose to the occasion. No one had ever looked at Hamish Hamlayton as the type of man who would rule effectively, but he was the one who stepped forward with a plan and a system and the strength of will to see it through. Under his leadership, not as governor ruling as regent of the Empire but as the rightfully elected prime minister of a free nation, Lunar Island grew to be stable and prosperous—both in the south and the north. Authentic iron rings from Lunar Island became a popular fashion thanks to their dual association with rebellion.

Grey and I saw none of it.

Grey took the money Hamish offered him as reward for services rendered, and we bought a small ship. We set sail from Blackdocks before news of the Emperor's death reached Miraband. We went east first. The Empire could fight its battles without us.

Sometimes, I hold my hand over my chest. The black stain of Wellebourne's soul has disappeared, but there is a scar over my heart where I clutched the pieces of my broken crucible. The edges of the scar are as ragged and uneven as the shards of iron were, but I like to trace them with my finger and remind myself that life, too, is not perfectly formed.

On the first night, I discovered the greatest gift Grey had ever given me. Hanging in the main cabin, framed in elegantly carved mahogany, was the map Papa had given me when I first left for Yūgen. I had no idea how Grey had retrieved it from my dormitory.

We'll see the whole world, just the two of us. We'll go to every city on the map.

We will live all the life that we can live.

ACKNOWLEDGMENTS

WITHOUT MY MOTHER'S love, this story could not exist. Without my father's loss, this story could not have been true. Without my husband and son, Nedra could not have found peace or hope. This work is the sum impact their love has had on my life.

My thanks to my agent, Merrilee Heifetz, and her assistant Rebecca Eskildsen, for their help as the book developed in guiding the story, and to Cecilia de la Campa and Alessandra Birch for helping to tell the story in different languages around the world.

Kati Gardner and Angel Giuffria both gave me keen insight into making Nedra's character more realistic, and I would not have been able to create her as vividly without their advice.

Marissa Grossman pushed me to take Nedra and Grey off Lunar Island, and suddenly the world became much larger. Alex Sanchez suggested to me that, while the dead cannot die, they can be ripped apart, and suddenly the book contained much more blood. Both of these editors helped me to form Nedra's story and world and make them real, and I am eternally grateful.

So many people work to make a book reach a reader's hands. My thanks to everyone on the Razorbill and Penguin Teen teams, including Maggie Edkins for the cover design, Bridget Hartzler and Lizzie Goodell for publicity, Krista Ahlberg and Samantha Hoback for copyediting, and Felicity Vallence in marketing.

Author Emily B. Martin told me about a song by Alan Doyle called "Laying Down to Perish." I listened to that song hundreds of times while writing this book, and if you listen to it, too, you'll notice something familiar. My thanks to both these artists for introducing me to a new favorite. Another artistic influence lay in Lin-Manuel Miranda's *Hamilton*, whose songs led me to the epigraph you'll see at the beginning of the book.

I am grateful to every library, school, and bookstore that has supported me, with special love to Malaprops bookstore in Asheville, North Carolina, my home on the shelves.

And, finally, thank *you*. Without readers, books are nothing but ink and paper. You are what makes the story real. You are the fifth alchemy.